# The Body

Hanif Kureishi was born and brought up in Kent. He read philosophy at King's College, London. In 1981 he won the George Devine Award for his plays *Outskirts* and *Borderline*, and in 1982 he was appointed Writer-in-Residence at the Royal Court Theatre. In 1984 he wrote *My Beautiful Laundrette*, which received an Oscar nomination for Best Screenplay. His second screenplay *Sammy and Rosie get Laid* (1987) was followed by *London Kills Me* (1991) which he also directed. *The Buddha of Suburbia* won the Whitbread Prize for Best First Novel in 1990 and was made into a four-part drama series by the BBC in 1993. His version of Brecht's *Mother Courage* has been produced by the Royal National Theatre and by the Royal Shakespeare Company. His second novel, *The Black Album*, was published in 1995. With Jon Savage he edited *The Faber Book of Pop* (1995). His first collection of short stories, *Love in a Blue Time*, was published in 1997. His story *My Son the Fanatic*, from that collection, was adapted for film and released in 1998. *Intimacy*, his third novel, was published in 1998, and a film of the same title, based on the novel and other stories by the author, was released in 2001 and won the Golden Bear award at the Berlin Film Festival. His play *Sleep With Me* premièred at the Royal National Theatre in 1999. His second collection of stories, *Midnight All Day*, was published in 2000. *Gabriel's Gift*, his fourth novel, was published in 2001. *Dreaming and Scheming*, a collection of essays, was published in 2002. A film of his most recent script, *The Mother*, directed by Roger Michell, will be released in 2003. He has been awarded the Chevalier de l'Ordre des Arts et des Lettres.

# HANIF KUREISHI

# The Body

*and*

*Seven Stories*

*faber and faber*

First published in 2002
by Faber and Faber Limited
3 Queen Square London WC1N 3AU

Typeset by Faber and Faber Limited
Printed in England by Mackays of Chatham plc, Chatham, Kent

'Hullabaloo in the Tree' was first published in the *Guardian*
'Face to Face with You' was first published in *The Black Book*
'Goodbye, Mother' was first published in *Granta*
'Remember This Moment, Remember Us' was first published in *Red*
'Touched' was first published in *The New Yorker*

A CIP record for this book
is available from the British Library

ISBN 0–571–20972–6

2 4 6 8 10 9 7 5 3 1

# Contents

# THE BODY

# 1

He said, 'Listen: you say you can't hear well and your back hurts. Your body won't stop reminding you of your ailing existence. Would you like to do something about it?'

'This half-dead old carcass?' I said. 'Sure. What?'

'How about trading it in and getting something new?'

It was an invitation I couldn't say no to, or yes, for that matter. There was certainly nothing simple or straightforward about it. When I had heard the man's proposal, although I wanted to dismiss it as madness, I couldn't stop considering it. All that night I was excited by an idea that was – and had been for a while, now I was forced to confront it – inevitable.

This 'adventure' started with a party I didn't want to go to.

Though the late 1950s and early 1960s were supposed to be my heyday, I don't like the assault of loud music, and I have come to appreciate silence in its many varieties. I am not crazy about half-raw barbecued food either.

Want to hear about my health? I don't feel particularly ill, but I am in my mid-sixties; my bed is my boat across these final years. My knees and back give me a lot of pain. I have haemorrhoids, an ulcer and cataracts. When I eat, it's not unusual for me to spit out bits of tooth as I go. My ears seem to lose focus as the day goes on and people have to yell into me. I don't go to parties because I don't like to stand up. If I sit down, it makes it difficult for others to speak to me. Not that I am always interested in what they have to say; and if I am bored, I don't want to hang around, which might make me seem abrupt or arrogant.

I have friends in worse shape. If you're lucky, you'll be hearing about them. I do like to drink, but I can do that at home. Fortunately, I'm a cheap drunk. A few glasses and I can understand Lacan.

My wife Margot has been a counsellor for five years, training now to be a therapist. She listens to people for a living, in a room in the house. We have been fortunate; each of us has always envied the other's profession. She has wanted to make from within; I need to hear from without.

Our children have left home, the girl training to be a doctor and the boy working as a film editor. I guess my life has had a happy ending. When my wife, Margot, walks into a room, I want to tell her what I've been thinking, some of which I know she will attend to. Margot, though, enjoys claiming that men start to get particularly bad-tempered, pompous and demanding in late middle age. According to her, we stop thinking that politeness matters; we forget that other people are more important than ourselves. After that, it gets worse.

I'd agree that I'm not a man who has reached some kind of Buddhist plateau. I might have some virtues, such as compassion and occasional kindness; unlike several of my friends, I've never stopped being interested in others, or in culture and politics – in the general traffic of mankind. I have wanted to be a good enough father. Despite their necessary hatred of me at times, I enjoyed the kids and liked their company. So far, I can say I've been a tolerable husband overall. Margot claims I have always written for fame, money and women's affection. I would have to add that I love what I do, too, and it continues to fascinate me. Through my work I think about the world, about what matters to me and to others.

Beside my numerous contradictions – I am, I have been told, at least three different people – I am unstable, too, lost in myself, envious and constantly in need of reassurance. My wife says that I have craziness, bewildering moods and 'internal disappearances' I am not even aware of. I can go into the shower as one man and emerge as another, worse, one. My pupils enlarge, I move around obsessively, I yell and stamp my feet. A few words of criticism and I can bear a grudge for three days at a time, convinced she is plotting against me. None of this has diminished, despite years of self-analysis, therapy and 'writing as healing', as some of my students used to call the attempt to make art. Nothing has cured me of myself, of the self I cling to. If you asked me, I would probably say that my problems are myself; my life is my dilemmas. I'd better enjoy them, then.

I wouldn't have considered attending this party if Margot hadn't gone out to dinner with a group of women friends, and if I hadn't envied what I saw as the intimacy and urgency of their conversation, their pleasure in one another. Men can't be so direct, it seems to me.

But if I stay in alone now, after an hour I am walking about picking things up, putting them down and then searching everywhere for them. I no longer believe or hope that book knowledge will satisfy or even entertain me, and if I watch TV for too long I begin to feel hollow. How out of the world I already believe myself to be! I am no longer familiar with the pop stars, actors or serials on TV. I'm never certain who the pornographic boy and girl bodies belong to. It is like trying to take part in a conversation of which I can only grasp a fraction. As for the politicians, I can barely make out which side they are on. My age, education and experience seem to be no advantage. I imagine that to participate in the world with curiosity and pleasure, to see the point of what is going on, you have to be young and uninformed. Do I want to participate?

On this particular evening, with some semi-senile vacillation and nothing better to do, I showered, put on a white shirt, opened the front door, and trotted out. It was the height of summer and the streets were baking. Although I have lived in

London since I was a student, when I open my front door today I am still excited by the thought of what I might see or hear, and by who I might run into and be made to think about. London seems no longer part of Britain – in my view, a dreary, narrow place full of fields, boarded-up shops and cities trying to imitate London – but has developed into a semi-independent city-state, like New York, and has begun to come to terms with the importance of gratification. On the other hand, I had been discussing with Margot the fact that it was impossible to get to the end of the street without people stopping you to ask for money. Normally, I looked so shambolic myself the beggars lost hope even as they held out their hands.

It was a theatre party, given by a friend, a director who also teaches. Some of her drama school pupils would be there, as well as the usual crowd, my friends and acquaintances, those who were still actively alive, not in hospital or away for the summer.

As my doctor had instructed me to take exercise, and still hoping I had the energy of a young man, I decided to walk from west London to the party. After about forty-five minutes I was breathless and feeble. There were no taxis around and I felt stranded on the dusty, mostly deserted streets. I wanted to sit down in a shaded park, but doubted whether I'd be able to get up again, and there was no one to help me. Many of the boozers I'd have dropped into for a pint of bitter and a read of the evening paper, full of local semi-derelicts escaping their families – alcoholics, they'd be called, now everyone has been pathologized – had become bars, bursting with hyperactive young people. I wouldn't have attempted to get past the huge doormen. At times, London appeared to be a city occupied by cameras and security people; you couldn't go through a door without being strip-searched or having your shoes and pockets examined, and for all your own good, though it seemed neither safer nor more dangerous than before. There was no possibility of engaging in those awful pub conversations with wretched strangers which connected you to the impressive singularity of other people's lives. The elderly seem to have been swept from the streets; the young appear to have wires coming out of their heads, supplying either music, voices on the phone or the electricity which makes them move.

Yet I've always walked around London in the afternoons and evenings. These are relatively long distances, and I look at shops, obscure theatres and strange museums, otherwise my body feels clogged up after a morning's desk work.

The party was held not in my friend's flat, but in her rich brother's place, which turned out to be one of those five-floor, wide stucco houses near the zoo.

When at last I got to the door, a handful of kids in their twenties turned up at the same time.

'It's you,' said one, staring. 'We're doing you. You're on the syllabus.'

'I hope I'm not causing you too much discomfort,' I replied.

'We wondered if you might tell us what you were trying to do with –'

'I wish I could remember,' I said. 'Sorry.'

'We heard you were sour and cynical,' murmured another, adding, 'and you don't look anything like your picture on the back of your books.'

My friend whose party it was came to the door, took my arm and led me through the house. Perhaps she thought I might run away. The truth is, these parties make me as anxious now as they did when I was twenty-five. What's worse is knowing that these terrors, destructive of one's pleasures as they are, are not only generated by one's own mind, but are still inexplicable. As you age, the source of your convolutedly self-stymieing behaviour seems almost beyond reach in the past; why, now, would you want to untangle it?

'Don't you just hate the young beautiful ones with their vanity and sentences beginning with the words "when I left Oxford", or "RADA"?' she said, getting me a drink. 'But they're a necessity at any good party. A necessity anywhere anyone fancies a fuck, wouldn't you say?'

'Not that they'd want either of us too close to them,' I said.

'Oh, I don't know,' she said.

She took me out into the garden, where most people had gathered. It was surprisingly large, with both open and wooded areas, and I couldn't see the limits of it. Parts were lit by lanterns hung from trees; other areas were invitingly dark. There was a jazz combo, food, animated conversation and everyone in minimal summer clothing.

I had fetched some food and a drink and was looking for a place to sit when my friend approached me again.

'Adam,' she said. 'Now, don't make a fuss, dear.'

'What is it?'

My heart always sinks when I hear the words 'there's someone who wants to meet you'.

'Who is it?'

I sighed inwardly, and, no doubt, outwardly, when it turned out to be a young man at drama school, a tyro actor. He was standing behind her.

'Would you mind if I sat with you for a bit?' he said. He was going to ask me for a job, I knew it. 'Don't worry, I don't want work.'

I laughed. 'Let's find a bench.'

I wouldn't be curmudgeonly on such a delightful evening. Why shouldn't I listen to an actor? My life has been spent with those who transform themselves in the dark and make a living by calculating the effect they have on others.

My friend, seeing we were okay, left us.

I said, 'I can't stand up for long.'

'May I ask why?'

'A back problem. Only age, in other words.'

He smiled and pointed. 'There's a nice spot over there.'

We walked through the garden to a bench surrounded by bushes where we could look out on the rest of the party.

'Ralph,' he said. I put down my food and we shook hands. He was a beautiful young man, tall, handsome and confident, without seeming immodest. 'I know who you are. Before we talk, let me get us more champagne.'

Whether it was the influence of Ralph, or the luminous, almost supernatural quality that the night seemed to have, I couldn't help noticing how well groomed everyone seemed, particularly the pierced, tattooed young men, as decorated as a jeweller's window, with their hair dyed in contrasting colours. Apart from the gym, these boys must have kept fit twisting and untwisting numerous jars, tubs and bottles. They dressed to show off their bodies rather than their clothes.

One of the pleasures of being a man has been that of watching women dress and undress, paint and unpaint. When it comes to their bodies, women believe they're wearing the inside on the outside. However, the scale of the upkeep, the shop scouring and forethought, the possibilities of judgement, criticism and sartorial inaccuracy as, in contrast, the man splashes water on his face and steps without fear into whatever he can find at the end of the bed and then out into the street, have never been enviable to me.

When Ralph returned and I busied myself eating and looking, he praised my work with enthusiasm and, more importantly, with extensive knowledge, even of its obscurer aspects. He'd seen the films I'd written and many productions of my numerous plays. He'd read my essays, reviews and recently published memoirs *Too Late*. (What a dismal business that final addition and subtraction had been, like writing an interminable will, and nothing to be done about any of it, except to turn and torture it in the hope of a more favourable outlook.) He knew my work well; it seemed to have meant a lot to him. Praise can be a trial; I endured it.

I was about to go to the trouble of standing up to fetch more food when Ralph mentioned an actor who'd played a small part in one of my plays in the early 1970s, and had died of leukaemia soon after.

'Extraordinary actor,' he said. 'With a melancholy we all identified with.'

'He was a good friend,' I said. 'But you wouldn't remember his performance.'

'But I do.'

'How old were you, four?'

'I was right there. In the stalls. I always had the best seats.'

I studied his face as best I could in the available light. There was no doubt that he was in his early twenties.

'You must be mistaken,' I said. 'Is it what you heard? I've been spending time with a friend, someone I consider Britain's finest post-war director. Where is his work now? There can be no record of how it felt to watch a particular production. Even a film of it will yield no idea of the atmosphere, the size, the feeling of the work. Mind you,' I added, 'there are plenty of directors who'd admit that that was a mercy.'

He interrupted. 'I was there, and I wasn't a kid. Adam, do you have a little more time?'

I looked about, recognizing many familiar faces, some as wrinkled as old penises. I'd worked and argued with some of these people for more than thirty years. These days, when we met it was less an excited human exchange than a litany of decline; no one would put on our work, and if they did it wasn't sufficiently praised. Such bitterness, more than we were entitled to, was enervating. Or we would talk of grandchildren, hospitals, funerals and memorial services, saying how much we missed so-and-so, wondering, all the while, who would be next, when it would be our turn.

'Okay,' I said. 'Why would I be in a hurry? I was only thinking recently that after a certain age one always seems to be about to go to bed. But it's a relief to be done with success. I can lie down with the electric blanket on, listening to opera and reading badly. What a luxury reading badly can be, or doing anything badly for that matter.'

Two young women had stationed themselves out of earshot, but close enough to observe us, turning occasionally to glance and giggle in our direction. I knew that the face out of which I looked was of no fascination to them.

He leaned towards me. 'It's time I explained myself. Let's say . . . once there was a young man, not the first, who felt like Hamlet. As baffled, as mad and mentally chaotic, and as ruined by his parents. Still, he pulled himself together and became successful, by which I mean he made money doing something necessary but stupid. Manufacturing toilet rolls, say, or a new kind of tinned soup. He married, and brought up his children.

'In his middle age, as sometimes happens, he felt able to fall in love at last. In his case it was with the theatre. He bought a flat in the West End so he could walk to the theatre every night. He did this for years, but though he loved the gilt, the plush seats, the ice-creams, the post-show discussions in expensive restaurants, it didn't satisfy him. He had begun to realize that he wanted to be an actor, to stand electrified before a large crowd every night. How could anything else fulfil him?

'But he was too old. He couldn't possibly go to drama school, without feeling ridiculous. He was destined to be one of those unlucky people who realize too late what they want to do. A vocation is, after all, the backbone of a life.

'At the same time,' he went on, 'something terrible was happening. His wife, with whom he had been in love, suffered from a degenerative illness that destroyed her body but left her mind

11

unharmed. She was, as she described it, a healthy driver in a car that wouldn't respond, that was deteriorating and would crash, killing her. She said that all she needed was a new body. They tried many treatments in several countries, but in the end she was begging for death. In fact, she asked her husband to take her life. He did not do this, but was considering it when she saved him the trouble.'

'I'm sorry,' I said.

'These days, dying can be a nightmare. People hang on for years, long after they've got anything to talk about.'

He went on, 'The man, who had been looking after his wife for ten years, retired and went on a trip to recuperate. However, he didn't feel that he had long to live. He was exhausted, old and impotent. He was preparing for death too.

'One day, in South America, where he knew other wealthy but somewhat dreary people, he heard a fantastic story from a young man he trusted, a doctor who, like him, was interested in the theatre, in culture. Together – can you imagine? – they put on an amateur production of *Endgame*. This doctor was moved by the old man's wish for something unattainable. He confided in him, saying that an amazing thing was taking place. Certain old, rich men and women were having their living brains removed and transplanted into the bodies of the young dead.'

Ralph became quiet here, as if he needed to know my reaction before he could continue.

I said, 'It seems logical that technology and medical capability only need to catch up with the human imagination or will. I know nothing about science, but isn't this usually the way?'

Ralph went on, 'These people might not exactly live for ever, but they would become young again. They could be twenty-year-olds if they wanted. They could live the lives they believed they'd missed out on. They could do what everybody dreams of, have a second chance.'

I murmured, 'After a bit you realize there's only one invaluable commodity. Not gold or love, but time.'

'Who hasn't asked: why can't I be someone else? Who, really, wouldn't want to live again, given the chance?'

'I'm not convinced of that,' I said. 'Please continue. Were there people you met who had done this?'

'Yes.'

'What were they like?'

'Make up your own mind.' I turned to him again. 'Go on,' he said. 'Have a good stare.' He leaned into the light in order to let me see him. 'Touch me if you want.'

'It's all right,' I said, prissily, after stroking his cheek, which felt like the flesh of any other young man. 'Go on.'

'I have followed your life from the beginning, in parallel to my own. I've spotted you in restaurants, even asked for your auto-graph. You have spoken my thoughts. My audition speech at drama school was a piece by you. Adam, I am older than you.'

'This conversation is difficult to believe,' I said. 'Still, I always enjoyed fairy stories.'

He continued, 'As I told you, I had made money but my time was running out. You know better than me, an actor walks into a room and immediately you see – it's all you see – he's too old for the part. Yet one's store of desire doesn't diminish with age, with many it increases; the means to fulfil it become weakened. I didn't want a trim stomach, woven hair or less baggy eyes, or any of those . . . trivial repairs.' Here he laughed. It was the first time he hadn't seemed earnest. 'What I wanted was another twenty years, at least, of health and youth. I had the operation.'

'You had your brain removed . . . to become a younger man?'

'What I am saying sounds deranged. It is unbelievable.'

'Let us pretend, for the sake of this enjoyable fantasy, that it really is true. How does it work?'

He said the procedure was terrifying, but physically not as

awful as open-heart surgery, which we'd both had. When you come round from the anaesthetic in this case, you feel fit and optimistic. 'Ready to jump and run', as he put it. The operation wasn't exactly common yet. There were only a handful of surgeons who could do it. The procedure had been done hundreds of times, perhaps a thousand, he didn't know the exact figure, in the last five years. But it was still, as far as he knew, a secret. Now was the time to have it, at the beginning, before there was a rush; when it was still in everyone's interest to keep the secret.

He went on to say that there were certain people whom he believed needed more time on earth, for whom the benefit to mankind could be immense. To this, I replied that although I didn't know him, it was his mildness that struck me. He didn't seem the type to lead some kind of master-race. He wasn't Stalin, Pol Pot or even Mother Teresa returning for another fifty years.

'That's right,' he said. 'Needless to say, I don't include myself in this. I had children and I worked hard. I needed another life in order to catch up on my sleep. If I'm back, it's for the crack!'

I asked, 'If you really were one of these women or men, what would you want to do with your new time?'

'For years, all I've wanted is to play Hamlet. Not as a seventy-year-old but as a kid. That is what I'm going to do,' he said. 'At drama school, first. It's already been cast and I've got the part. I've known the lines for years. In my various factories, I'd walk about, speaking the verse, to keep sane.'

'I hope you don't mind me pointing this out, but what's wrong with Lear or Prospero?'

'I will approach those pinnacles eventually. Adam, I can do anything now, anything!'

I said, 'Is that what you are intending to do after you've played Hamlet?'

'I will continue as an actor, which I love. Adam, I have money, experience, health and some intelligence. I've got the friends I want. The young people at the school, they're full of enthusiasm and ardour. Something you wrote influenced me. You said that unlike films, plays don't take place in the past. The fear, anxiety and skill of the actors is happening now, in front of you. If performing is risky, we identify with the possibility of grandeur and disaster. I want that. I can tell you that what has happened to me is an innovation in the history of humankind. How about joining me?'

I was giggling. 'I'm no saint, only a scribbler with an interest, sometimes, in how people use one another. I don't feel entitled to another go at life on the basis of my "nobility".'

'You're creative, contrary and articulate,' he said. 'And, in my opinion, you've only just started to develop as an artist.'

'Jesus, and I thought I'd had my say.'

'You deserve to evolve. Meet me tomorrow morning.' As he picked up his plate and glass from the floor, the two observing women, who had not lost patience, began to flutter. 'We'll take it further then.'

He touched me on the arm, named a place and got up.

'What's the rush?' I said. 'Can't we meet in a few days?'

'There is the security aspect,' he said. 'But I also believe the best decisions are taken immediately.'

'I believe that too,' I said. 'But I don't know about this.'

'Dream on it,' he said. 'You've heard enough for one evening. It would be too much for anyone to take in. See you tomorrow. It's getting late. I really want to dance. I can dance all night, without stimulants.'

He pressed my hand, looked into my eyes as if we already had an understanding, and walked away.

The conversation had ended abruptly but not impolitely. Perhaps he had said all there was to say for the moment. He had certainly left me wanting to know more. Hadn't I, like everyone else, often thought of how I'd live had I known all that I know

now? But wasn't it a ridiculous idea? If anything made life and feeling possible, it was transience.

I watched Ralph join a group of drama students, his 'contemporaries'. Like him, presumably, but unlike me, they didn't think of their own death every day.

I got up and briefly talked to my friends – the old fucks with watery eyes; some of them quite shrunken, their best work long done – finished my drink, and said goodbye to the host.

At the door, when I looked back, Ralph was dancing with a group of young people among whom were the two women who'd been watching him. Walking through the house, I saw the kids I'd met at the front door sitting at a long table drinking, playing with one another's hair. I was sure I could hear someone saying they preferred the book to the film, or was it the film to the book? Suddenly, I longed for a new world, one in which no one compared the book to the film, or vice versa. Ever.

In order to think, I walked home, but this time I didn't feel tired. As I went I was aware of groups of young men and women hanging around the streets. The boys, in long coats and hoods that concealed most of their faces, made me think of figures from *The Seventh Seal*. They made me recall my best friend's painful death, two months before.

'It won't be the same without me around,' he had said. We had known each other since university. He was a bad alcoholic and fuck-up. 'Look at your life and all you've done. I've wasted my life.'

'I don't know what waste means.'

'Oh, I know what it is now,' he had said. 'The inability to take pleasure in oneself or others. Cheerio.'

The chess pieces of my life were being removed one by one. My friend's death had taken me by surprise; I had believed he would never give up his suffering. The end of my life was approaching, too; there was a lot I was already unable to do, soon there would be more. I'd been alive a long time but my life, like most lives, seemed to have happened too quickly, when I was not ready.

The shouts of the street kids, their incomprehensibly hip vocabulary and threatening presence reminded me of how much the needs of the young terrify the old. Maybe it would be interesting to know what they felt. I'm sure they would be willing to talk. But there was no way, until now, that I could actually have 'had' their feelings.

At home, I looked at myself in the mirror. Margot had said that with my rotund stomach, veiny, spindly legs and left-leaning posture I was beginning to resemble my father just before his death. Did that matter? What did I think a younger body would bring me? More love? Even I knew that that wasn't what I required as much as the ability to love more.

I waited up for my wife, watched her undress and followed her instruction to sit in the bathroom as she bathed by candle-light, attending to her account of the day and – the highlight for me – who had annoyed her the most. She and I also liked to discuss our chocolate indulgences and bodies: which part of which of us, for example, seemed full of ice-cream and was expanding. Various diets and possible types of exercise were always popular between us. She liked to accuse me of not being 'toned', of being, in fact, 'mush', but threatened murder and suicide if I mentioned any of her body parts without reverence. As I looked at her with her hair up, wearing a dressing gown and examining and cleaning her face in the mirror, I wondered how many more such ordinary nights we would have together.

A few minutes after getting into bed, she was slipping into sleep. I resented her ability to drop off. Although sleeping had come to seem more luxurious, I hadn't got any better at it. I guess children and older adults fear the separation from consciousness, as though it'll never return. If anyone asked me, I said that consciousness was the thing I liked most about life. But who doesn't need a rest from it now and again?

Lying beside Margot, chatting and sleeping, was exceptional every night. To be well married you have to have a penchant for the intricacies of intimacy and larval change: to be interested, for instance, in people dreaming together. If the personality is a spider's web, you will want to know every thread. Otherwise, after forty, when the colour begins to drain from the world, it's either retirement or reinvention. Pleasures no longer come to you, but there are pickings to be had if you can learn to scavenge for them.

Later, unusually – it had been a long time – she woke me up to make love, which I did happily, telling her that I'd always loved her, and reminiscing, as we often did, about how we met and got together. These were our favourite stories, always the same and also slightly different so that I listened out for a new feeling or aspect.

For the rest of the night I was awake, walking about the house, wondering.

## 2

The following morning there was no question of not meeting Ralph at the coffee shop he'd suggested. At the same time I didn't believe he'd show up; perhaps that was my wish. He had made me think so hard, the scope of my everyday life seemed so mundane and I had become so excited about this possible adventure and future that I was already beginning to feel afraid.

He arrived on a bicycle, wearing few clothes, and told me he'd stayed up late dancing, woken up early, exercised and studied a 'dramatic text' before coming here. It was common, he said, that people living a 'second' life, like people on a second marriage, took what they did more seriously. Each moment seemed even more precious. There was no doubt he looked fit, well and ready to be interested in things.

I found myself studying his face. How should I put it? If the body is a picture of the mind, his body was like a map of a place that didn't exist. What I wanted was to see his original face, before he was reborn. Otherwise it was like speaking on the phone to someone you'd never met, trying to guess what they were really like.

But it was me, not him, we were there for, and he was businesslike, as I guessed he must have been in his former life. He went through everything as though reading from a clipboard in his mind. After two hours we shook hands, and I returned home.

Margot and I always talked and bickered over lunch together, soup and bread, or salad and sandwiches, before our afternoon nap on separate sofas. Today, I had to tell her I was going away.

Earlier in the year Margot had gone to Australia for two months to visit friends and travel. We needed each other, Margot and I, but we didn't want to turn our marriage into more of an enclosure than necessary. We had agreed that I, too, could go on 'walkabout' if I wanted to. (Apparently, 'walkabout' was called 'the dreaming' by some Aboriginals.) I told her I wanted to leave in three days' time. I asked for 'a six-month sabbatical'. As well as being upset by the suddenness of my decision, she was shocked and hurt by the length of time I required. She and I are always pleased to part, but then, after a few days, we need to share our complaints. I guess that was how we knew our marriage was still alive. Yet she knew that when I make up my mind, I enter a tunnel of determination, for fear that vacillation is never far away.

She said, 'Without you here to talk about yourself in bed, how will I go to sleep?'

'At least I am some use, then.'

She acquiesced because she was kind. She didn't believe I'd last six months. In a few weeks I'd be bored and tired. How could anyone be as interested in my ailments as her?

It took me less time than I would have hoped to settle my

affairs before the 'trip'. I had a circle of male friends who came to the house once a fortnight to drink, watch football and discuss the miseries of our work. Margot would inform them I was going walkabout and we would reconvene on my return. I made the necessary financial arrangements through my lawyer, and followed the other preparations Ralph had insisted on.

When Ralph and I met up again he took one look at me and said, 'You're my first initiate. I'm delighted that you're doing this. You live your life trying to find out how to live a life, and then it ends. I don't think I could have picked a better person.'

'Initiate?'

'I've been waiting for the right person to follow me down this path, and it's someone as distinguished as you!'

'I need to see what this will bring me,' I murmured, mostly to myself.

'The face you have must have brought you plenty,' he said. 'Didn't you see those girls watching you at the party? They asked me later if you were really you.'

'They did?'

'Now – ready?'

He was already walking to his car. I followed. Ralph was so solicitous and optimistic, I felt as comfortable as anyone could in the circumstances. Then I began to look forward to 'the change' and fantasized about all that I would do in my new skin.

By now we'd arrived at the 'hospital', a run-down warehouse on a bleak, wind-blown industrial estate outside London (he had already explained that 'things would not be as they seemed'). I noticed from the size of the fence and the number of black-uniformed men that security was tight. Ralph and I showed our passports at the door. We were both searched.

Inside, the place did resemble a small, expensive private hospital. The walls, sofas and pictures were pastel coloured and the building seemed almost silent, as if it had monumental walls. There were no patients moving about, no visitors with flowers, books and fruit, only the occasional doctor and nurse. When I did glimpse, at the far end of a corridor, a withered old woman in a pink flannel night-gown being pushed in a wheel-chair by an orderly, Ralph and I were rapidly ushered into a side office.

Immediately, the surgeon came into the room, a man in his mid-thirties who seemed so serene I could only wonder what kind of yoga or therapy he had had, and for how long.

His assistant ensured the paperwork was rapidly taken care of, and I wrote a cheque. It was for a considerable amount, money that would otherwise have gone to my children. I hoped scarcity would make them inventive and vital. My wife was already pro-vided for. What was bothering me? I couldn't stop suspecting that this was a confidence trick, that I'd been made a fool of in my most vulnerable areas: my vanity and fear of decline and death. But if it was a hoax, it was a laboured one, and I would have parted with money to hear about it.

The surgeon said, 'We are delighted to have an artist of your calibre join us.'

'Thank you.'

'Have you done anything I might have heard of?'

'I doubt it.'

'I think my wife saw one of your plays. She loves comedy and now has the leisure to enjoy herself. Ralph has told me that it's a short-term body rental you require, initially? The six-months minimum – is that correct?'

'That is correct,' I said. 'After six months I'll be happy to return to myself again.'

'I have to warn you, not everyone wants to go back.'

'I will. I am fascinated by this experiment and want to be involved, but I'm not particularly unhappy with my life.'

'You might be unhappy with your death.'

'Not necessarily.'

He countered, 'I wouldn't leave it until you're on your death-bed to find out. Some people, you know, lose the power of speech then. Or it is too late for all kinds of other reasons.'

'You're suggesting I won't want to return to myself?'

'It's impossible for either of us to predict how you will feel in six months' time.'

I nodded.

He noticed me looking at him. 'You are wondering if –'

'Of course.'

'I am,' he replied, glancing at Ralph. 'We both are. Newbodies.'

'And ordinary people going about their business out there' – I pointed somewhere into the distance – 'are called Oldbodies?'

'Perhaps. Yes. Why not?'

'These are words that will eventually be part of most people's everyday vocabulary, you think?'

'Words are your living,' he said. 'Bodies are mine. But I would imagine so.'

'The existence of Newbodies, as you call them, will create considerable confusion, won't it? How will we know who is new and who old?'

'The thinking in this area has yet to be done,' he said. 'Just as there has been argument over abortion, genetic engineering, cloning and organ transplants, or any other medical advances, so there will be over this.'

'Surely this is of a different order,' I said. 'Parents the same age as their children, or even younger, for instance. What will that mean?'

'That is for the philosophers, priests, poets and television pundits to say. My work is only to extend life.'

'As an educated man, you must have thought this over.'

'How could I work out the implications alone? They can only be lived.'

'But –'

We batted this subject back and forth until it became clear even to me that I was playing for time.

'I was just thinking . . .' said Ralph. He was smiling. 'If I were dead we wouldn't be having this conversation.'

The doctor said, 'Adam's is a necessary equivocation.' He turned to me. 'You have to make a second important decision.'

I guessed this was coming. 'It won't be so difficult, I hope.'

'Please, follow me.'

The doctor, accompanied by a porter and a young nurse, took me and Ralph down several corridors and through several locked doors. At last we entered what seemed like a broad, low-ceilinged, neon-lit fridge with a tiled floor.

I was shivering as I stood there, and not only because of the temperature. Ralph took my arm and began to murmur in my ear, but I couldn't hear him. What I saw was unlike anything I had seen before; indeed, unlike anything anyone had ever seen. This was no longer amusing speculation or inquisitiveness. It was where the new world began.

'Where do you get them?' I asked. 'The bodies.'

'They're young people who have, unfortunately, passed away,' said the doctor.

Stupidly, I said, as though I were looking at the result of a massacre, 'All at once?'

'At different times, naturally. And in different parts of the world. They're transported in the same way as organs are now. That's not difficult to do.'

'What is difficult about this process now?'

'It takes time and great expertise. But so does cleaning a great painting. The right person has to do it. There are not many of those people yet. But it can be done. It is, of course, something that was always going to happen.'

Suspended in harnesses, there were rows and rows of bodies: the pale, the dark and the in-between; the mottled, the clear-skinned, the hairy and the hairless, the bearded and the large-breasted; the tall, the broad and the squat. Each had a number in a plastic wallet above the head. Some looked awkward, as though they were asleep, with their heads lolling slightly to one side, their legs at different angles. Others looked as though they were about to go for a run. All the bodies, as far as I could see, were relatively young; some of them looked less like young adults than older children. The oldest were in their early forties. I was reminded of the rows of suits in the tailors I'd visit as a boy with my father. Except these were not cloth coverings but human bodies, born alive from between a woman's legs.

'Why don't you browse?' said the surgeon, leaving me with the nurse. 'Choose a short list, perhaps. Write down the numbers you fancy. We can discuss your choices. This is the part I enjoy. You know what I like to do? Guess in advance who I think the person will choose, and wait to see whether I am right. Often I am.'

Shopping for bodies: it was true that I had some idea what I was looking for. I knew, for instance, that I didn't want to be a fair, blue-eyed blond. People might consider me a beautiful fool.

'Can I suggest something?' said Ralph. 'You might, for a change, want to come back as a young woman.'

I said, 'A change is as good as a rest, as my mother used to say.'

'Some men want to give birth. Or they want to have sex as a woman. You do have one of your male characters say that in his sexual fantasies he's always a woman.'

'Yes . . . I see what you mean . . .'

'Or you could choose a black body. There's a few of those,' he said with an ironic sniff. 'Think how much you'd learn about society and . . . all that.'

'Yes,' I said. 'But couldn't I just read a novel about it?'

'Whatever. All I want is for you to know that there are

options. Take your time. The race, gender, size and age you prefer can only be your choice. I would say that in my view people aren't able to give these things enough thought. They take it for granted that tough guys have all the fun. Still, you could give another body a run-out in six months. Or are you particularly attached to your identity?'

'It never occurred to me not to be.'

He said, 'One learns that identities are good for some things but not for others. Here.'

'Jesus. Thanks.'

I took the bag but wasn't sick. I did want to get out of that room. It was worse than a mortuary. These bodies would be reanimated. The consequences were unimaginable. Every type of human being, apart from the old, seemed available. The young must have been dying in droves; maybe they were being killed. I would make a good but expeditious choice and leave.

When the others fell back discreetly I walked beside this stationary army of the dead, this warehouse of the lost, examining their faces and naked bodies. I looked, as one might look too long at a painting, until its value – the value of life – seemed to evaporate, existing only as a moment of embodied frustration between two eternities. Then I began to think of poetry and children and the early morning, until it came back to me, why I wanted to go on living and why it might, at times, seem worth it.

I considered several bodies but kept moving, hoping for something better. At last, I stopped. I had seen 'my guy'. Or rather, he had seemed to choose me. Stocky and as classically handsome as any sculpture in the British Museum, he was neither white nor dark but lightly toasted, with a fine, thick penis and heavy balls. I would, at last, have the body of an Italian footballer: an aggressive, attacking midfielder, say. My face resembled that of the young Alain Delon with, naturally, my own brain leading this combination out to play for six months.

'That's him,' I said, across the lines of bodies. 'My man. He looks fine. We like each other.'

'Do you want to see his eyes?' said the nurse, who'd been waiting by the door. 'You'd better.'

'Why not?'

'Look, then,' she said.

She prised open my man's eyelids. The room was scrupulously odourless, but as I moved closer to him I detected an antiseptic whiff. However, I liked him already. For the first time, I would have dark brown eyes.

'Lovely.' I considered patting him on the head, but realized he would be cold. I said to him, 'See you later, pal.'

On the way out, I noticed another heavy, locked door. 'Are there more in there? Is that where they keep the second division players?'

'That's where they keep the old bodies,' she said. 'Your last facility will be in there.'

'Facility?' I asked. The necessity for euphemism always alerted me to hidden fears.

'The body you're wearing at the moment.'

'Right. But only for a bit.'

'For a bit,' she repeated.

'No harm will come to it in there, will it?'

'How could it?'

'You won't sell it?'

'Er . . . why should we?' She added, 'No disrespect intended. If, after six months, you change your mind, or you just don't turn up, we will nullify the facility, of course.'

'Right. But I would like to see where I'm going to be hanging out – or up, rather.'

I moved towards the door of this room. The porter barred my way with his strong arm.

The nurse said, 'Confidential.'

26

Ralph intervened. 'It's unlikely, Adam, but you might know the people. Some say they're emigrating, others "seem" to have died. Others have disappeared, but they come here and re-emerge as Newbodies.'

'How much of this "coming and going" is there about?' I asked.

Ralph didn't reply. I felt myself becoming annoyed.

I said, 'It is curious, inquisitive types like me you claimed you wanted as "initiates". Now you won't answer my questions.'

'Be a patient patient. Soon you'll have as much time on your hands as you could want. You will come to understand much more then.' He embraced me. 'I'll leave you now. I will visit you when it's done.'

'I'll feel like a new man.'

'That's right.'

I was put into bed then, in my room, and examined by the doctor and his assistant. The doctor was whistling, and I closed my eyes. My body had already become just an object to be worked on. I imagined my new body being taken from its rack and prepared in another room.

After a while, the doctor said, 'We're ready to go ahead now. You made a good choice. Your new facility has almost been picked out a few times now. He's been waiting a while for his outing. I'm glad his day has finally come.'

Insofar as it was possible, I had got used to the idea that I might die under the anaesthetic, that these might be my last moments on earth. The faces of my children as babies floated before me as I went under. This time, though, I was afraid in a new way: not only of death, but of what might come out of it – new life. How would I feel? Who would I be?

# 3

A theory-loving friend of mine has an idea that the notion of the self, of the separate, self-conscious individual, and of any auto-biography which that self might tell or write, developed around the same time as the invention of the mirror, first made en masse in Venice in the early sixteenth century. When people could consider their own faces, expressions of emotion and bodies for a sustained period, they could wonder who they were and how they were different from and similar to others.

My children, around the age of two, became fascinated by their own images in the looking-glass. Later, I can remember my son, aged six, clambering onto a chair and then onto the dining table in order to see himself in the mirror over the fireplace, kissing his fingers and saying, as he adjusted his top hat, 'Masterpiece! What a lucky man you are, to have such a good-looking son!' Later, of course, they and their mirrors were inseparable. As I said to them: make the most of it, there'll be a time when you won't be able to look at yourself without flinching.

According to my friend, if a creature can't see himself, he can't mature. He can't see where he ends and others begin. This process can be aided by hanging a mirror in an animal's cage.

Still only semi-conscious, I began to move. I found I could stand. I stood in front of the full-length mirror in my room, look-ing at myself – or whoever I was now – for a long time. I noticed that other mirrors had been provided. I adjusted them until I obtained an all-round view. In these mirrors I seemed to have been cloned as well as transformed. Everywhere I turned there were more me's, many, many more new me's, until I felt dizzy. I sat, lay down, jumped up and down, touched myself, wiggled my fingers and toes, shook my arms and legs and, finally, placed my head carefully on the floor before kicking myself up and standing on it – something I hadn't done for twenty-five years. There was a lot to take in.

It was a while ago, in my early fifties, that I began to lose my physical vanity, such as it was. I've been told that as a young man I was attractive to some people; I spent more time combing my hair than I did doing equations. Certainly I took it for granted that, at least, people wouldn't be repelled by my appearance. As a child, I lived among open fields and streams, and ran and explored all day. For the past few years, however, I have been plump and bald; my heart condition has given me a continuously damp upper lip. By forty I was faced with the dilemma of whether my belt should go over or under my stomach. Before my children advised me against it, I became, for a while, one of those men whose trousers went up to their chest.

When I first became aware of my deterioration, having had it pointed out by a disappointed lover, I dyed my hair and even signed on at a gym. Soon I was so hungry I ate even fruit. It didn't take me long to realize there are few things more risible than middle-aged narcissism. I knew the game was up when I had to wear my reading glasses in order to see the magazine I was masturbating over.

None of the women I knew could give up in this way. It was rare for my wife and her friends not to talk about botox and detox, about food and their body shape, size and relative fitness, and the sort of exercise they were or were not taking. I knew women, and not only actresses, who had squads of personal trainers, dieticians, nutritionists, yoga teachers, masseurs and beauticians labouring over their bodies daily, as if the mind's longing and anxiety could be cured via the body. Who doesn't want to be more desired and, therefore, loved?

In contrast, I tried to dissociate myself from my body, as if it were an embarrassing friend I no longer wanted to know. My pride, my sense of myself, my identity, if you will, didn't disappear; rather, it emigrated. I noticed this with my friends. Some of them had gone to the House of Lords; they sat on committees. They were given 'tribute' evenings; they picked up awards, medals, prizes and doctorates. The end of the year, when these things were handed out, was an anxious time for the elderly and their doctors. Prestige was more important than beauty. I imagined us, as if in a cartoon, sinking into the sludge of old age, dragged down by medals, our only motion being a jealous turn of the head to see what rewards our contemporaries were receiving.

Some of this, you will be delighted to hear, happened to me. My early plays were occasionally revived, most often by arthritic amateurs, though my latest play hadn't been produced: it was considered 'old-fashioned'. Someone was working on a biography which, for a writer, is like having a stone-mason begin to chisel one's name into a tombstone. My biographer seemed to know, better than I did, what had been important to me. He was young; I was his first job, a try-out. Despite my efforts, we both knew my life hadn't been scandalous enough for his book to be of much interest.

However, I'd written my memoirs and made money out of two houses I'd bought, without much thought, in the early 1960s, one for my parents and one for myself, which turned out to have been situated in an area which became fashionable.

Lately, what I have wanted to be cured of, if anything, was indifference, slight depression or weariness; of the feeling that my interest in things – culture, politics, other people, myself – was running down. A quarter of me was alive; it was that part which wanted a pure, unadulterated 'shot' of life.

I wasn't the only one. A successful but melancholic friend, ten years older than me, described his head as a 'raw wound'; he was as furious, pained and mad as he had been at twenty-five. No Nirvanic serenity for him; no freedom from ambition and envy.

He said, 'I wouldn't know whether you should go gentle into that night or rage against the dying of the light. I think, on reflection, that I'd prefer the gentle myself.' But it is as if your mind is inhabited by a houseful of squabbling relatives, all of whom one could gladly eject, but cannot.

But where to find consolation? Who will teach us the wisdom we require? Who has it and could pass it on? Does it even exist?

There was religion, once, now replaced by 'spirituality', or, for a lot of us, politics – of the 'fraternal' kind; there was culture, now there is shopping.

When I came round after the operation these weary thoughts, which I'd carried around for months, weren't with me. I had more important things to do, like standing on my head! Without Ralph telling me this – he had become an optimist – I had expected to feel, at least, as if I'd been beaten up. I had anticipated days of recovery time. However, even though I was only semi-conscious, I found I could move easily.

Nevertheless, as soon as I lay down on the bed, I fell asleep again. This time I dreamed I was at a railway station. When I take a train I like to get to the station early so as to watch the inhabited bodies move around one another. Yet I have become slightly phobic about others' bodies. I don't like them too close to me; I can't touch strangers, friends or even myself. In the dream, when I arrived at the station, everyone wanted to meet me; they crowded around me, shaking my hand, touching, kissing and stroking me in congratulation.

This semi-sleep continued. Somehow, I became aware that I was without my body. It might be better to say I was suspended between bodies: out of mine and not yet properly in another. I was assaulted by what I thought were images but which I realized were really bodily sensations, as if my life were slowly returning, as physical feeling. I had always taken it for granted that I was a person, which was a good thing to be. But now I was being reminded that first and foremost I was a body, which wanted things.

In this strange condition, I thought of how babies are close to their mother's skin almost the whole time. A body is the child's first playground and his first experiences are sensual. It doesn't take long for children to learn that you can get things from other bodies: milk, kisses, bottles, caresses, slaps. People's hands are useful for this, as they are for exploring the numerous holes bodies have, out of which leaks different stuff, whether you like it or not: sweat, shit, semen, pus, breath, blood, saliva, words. These are holes into which you can put things, too, if you feel like it.

My mother, a librarian, was fat and couldn't walk far. Movement disturbed her. Her clothes were voluminous. She had no dealings with diets, except once, when she decided to go on a fast. She eschewed breakfast. By lunchtime she had a headache and dizziness; she was 'starving' and had a cream bun to cheer herself up.

Mother was always hungry, but I guess she didn't know what she was hungry for. She replied, when I asked her why she consumed so much rubbish, 'You never know where your next meal is coming from, do you?' Things can seem like that to some people, as if there is only scarcity and you should get as much down you as you can, though it never satisfies you.

Mother never let me see her body or sleep beside her; she didn't like to touch me. She didn't want anyone's hands on her, saying it was 'unnecessary'. Perhaps she made herself fat to discourage temptation.

As you get older, you are instructed that you can't touch just anyone, nor can they touch you. Although parents encourage their children in generosity, they don't usually share their genitals, or those of their partner, with you. Sometimes you are not even allowed to touch parts of your own body, as if they don't quite belong to you. There are feelings your body is forbidden to generate, feelings the elders don't like anyone having. We consider ourselves to be liberals; it is the others who have inexplicable customs. Yet the etiquette of touching bodies is strict everywhere.

Every body is different, but all are identical in their uncontrollability: bodies do various involuntary things, like crying, sneezing, urinating, growing or becoming sexually excited. You soon find that bodies can get very attracted and repelled by other bodies, even – or particularly – when they don't want to be.

I grew up after the major European wars, playing soldier games on my father's farm. My mind was possessed by images of millions of upright male bodies in identical clothes and poses. The world these men made was mayhem and disorder, but at least, as my father used to say, they were 'well turned out' for it. At school, it seemed that each teacher had a particular disability – one ear, one leg or testicle, or some war-wound – which fascinated us. None of us thought we'd ever be down to just one of anything where there was supposed to be two, but we couldn't stop thinking about it. This was the misunderstanding of education: the teachers were interested in minds, and we were interested in bodies. It was the bodies I wanted when I grew up.

I became aware of the reality of my own death at the same time I became aware of the possibility of having real sex with others. Each made the other possible. You might die, but you could say 'hello' before you went.

In the countryside, there are fewer bodies and more distance between them. I came to the city because the bodies are closer; there is heat and magnetism. The bodies jostle; is that for space, or for touching? The tables in the restaurants and pubs are more adjacent. On the trains and in the tubes, of course, the bodies seem to breathe one another in, which must be why people go to work. The bodies seem anonymous, but sometimes any body will do. Why would anyone want this, particularly a semi-claustrophobic like me?

If other people's bodies get too much for you, you can stop them by stabbing or crucifixion. You can shoot or burn them to make them keep still or to prevent them saying words which displease you. If your own body gets too much – and whose doesn't? – you might meditate yourself into desirelessness, enter a monastery or find an addiction which channels desire. Some bodies are such a nuisance to their owners – they can seem as unpredictable as untamed animals, or the feeling can overheat and there's no ther-mostat – that they not only starve or attempt to shape them, but they flagellate or punish them.

As a young man, I wanted to get inside bodies, not just with a portion of my frame, but to burrow inside them, to live in there. If this seems impractical, you can at least get acquainted with a body by sleeping next to it. Then you can put bits of your body into the holes in other bodies. This is awful fun. Before I met my present wife, I spent a while putting sensitive areas of my body as close to the sensitive areas of other bodies as I could, learning all I could about what bodies wanted. I never lost my fearful fas-cination with women's bodies. The women seemed to under-stand this: that the force of our desire made us crazy and terrified. You could kill a woman for wanting her too much.

The older and sicker you get, the less your body is a fashion item, the less people want to touch you. You will have to pay. Masseurs and prostitutes will caress you, if you give them money. How many therapies these days happen to involve the 'laying-on of hands'? Nurses will handle the sick. Doctors spend their lives touching bodies, which is why young people go to medical school. Dentists and gynaecologists love the dark inside. Some workers, as in shoe shops, can get to hold body parts without having had to attend anatomy lectures. Priests and politicians tell people what to do with their bodies. People always choose their work according to their preferences about bodies. Careers advisors should bear this in mind. Behind every vocation there is a fetish.

34

Around puberty, people begin to worry – some say women do this more than men, but I'm not convinced – about the shape and size of their bodies. They think about it a lot, though the sensible know their bodies will never provide the satisfaction they desire because it is their appetite rather than their frame that bothers them. Having an appetite, of course, alters the shape of your body and how others see it. Starvation; fasting; dieting. These can seem like decent solutions to the problem of appetite or of desire.

The appetite of my new body seemed to be reviving, too. I was coming round because I was aware of a blaze of need. But my form felt like a building I'd never before been in. Where exactly was this feeling coming from? What did I want? At least I knew that my stomach must have been empty. First, I would wake up properly; then I could eat.

My watch was on the bedside table. I could see the numbers with perfect vision, but the strap wouldn't fit round my thick new wrist. At least I knew it was morning and I'd slept through the night. It was time for breakfast. I could not walk out of the room in my new body without preparation.

I continued to examine myself in the mirror, stepping forwards and backwards, examining my hairy arms and legs, turning my head here and there, opening and closing my mouth, looking at my good teeth and wide, clean tongue, smiling and frowning, trying different expressions. I wasn't just handsome, with my features in felicitous proportion. The nurse had asked me to examine my eyes. I saw what she meant. There was a softness in me, a wistfulness; I detected a yearning, or even something tragic, in the eyes.

I was falling in love with myself. Not that beauty, or life itself, means much if you're in a room on your own. Heaven is other people.

The door opened and the surgeon came in.

'You look splendid.' He walked around me. 'Michelangelo has made David!'

35

'I was going to say Frankenstein has just –'

'No joins or bumps either. Do you feel well?'

'I think so.'

But my voice sounded unfamiliar to me. It was lighter in tone, but had more force and volume than before.

'Go and have a pee,' he said.

In the toilet, I touched my new penis and became as engrossed in it as a four-year-old. I weighed and inspected it. I raised my arms and wriggled my hips; no doubt I pouted, too. Elvis, of course, had been one of my earliest influences, along with Socrates. When I peed, the stream was full, clear and what I must describe as 'decisive'. Putting my prick away, I gave it a final squeeze. Who wouldn't want to see this! My, what a lot I had to look forward to! My appetite – all my appetites, I suspected – had reached another dimension.

'Okay?' he said.

I nodded. We went into another room where the doctor fixed various parts of me to machines, giving me, or my new body, a thorough check-up. As he did so, I babbled away in my new voice, mostly childhood memories, listening to myself in the attempt to draw myself back together again.

'I'm through,' he said at last. Denying me the privacy of a natural born being, he watched me clumsily put on the clothes Ralph had bought me. 'Good. Good. This is incredible. It has worked.'

'Why the surprise? Haven't you done this before?'

'Of course. But each time it seems to be a miracle. We have another success on our hands. Everything is complete now. Your mind and the body's nervous system are in perfect co-ordination. You have your old mind in a new body. New life has been made.'

'Is that it?' I said. 'Don't I require more preparation?'

'I expect you do,' he said. 'Mentally. There will be shocks ahead, adjustments to be made. It would be a good idea to discuss it with

Ralph, your mentor. It goes without saying that you cannot talk freely about this. Otherwise you are free to go, sir. Your clock has been restarted, but it is still ticking. See you in six months. You know where we are.'

'But do I know where I am?'

'I hope you will find out. I look forward to hearing how it went.'

The nurse, in reception, handed me my wallet and the bag of things Ralph had told me I'd need for the first few hours after my 'transformation'. She took a copy of my memoirs from under the desk and asked me to sign it.

'I've long been an admirer, sir.'

Writing my old name with my new fingers I had to bend over from a different height. For the first time in years, I did so without having to adjust my posture to avoid an expected pain. I stood back and stared at my signature, which resembled a bad forgery of my own scrawl. I took another piece of paper and scribbled my name again and again. However hard I tried, I couldn't make it come out like the old one.

The amused nurse called a cab for me.

I waited on the couch with my new long legs stuck out in front of me, taking up a lot of room and touching my face. Watching her work in reception, it occurred to me that the desirable nurse – whose attractiveness was, really, only lack of any flaw – might be seventy or ninety years old. Like people who work at a dentist's, and always have perfect teeth, she was bound to be a Newbody herself. But why would she be doing such a job?

A long-haired, model-like young woman approached the desk, requesting a taxi. Her hip, slightly Hispanic look was so ravishing I must have audibly sighed, because she smiled. It was difficult to tell whether she was in her late teens or early thirties. It occurred to me that we were making a society in which everyone would be the same age. I noticed that the woman was carrying an open bag in which I glimpsed what looked like the corner of a pink flannel night-gown. She sat opposite me, waiting too, nervously. In fact, she seemed to relate strangely to herself, as I must have done, moving different parts of herself experimentally, at first diffidently, and then with some internal celebration. Then she smiled in my direction with such radiant confidence I thought of suggesting we share a cab. What a perfect couple we would make!

But I wanted to be back among ordinary people, those who decayed and were afraid of death. I got up and cancelled the cab. I would enjoy walking. A marathon would be nothing. The nurse seemed to understand.

'Good luck,' I said to the woman.

I headed for the main road. I must have walked for five miles, taking considerable strides and loving the steady motion. My new body was taller and heavier than my last 'vessel', but I felt lighter and more agile than I could recall, as though I were at the wheel of a luxury car. I could see over the heads of others on the street. People had to look up to me. I'd been bullied as a kid. Now, I could punch people out. Not that a fight would be the best start to my new incarnation.

I found a cheap café and ate a meal. I ate another meal. I checked into a big anonymous hotel where a reservation had already been made. I found a good position in the bar where I could look out for people looking at me. Was that woman smiling in my direction? People did glance at me, but with no more obvious interest than they had before. My mind felt disturbingly clear. What defined edges the world had! It had been a long time since I'd had such undeviating contact with reality. After a couple of drinks, I gained even more clarity along with a touch of ecstasy, but I didn't want to get blotto on my first day as a Newbody.

I was waiting in the crowded hotel foyer when Ralph hurried in and stood there looking about. It was disconcerting when he didn't recognize the writer he'd worshipped, whose words he'd memorized, the one he believed deserved immortality! It took him a few distracted moments to pick my body out among the others, and he still wasn't certain it was me.

I went over. 'Hi, Ralph, it's me, Adam.'

He embraced me, running his hands over my shoulders and back; he even patted my stomach.

'Great hard body, pal. You look superb. I'm proud of you. You've got guts. How do you feel?'

'Never better,' I said. They were my words, but my voice was strong. 'Thanks, Ralph, for doing this for me.'

'By the way,' he said. 'What's your name?'

'Sorry?'

'You'll need a new name. You could keep your old name, of course, or a derivative. But it might cause confusion. You're not really Adam any more. What do you think?'

My instinct was to change my name. It would help me remember that I was a new combination. Anyway, hybrids were hip.

'What will it be?' he asked.

'I'll be called Leo Raphael Adams,' I said at last. 'Does that sound grand enough?'

'Up to you,' he said. 'Good. I'll tell them. You have money, don't you?'

'As you insisted, enough for six months.'

'I'll make sure you receive a passport and driving licence in your new name.'

'That must be illegal,' I said.

'Does that worry you?'

'I'm afraid so. I'm not a good man by any means, but I do tend towards honesty in trivial matters.'

'That's the least of it, man. You're in a place that few other humans have ever been before. You're a walking laboratory, an experiment. You're beyond good and evil now.'

'Right, I see,' I said. 'The identity theorists are going to be busy worrying about this one.'

He touched my shoulder. 'You need to get laid. It works, doesn't it – your thing?'

'I can't tell you how good it feels not to piss in all directions at once or over your own new shoes. As soon as I get an erection, I'll call.'

'The first time I had sex in my new body, it all came back. I was with a Russian girl. She was screaming like a pig.'

'Yeah?'

'I knew, that night, it had been worth it. That all those years, day after day, watching my wife die, were over. This was moving on in glory.'

'My wife isn't dead. I hope she doesn't die while I'm "away".'

'It's okay to be unfaithful,' he said. 'It isn't you doing it.'

We talked for a bit, but I felt restless and kept bouncing on my toes. I said I wanted to get out and walk, shake my new arse, and show off. Ralph said he had done the same. He would let me go my own way as soon as he could. First, we had to do some shopping. Ralph had brought a suit, shirt, underwear and shoes to the hospital, but I would need more.

'My son only seems to possess jeans, T-shirts and sunglasses,' I said. 'Otherwise I have no idea what twenty-five-year-olds wear.'

'I will help you,' he said. 'I only know twenty-five-year-olds.'

I was photographed for my new passport, and then Ralph took me to a chain-store. Each time I saw myself in the changing-room mirror I thought a stranger was standing in front of me. My feet were an unnecessary distance from my waist. Recently, I'd found it difficult to get my socks on, but I'd never been unfamiliar with the dimensions of my own body before. I'd always known where to find my own balls.

I dressed in black trousers, white shirt and raincoat, nothing fashionable or ostentatious. I had no desire to express myself. Which self would I be expressing? The only thing I did buy, which I'd always wanted but never owned before, was a pair of tight leather trousers. My wife and children would have had hysterics.

Ralph left to go to a rehearsal. He was busy. He was pleased with me and with himself, but his job was done. He wanted to get on with his own new life.

Staring at myself in the mirror again, attempting to get used to my new body, I realized my hair was a little long. Whichever 'me' I was, it didn't suit me. I would customize myself.

There was a hairdresser's near my house, which I had walked past most days for years, lacking the courage to go in. The people were young, the women with bare pierced-bellies, and the noise horrendous. Now, as the girl chopped at my thick hair and chattered, my mind teemed with numerous excitements, wonderments and questions. I had quickly agreed to become a Newbody in order not to vacillate. Since the operation, I had felt euphoric; this second chance, this reprieve, had made me feel well and glad to be alive. Age and illness drain you, but you're never aware of how much energy you've lost, how much mental preparation goes into death.

What I didn't know, and would soon find out, was what it was like to be young again in a new body. I enjoyed trying out my new persona on the hairdresser, making myself up. I told her I was single, had been brought up in west London and had been a philosophy and psychology student; I had worked in restaurants and bars, and now I was deciding what to do.

'What do you have in mind?' she asked.

I told her I was intending to go away; I'd had enough of London and wanted to travel. I would be in the city for only a few more days, before setting off. As I spoke, I felt a surge or great push within, but towards what I had no idea, except that I knew they were pleasures.

Walking out of the hairdresser's, I saw my wife across the road pulling her shopping trolley on wheels. She looked more tired and frailer than my mental picture of her. Or perhaps I was reverting to the view of the young, that the old are like a race all of whom look the same. Possibly I needed to be reminded that age in itself was not an illness.

I recalled talking in bed with her last week, semi-asleep, with one eye open. I could see only part of her throat and neck and shoulder, and I had stared at her flesh thinking I had never seen anything more beautiful or important.

She glanced across the street. I froze. Of course her eyes moved over me without recognition. She walked on.

Being, in a sense, invisible, and therefore omniscient, I could spy on those I loved, or even use and mock them. It was an unpleasant loneliness I had condemned myself to. Still, six months was a small proportion of a life. What would be the purpose of my new youth? I had led a perplexed and unnecessarily pained inner life, but unlike Ralph, I had not felt unfulfilled, or wished to be a violinist, pioneering explorer or to learn the tango. I'd had projects galore.

My bewilderment was, I guessed, the experience of young people who'd recently left home and school. When I taught young people 'creative' writing, their excessive concern about 'structure' puzzled me. It was only when I saw that they were referring to their lives as well as to their work that I began to understand them. Looking for 'structure' was like asking the question: what do you want to do? Who would you like to be? They could only take the time to find out. Such an experiment wasn't something I'd allowed myself to experience at twenty-five. At that age I moved between hyperactivity and enervating depression – one the remedy, I hoped, for the other.

If my desire pointed in a particular direction this time around, I would have to discover what it was – if there was, in fact, something to find. Perhaps in my last life I'd been over-constrained by ambition. Hadn't my needs been too narrow, too concentrated? Maybe it was not, this time, a question of finding one big thing, but of liking lots of little ones. I would do it differently, but why believe I'd do it better?

That evening I changed hotels, wanting somewhere smaller and less busy. I ate three times and went to bed early, still a little groggy from the operation.

The next day was a fine one, and I awoke in an excellent mood. If I lacked Ralph's sense of purpose, I didn't lack enthusiasm. Whatever I was going to do, I was up for it.

There I was, walking in the street, shopping for the trip I had finally decided to take, when two gay men in their thirties started waving and shouting from across the road.

'Mark, Mark!' they called, straight at me. 'It's you! How are you! We've missed you!'

I was looking about. There was no one else they could have been motioning to. Perhaps my leather trousers were already having an effect on the general public. But it was more than that: the couple were moving through the traffic, their arms extended. I considered running away – I thought I might pretend to be jogging – but they were almost on me. I could only face them as they greeted me warmly. In fact, they both embraced me.

Luckily, their talk was relentless and almost entirely about themselves. When I managed to inform them that I was about to go on holiday, they told me they were going away, too, with friends, an artist and a couple of dancers.

'Your accent's changed, too,' they said. 'Very British.'

'It's London, dear. I'm a new man now,' I explained. 'A reinvention.'

'We're so pleased.'

I understood that the last time we met, in New York, my mental state hadn't been good, which was why they were pleased to see me out shopping in London. They and their circle of friends had been worried about me.

I survived this, and soon we were saying our farewells. The two men kissed and hugged me.

'And you're looking good,' they added. 'You're not modelling any more, are you?'

'Not at the moment,' I said.

One of them said, 'But you're not doing the other thing, are you, for money?'

'Oh, not right now.'

'It was driving you crazy.'

'Yes, yes,' I said. 'I believe it was.'

'Shame the boy band idea didn't work out. Particularly after you got through the audition with that weird song.'

'Too unstable, I guess.'

'Would you like to join us for a drink – of orange juice, of course? Why not?'

'Yes, yes,' said the other. 'Let's go and talk somewhere.'

'I'm sorry, but I must go,' I said, moving away. 'I'm already late for my psychiatrist! He tells me there's much to be done!'

'Enjoy!'

I rang Ralph straight away.

'You got your erection, eh?' he said.

I insisted on seeing him. He was rehearsing. He made me go to the college canteen during his tea break and wait. When he did turn up, he seemed preoccupied, having had an argument with Ophelia. I didn't care. I told him what had happened to me on the street.

'That shouldn't have occurred,' he said, with some concern. 'It's never happened to me, though I guess I'll start to get recognized when I've played Hamlet.'

'What is going on? Don't they do any checks first?'

'Of course,' he said. 'But the world's a small place now. Your guy's from LA.'

'Mark. That's his name. That's what they called me.'

'So? How can anyone be expected to know he's got friends in Kensington?'

'Suppose he's wanted by the police somewhere?'

He shook his head. 'It won't happen again,' he said confidently. 'The chances of such a repeat are low, statistically.'

'There have been other weird occurrences.'

'For example?' He didn't want to hear, but he had to.

'Tell me, first, how did he die, my body, my man?'

Ralph hesitated. 'Why do you want to know?'

'Why, are you not allowed to tell me?'

'This is a new area.'

I went on, 'In bed, I was aware of these twinges, or sensations. There were times in my Oldbody life, particularly as I got older, or when I was meditating, when I felt that the limits of my mind and body had been extended. I felt, almost mystically, part of others, an "outgrowth of the One".'

'Really?'

'This is different. It's as if I have a ghost or shadow-soul inside me. I can feel things, perhaps memories, of the man who was here first. Perhaps the physical body has a soul. There's a phrase of Freud's that might apply here: the bodily ego, he calls it, I think.'

'Isn't it a little late for this? I'm an actor, not a mystic.'

I noticed a lack of respect in Ralph. I was a puling twenty-five-year-old rather than a distinguished author. It hadn't taken long before I was confronted with the losses involved in gaining pro-longed youth.

I said, 'I need to know more about my body. It was Mark's face they were seeing when they looked at me. It was his childhood experience they were partly taking in, not yours or mine.'

45

'You want to know why he snuffed himself out? I'm telling you, Leo, face it, this is the truth and you know it already. Your guy's going to have died in some grisly fashion.'

'What sort of thing are we talking about?'

'If he's young, it's not going to be pleasant. No young death is a relief. The whole world works by exploitation. We all know the clothes we wear, the food, it's packed by Third World peasants.'

'Ralph, I am not just wearing this guy's shoes.'

'He was definitely "obscure", your man. There's no way I'm going to let them give you shoddy goods. Anyway, it's impossible, at the moment, to just go and kill someone for their body. Their family, the police, the press, everyone's going to be looking for them. The body has to be "cleared", and then it has to be prepared for new use by a doctor who knows what he is doing. It's a long and complicated process. You can't just plug your brain into any skull, thank Christ. Imagine what a freak show we'd have then.'

'If he's been "cleared", I think that at least you should tell me what you know,' I said. 'I presume he was homosexual.'

'Why else would he be in such good shape? Most hets, apart from actors, have the bodies of corpses. You object to homosexuality?'

'Not in principle, and not yet. I haven't had time to take it in. I'm at the beginning here. I need to know what all this might mean.'

Ralph said, 'As far as I know, he was nutty but not druggy. A suicide, I think, by carbon monoxide poisoning. They had to fix up his lungs. I looked into it, for you. Adam – Leo, I mean. I asked them to give you the best. Some of those women were in great shape.'

'I told you, I'm not ready to be a woman. I'm not even used to being a man.'

'That was your choice, then. Your man had something like clinical depression. Obviously a lot of young people suffer from it. They can't get the help they need. Even in the long run they don't come round. Anti-depressants, therapy, all that, it never works. They're never going to be doers and getters like us, man. Better to be rid of them altogether and let the healthy ones live.'

'Live in the bodies of the discarded, you mean? The neglected, the failures?'

'Right.'

'I see what you're getting at. "Mark" might have suffered in his mind. He might not have lived a "successful" life, but his friends seemed to like him. His mother would like to see him.'

'What are you saying?'

'What if I –'

'Don't think about pulling that kind of stunt in front of his mother,' he said. 'She'd go mad if you walked in there with that face on. His whole family! They'd think they'd seen a fucking ghost!'

'I'm not about to do that,' I said. 'I don't know where she lives. That's not quite what I mean.'

Ralph said, 'My guy was struck by lightning while lying drunk under a tree. Nothing unusual about my man, thank Christ, though I keep away from AA meetings.'

There wouldn't be much more I could get out of Ralph. I had to live with the consequences of what I'd done. Except that I had no idea what those consequences might turn out to be.

Ralph said, 'You will come and see me as Hamlet?'

'Only if you come and see me as Don Giovanni.'

'Yeah? Is that what you're going to do? I can see you as the Don. Got laid yet?'

'No.' He gave me my new passport and driving licence. 'Listen, Ralph,' I said as we parted. 'I need you to know I'm grateful for this opportunity. Nothing quite so odd has ever happened to me before.'

'Good,' he said. 'Now go and have a walk and calm down.'

I was, I noticed, becoming used to my body; I was even relaxing in it now. My long strides, the feel of my hands and face, seemed natural. I was beginning to stop expecting a different, slower response from my limbs.

There was something else.

For the first time in years, my body felt sensual and full of intense yearning; I was inhabited by a warm, inner fire, which nonetheless reached out to others – to anyone, almost. I had forgotten how inexorable and indiscriminate desire can be. Whether it was the previous inhabitant of this flesh, or youth itself, it was a pleasure that overtook and choked me.

From the start of our marriage I had decided to be faithful to Margot, without, of course, having enough idea of the difficulty. It is probably false that knowing is counter-erotic and the mundane designed to kill desire. Desire can find the smallest gap, and it is a hell to live in close proximity to and enforced celibacy with someone you want and with whom contact, when it occurs, is of an intimacy that one has always been addicted to. I learned that sexual happiness of the sort I'd envisaged, a constant and deep satisfaction – the romantic fantasy we're hypnotized by – was as impossible as the idea that you could secure everything you wanted from one person. But the alternative – lovers, mistresses, whores, lying – seemed too destructive, too unpredictable. The overcoming of bitterness and resentment, as well as sexual envy of the young, took as much maturity as I could muster, as did the realization that you have to find happiness in spite of life. I became a serial substitutor: property, children, work, raking the garden leaves, kept the rage of failure at bay. Illness, too, was helpful. I became so phobic of others I couldn't even have a stranger cut my hair. My daughter would do it. This is how I survived my life and mind without murdering anyone. Enough! It was not enough.

Now I found myself looking at young women and even

young men on the street and in cafés. When, on my way down an escalator, a woman on her way up smiled and gestured at me, I pursued her into the street. I would, this time, follow my impulses. I approached her with a courage I'd never had as a young man. Then, my desire had been so forceful and strange – which I experienced as a kind of chaos – I'd found it difficult to contain or enjoy. For me to want someone had meant to get involved in maddening and intense negotiations with myself.

I asked the girl to join me for a drink. Later, we walked in the park before retiring to her room in a cheap hotel. Later still, we ate, saw a film and returned to her room. She loved my body and couldn't get enough of it. Her pleasure increased mine. She and I looked at and admired each other's bodies – bodies which did as much as two willing bodies could do, several times, before parting for ever, a perfect paradigm of impersonal love, both generous and selfish. We could imagine around each other, playing with our bodies, living in our minds. We became machines for making pornography of ourselves. I hoped there'd be many more occasions like it. How fidelity interferes with love, at times! What were refinement and the intellect compared to a sublime fuck?

As we lay in each other's arms, and, when she was asleep, I kissed her and said, 'Goodbye, whoever you are', creeping out at dawn to walk the streets for a couple of hours, it occurred to me that this was an excellent way to live.

# 4

Next morning I was on the train to Paris, my new rucksack on the rack above me. Before we reached Dover I had helped people with their heavy luggage, eaten two breakfasts and read the newspapers in two languages. For the rest of the journey I studied guidebooks and timetables.

For a few weeks before I became a Newbody, I had been in what I called an 'experimental' frame of mind. After finishing *Too Late*, I'd been failing as a writer. I'd become more skilful, but not better. I wouldn't have minded the work getting worse if I'd been able to find interesting ways to make it more difficult. Urgency and contemporaneity make up for any amount of clumsiness, in literature as in love. I had stopped work and had been drawing, taking photographs and talking to people I'd normally flee. I would see what occurred, rather than hide in my room. Despite these efforts, there was no doubt I was becoming isolated, as if it were the solitude of my craft I had become attached to, and it was that I couldn't get away from.

There are few things more depressing than constant pain, and there were certain physical agonies I thought I would never be without. Flannery O'Connor wrote, 'Illness is a place where there is no company.' Perhaps I had been unconsciously preparing for death, as I recall preparing for my parents' deaths. I realized what a significant part of my life my own death had become. As a badly off young man I had constantly thought: do I have the money to do this? As an older man I had constantly thought: do I have the time for this; or, is this what I really want to do with my remaining days?

Now, a renewed physical animation, combined with mental curiosity, made me feel particularly energetic. In this incarnation I would go everywhere and see everything.

When I first had children I was inspired to think about my own childhood and parents; now, this transformation was making me reflect on the sort of young man I had been. I hadn't travelled much then. I had been too absorbed in the theatre, working in any capacity, reading scripts, running the box-office and serving tyrannical directors. The rest of the time I was having tragic, complicated affairs, and trying to write. I forfeited a lot of pleasure for my craft; at times I found the deferment and discipline intolerable. I'd break out and go mad, before retiring to my room for long periods – for too long, I'd say now. But those years of habit and repetition served me well: I gained invaluable experience of writing, not only of the practical difficulties, but of the terrors and inhibitions that seem to be involved in any attempt to become an artist.

My excitements then had never been pure; they had always been anxieties. In later life I wondered whether I had been too constrained and afraid for my future, too focused on the success I yearned for and too determined to become established. Travelling unworriedly through Europe had been the least of my concerns.

Did I regret it now, or wish it otherwise? At least I had the sense to understand that there couldn't be a life without foolishness, hesitation, breakdown, unbearable conflict. We are our mistakes, our symptoms, our breakdowns.

The thing I missed most in my new life was the opportunity to discuss – and, therefore, think about properly – the implications of becoming a Newbody. I doubted whether Ralph would have been interested in going into it further. Perhaps such a transformation, like face-lifts, worked better for people who didn't have theories of authenticity or the 'natural', people who didn't worry about its meaning at the expense of its obvious pleasures.

It was its pleasures I was in search of. Soon, I was tearing across Paris; then I went to Amsterdam, Berlin, Vienna. I did the churches and museums of Italy, and they did me. It wasn't long before I'd had my fill of degraded, orgasmically violated bodies strung from walls, and vaults full of old bones. On most days I woke up in a different place. I travelled by train and bus, in the slowest possible way. Sometimes I just walked across mountains, beaches or fields, or got off trains when I fancied the view from the window. If I liked a bus – the route, the thoughts it provoked, the width of the seat or a sentence in a book I was reading on it –

I'd sit there until the end of the line. There was no rush.

I stayed in cheap hotels, hostels and boarding houses. I had money, but I didn't want opulence. As a young man I'd wanted that – as a measure of success and of how far I had escaped my childhood. Now it seemed confining to be over-concerned with furnishings.

I talked only to strangers, making friends easily for the first time in years. I met people in cafés, museums and clubs, and went to their houses when I could. If I had been too fastidious before, now I stayed with anyone who would have me, to see how they lived. Unlike most young people, I was interested in people of all ages. I'd go to the house of a Dutch guy of my age, and end up chatting to his parents all weekend. It was the mothers I got along with because I was interested in children and how you might get through to them. The mothers talked about children, but I learned they were talking about themselves, too, and this moved me.

I did, at least, know how to look after myself. I could escape anyone boring. People were more generous than I had noticed. If you could listen, they liked to talk. Perhaps being ambitious and relatively well known from a young age had put the barrier of my reputation, such as it was, between me and others.

The days in each city were full. I could drink, have sex with people I picked up or with any prostitute whose body took my fancy, visit galleries, queue for cheap seats to the theatre or opera, or merely read and walk. In the former East Berlin all I did was walk and take photographs. In a bar in Paris, I met a young Algerian guy who modelled occasionally. The male models didn't earn anything like as much as the girls, and most of them had other jobs. My friend got me a catwalk show during Fashion Week, and I took my turn parading on the narrow aisle, as the flash-bulbs exploded and the unprepossessing journalists scribbled. Was it the clothes or really the bodies they were looking at?

Backstage, it was a chaos of semi-naked girls and boys, dressers, the designer and numerous assistants.

I enjoyed all of it, and, after chatting with the designer, whom I'd known slightly in my previous body, I was offered a job in one of his shops, with the prospect of becoming a buyer, which I declined. I did ask him, though, whether, by any chance, as I was a 'student', he'd read any of 'my' – Adam's – books or seen 'my' plays or films. If he had, he couldn't remember. He didn't have time for cultural frivolity. Making a decent pair of trousers was more important. He did say he liked 'me' – Adam – though he had found me shy at times. He said, to my surprise, that he envied the fact that women were attracted to me.

The following day, my new catwalk acquaintance thought it would be a good idea to take me shopping. I had told him I had a small inheritance to blow, and he knew where to shop. In our new gear we went to bars suitable for looking at others as we enjoyed them looking at us – those, that is, who didn't regard us dark-skinners with fear and contempt.

I didn't stay; I wasn't like these kids. I didn't want a place in the world and money. One day, because it rained, I thought I should go to Rome. There, as I attended a lecture and dozed in the front row in my new linen suit, the queer biographer of an important writer, leaning over me enormously, asked me out for a drink. At dinner, this British hack said he wanted me to be his assistant, which I did agree to try, while insisting, as I'd learned I had to, that I would not be his lover. He claimed that all he wanted was to lick my ears. I thought: why not share these fine pert ears around? They're not even mine, but a general asset. I closed my eyes and let his old tongue enjoy me. It was as pleasant as having a snail crawl across your eyeball. It was more difficult being a tart than I'd hoped. Tarts are trouble, mostly to themselves.

I could experiment because I was safe. If you know you're

going home, you can go anywhere first. I went with him, imagining tall, glass-fronted bookcases and long, polished library tables on which I would work on my version of *The Key to All Mythologies*, in the way I'd browsed in my father's books as a teenager. That, indeed, was what I was doing, 'browsing' or 'grazing' in the world. The job was less demanding than I'd hoped. Mostly it involved me wearing the clothes he bought for me to parties and dinners. I was his bauble or pornography, to be shown off to friends – intelligent, cultured queens I'd have liked to talk with. As a young man I didn't much enjoy the company of my peers; I liked being an admired boy in the theatre, surrounded by older men.

Therefore this fantasy of Greek life suited me, except that my 'employer' refused to let me out of his sight. When I did get the opportunity to read in his library, I could see his bald pate bobbing up and down outside, as he tried to watch me through the window from an uneven box. His adoration of me became nothing but suffering for him, until I began to feel like an imprisoned princess from *The Arabian Nights*. Beauty sets people dreaming of love. If you don't want to be in someone else's dream you have to clear off.

I got a job working as a 'picker' at the door of a club in Vienna. I tended to point at the inpulchritudinous and lame until a lunatic kicked me in the stomach. A few days later, having been taken to a casino by another acquaintance, I was boredly smoking a cigarette outside and wondering why people were so keen to rid themselves of their money when a woman came to me. She said she'd been watching me. She liked my eyes. She wanted to make love to me.

She was not old. I must have been looking doubtful. (I wasn't always sure whether my expression matched my feeling. I wasn't, yet, convinced of my ability to lie.)

'I will pay you,' she said.

'Have you paid for such love before?'

She shook her head. My deal with myself was not to turn down such offers. I looked at her more closely and said no one had ever offered me a better exchange.

'Come, then.'

She had a chauffeur, and she took me with her. I sat in the back of the car, being driven through the night to an unknown destination.

She was an American heiress with a partially collapsed villa outside Perugia. She hired an octogenarian pianist to play Mozart sonatas out of tune while she painted me nude looking out at the olive groves. Few portraits can have taken longer. I listened to her for days and strode about in shorts and workmen's boots, pretending I could mend things, though everything seemed fine as it was. (Is it only in Italy that ruin itself can seem like art?)

There were always her eyes to return to. I still liked having people fall in love with me. There are moments of life you get addicted to, that you want over and over, but then you get frustrated when you can't go any further, when the thing you've most wanted bores you.

My real labour was at night, in her room, where, after taking hours to prepare for me, she'd await my knock. I went at my employment seriously, limbering up, bathing, meditating, a proud professor of satisfaction. What internal trips I took, pretending to be a dancer or rock climber. It was dangerous work, sex, but, as always, it was the terrors and uncertainties which made it erotic. For her there had to be safety at the end, some hours of peace in her mind. I looked out for this on her face when she was asleep, like a blessing, and was pleased, waiting beside the bed to assess her temperature, her hand in mine. Then I would sleep well, alone. My pleasure was in her pleasure. After a few weeks, she wanted me to live with her in New York, if Italy got too slow for me. It did, but I didn't. I could satisfy her, but only at the cost of disappointing her. I walked away in my boots through the olive trees. Her eyes were on my back; she did not know where her next love would come from, if at all.

I was glad to have the time to walk around the cities, listening to music, always my greatest passion, on my headphones, particularly as, in my previous body, I'd been suffering from some deafness. I went to clubs and made the acquaintance of DJs. I talked about music. But to be honest, in my former guise I could get to meet more interesting people.

However, I loved this multiplicity of lives; I was delighted with the compliments about my manner and appearance, loved being told I was handsome, beautiful, good-looking. I could see what Ralph meant by a new start with old equipment. I had intelligence, money, some maturity and physical energy. Wasn't this human perfection? Why hadn't anyone thought of putting them together before?

Like many straights, I'd been intrigued by some of my gay friends' promiscuity, the hundreds or even thousands of partners. A gay actor I knew had once said to me, 'Anywhere I go in the world, one glance and I can see the need. A citizen of nowhere, I inhabit the Land of Fuck.' I'd long admired and coveted what I saw as the gay's innovative and experimental lives, their capacity for pleasure. They were reinventing love, keeping it close to instinct. Meanwhile, at least for the time being – though it was changing – the straights were stuck with the old model. I had, of course, envied all that sex without a hurting human face, and in my new guise I had plenty of open bodies in close proximity. On one particular day and night I had sex with six – or was it seven? – different people. It's not something you'd want to do often. Once in a lifetime might just do it.

In Switzerland, through a woman I'd been talking to in a bar, I became acquainted with a bunch of kids in their late twenties who were making a film about feckless young people like themselves. I helped the group move their equipment and was interested to see how they used the new lightweight cameras their parents had financed.

They began to shoot long scenes of banal, everyday dialogue. I was never one to believe that Andy Warhol's films could be a fruitful model, but I encouraged them to keep the camera still and photograph only the faces of their subjects, letting them speak while I sat behind the camera, asking questions about their childhood. I took these away to a studio, cut some of them together, and put music on. The best version was one where I took the sound of the voices off altogether, but kept the music going. The unreachable, silent, moving mouths – someone trying to be heard, or not being attended to – were oddly affecting. When it was my turn in front of the camera I had myself painted white, with a black stripe down the middle, and called it 'zebra piece'. One night, we showed the films in a club and the naked zebra danced on stage with a local thrash band.

Others in the group, operating from a collapsing warehouse, were curating shows of contemporary art. Some reasonable things did get done, though no one much noticed. It was irritating when I found myself interested in them as a teacher or parent – the extent of their minds; in how seriously they could take themselves. They didn't read much; there was a lot of cultural knowledge I took for granted and they didn't. My own son didn't start to read or watch decent films until he was almost twenty. He wouldn't allow us, but only a female teacher, to turn him on to these pleasures. Recently, on the radio I'd said I considered reading about as important as raising poodles. As intended, this had got me into wonderful trouble with the bookworms. The whispering, worshipful tones in which my parents referred to 'literature' and 'scholarship' had always made me wonder what more could be done with a body than pass information in and out of it.

I had been to a club once, in the early 1990s, to see Prince, with my son and the college lecturer who seemed to be educating him (in bed), Deedee Osgood. Despite the squalor and the fact that everyone but me was virtually naked and on drugs, I loved looking at everyone. Now, most evenings, my new pals took me to clubs. This soon bored me, so they gave me Ecstasy for the first time. Though I had smoked pot and taken LSD, and known people who'd become junkies or cocaine addicts, alcohol was the drug of my generation. It seemed the best drug. I'd never understood why anyone would want to waltz with mephitic alligators.

I doubted whether any of my new acquaintances went a day without a smoke or some other stimulant. As my friends knew, the 'E' hit me as a revelation and I wanted it served to the Prime Minister, and pumped into the water supply. I popped handfuls of it every day for a fortnight. It led me into my own body, and out into others', insofar as there was anyone real there at all. I couldn't tell. (I liked to call us E-trippers 'a loose association of solipsists'.) My ardour made my new pals laugh. They had learned that E wasn't the cure, and the last thing the world needed was another drug philosopher.

But after the purifications and substitutions of culture, I believed I was returning to something neglected: fundamental physical pleasure, the ecstasy of the body, of my skin, of movement, and of accelerated, spontaneous affection for others in the same state. I had been of puny build, not someone aware of his strength, and had always found it easier to speak of the most intimate things than to dance. As a Newbody, however, I began to like the pornographic circus of rough sex; the stuff that resembled some of the modern dance I had seen, animalistic, without talk. I begged to be turned into meat, held down, tied, blindfolded, slapped, pulled and strangled, entirely merged in the physical, all my swirling selves sucked into orgasm. 'Insights from the edge of consciousness', I'd have called it, had words come easily to me at that time. But they were the last thing on my mind.

By using others, I could get myself on to a sexual high for two or three days. It was indeed drug-like: a lucent, shivering pleasure not only in my own body but, I believed, in all existence at its most elemental. Narcissus singing into his own arse! Hello! I was also aware, as I danced naked on the balcony of a house overlooking Lake Como at daybreak after spending the night with a young couple who didn't interest me, of how many addicts I'd known and how tedious any form of addiction could be. The one thing I didn't want was to get stuck within.

For the group, there was sex of every variety, and the others' drug-taking had moved to heroin. At least two of the boys were HIV positive. Several of the others believed that that was their destiny. Because my contact with reality was, at the most, glancing, it took me a while to see how desperate the pleasures were, and how ridiculously romantic their sense of shared tragedy and doom was. My generation had been through it, with James Dean, Brian Jones, Jim Morrison and others. If I'd been a kid now, I'd have found poetic misery hard to resist. As it was, I knew I was not of them, because I couldn't help wondering what their parents would have thought.

What we used to call 'promiscuity' had always bothered me. Impersonal love seemed a devaluation of social intercourse. I couldn't help believing, no doubt pompously, that one of civilization's achievements was to give value to life, to conversation with others. Or was faithful love only an unnecessarily constraining bourgeois idiocy?

There would be a moment when the other, or 'bit of the other', as we used to say, would turn human. Some gesture, word or cry would indicate a bruised history or ailing mind. The bubble of fantasy was pricked (I came to understand fantasy as a fatal form of preconception and preoccupation). I saw another kind of opening then, which was also an opportunity for another kind of entry – into the real. I fled, not wanting my desire to take me too far into another person. Really, apart from with the woman who paid me, when it came to sex I was only interested in my own feeling.

It has, at least, become clear that it is our pleasures, rather than our addictions and vices, which are our greatest problems. Pleasure can change you in an instant; it can take you anywhere. If these gratifications were intoxicating and almost mystical in their intensity, I learned, when something stranger happened, that indulgence wasn't a full-time job and reality was a shore where dreams broke. It turned out I was seducible.

One of the artists in my group had a four-year-old son. The others were only intermittently interested in him, as I was in them, and mostly the kid watched videos. His loneliness reflected mine. If I'd been up partying and couldn't sleep the next day, I would, before I cured my come-down with another pill, take him to see the spiders in the zoo. Making him laugh was my greatest pleasure. We played football and drew and sang. I didn't mind ambling about at his speed, and I made up stories in cafés. 'Read another,' he'd say. He helped me recall moments with my own children: my boy, at four, fetching me an old newspaper from the kitchen, as he was used to my perpetual reading.

With his stubborn refusals, the kid reduced me twice to fury. I found myself actually stamping my feet. This jarring engagement made me see that otherwise I was like a spy, concealed and wary. If my generation had been fascinated by what it was like to be Burgess, or Philby or Blunt – the emotional price of a double life, of hiding in your mind – the kid reminded me of how much of one's useful self one locked away in the keeping of serious secrets.

The kid sent me into an unshareable spin. I wept alone, feeling guilty at how impatient I had been with my own children. I composed a lengthy email apologizing for omissions years ago, but didn't send it. Otherwise, I saw that most of my kids' childhood was a blank. I had either been somewhere else, or wanted to be, doing something 'important' or 'intellectually demanding'. Or I wanted the children to be more like adults – less passionate and infuriating, in other words. The division of labour between men and women had been more demarcated in my day: the men had the money and the women the children, a deprivation for both.

I came to like the kid more than the adults. One time, finding me puking on the floor, he was kind and tried to kiss me better. I didn't want him to consider me a fool. The whole thing shook me. I hadn't expected this Newbody experience to involve falling in love with a four-year-old whose narcissism far exceeded my own. When it came to youth and beauty, he had it all, as well as his emotional volume turned right up. It hadn't occurred to me that if I wanted to begin again as a human being, it would be as a father, or that I would have more energy with which to miss my children living at home, their voices as I entered the house, their concerns and possessions scattered everywhere. Ralph had failed to warn me of feeling 'broody'. I guessed such an idea would recommend 'eternal life' to no more than a few, just as you never hear anyone say that in heaven you have to do the washing up while suffering from indigestion. I had to shut the possibility of fatherhood out of my mind, kiss the kid goodbye and remind myself of what I had to look forward to, of what I liked and still wanted in my old life.

In my straighter moments, despite everything, I wanted to be close to my wife. I liked to watch her walk about the house, to hear her undress, to touch her things. She would lie in bed reading and I would smell her, moving up and down her body like an old dog, nose twitching. I still hadn't been all the way round her. Her flesh creased, folded and sagged, its colour altering, but I had never desired her because she was perfect, but because she was she.

After my journey through the cities and having to leave the kid, I decided to roam around the Greek islands. My own vanity bored even me and I craved warm sun, clear water and a fresh wind. I'd had two and a half months of ease and pleasure, and I wanted to prepare for my return – for illness and death, in fact. I began to think of what I'd tell my friends I'd been doing.

As the doctor had predicted, I wasn't looking forward to re-entering my old body. When I ate, would it still feel as though I were chewing nails and shitting screws? On some days, would I still only be able to swallow bananas and painkillers? But as my old body and its suffering stood for the life I had made, the sum total of my achievement made flesh, I believed I should re-inhabit it. I was no fan of the more rigid pieties, but it did seem to be my duty. Would most deaths soon feel like suicides? It was almost funny: becoming a Newbody made living a quagmire of deci-sion. In the meantime, I was looking forward to staying in the same place for a few weeks and finishing, or at least beginning again, *Under the Volcano*.

My father, the headmaster of a local school, said, before he died of heart failure, that he'd always regretted not becoming a postman. A gentle job, he believed, wandering the streets with nothing but dogs to worry about, would have extended his life. Idiotic, I considered this: worrying was an excitement I needed. But now I had some idea what he meant.

Not that he'd have survived on a postman's salary. I had begun to realize that I, too, wasn't used to today's financial world. I'd always bought my own milk, but had no idea of the price. I'd seriously underestimated what I'd need as a Newbody. The price of condoms! Apart from the cash I'd put aside for my return trip, I'd spent most of my money and couldn't use my bank accounts or credit cards. Until my return I needed a cheap place to stay and money for my keep.

It was in Greece, on a boat one morning, that I met a middle-aged woman with a rucksack who was going to study photography at a 'spiritual centre' on the island I was visiting. She had hitch-hiked from London to visit the Centre, which was known to be particularly rejuvenative for those suffering from urban breakdown. When I told her my sad story, she offered to take me along with her.

While I waited in a café in a nearby square, drinking wine and reading Cavafy, she went to the Centre and enquired whether there was any work I could do in exchange for food, a place to sleep and a little payment. Otherwise, I would find a job in a bar or disco, and crash on the beach. The woman returned and told me the Centre had been looking for an 'oddjob' to clean the rooms and work in the kitchen. Providing the leader didn't dislike me, I would eat for free, earn a little money and sleep on the roof.

We walked down to a handful of flower-dotted, whitewashed buildings on the edge of an incline, with a view of the sea. She opened the door in a long, high wall.

'Look,' she said. I did: the devil peeping into paradise. 'They must be between classes.'

It was a shaded garden where the women – naturally, it was mostly women – sat on benches. They talked, wrote earnestly in notebooks and read. In one corner, a woman was singing; another was doing yoga, another combing her hair; on a massage table, a body was being kneaded.

Here, these middle-aged, middle-class and, of course, divorced women from London took 'spiritual' nourishment, meditation, aromatherapy, massage, yoga, dream therapy. What baby with its mother ever had it better than in this modern equivalent of the old-style spa or sanatorium? The three men I saw were middle-aged, with hollow chests and varicose veins.

She asked, 'Will you be all right here?'

'I think I'll manage,' I replied.

After being shown around the kitchen, the 'work' rooms, and the dining room, I was taken to see the Centre's founder or leader, the 'wise woman', as she was called, without irony, or with none that I noticed. I had the impression that it would be wise for me, too, to lay off the irony. It was too much of a mature and academic pleasure.

Patricia came to the door of a small, shuttered house ten minutes' walk from the Centre. In her late fifties, she was big, with long, greying hair, in clothes with the texture and odour of cheap oriental carpets. She invited me in, and ordered me to sit on a cushion. As I dozed off, she talked loudly on the phone, read her correspondence ('Bastards! Bastards!'), scratched her backside and, from time to time, looked me over.

When I got up to inspect a picture, she turned. 'Sit down, don't fidget!' she said. 'Be still for five minutes!'

I sat down and bit my lip.

I could recall her variety of feminism from the first time around: its mad ugliness, the forced ecstasy of sisterhood, the whole revolutionary puritanism. I didn't loathe it – it seemed to me to be a strain of eccentric English socialism, like Shavianism – as long as I didn't have to live under or near it. It did, however, seem better being a young man these days: the women were less aggresive, earned their own money and didn't blame anyone with a cock for their nightmares.

I was irritated by what I considered to be this woman's high-handed approach, and was about to walk out – not that she would have minded – when it occurred to me that for her I was virtually a child as well as only a potential menial. I was neither an Oldbody nor a Newbody. I was a nobody.

I'd always had a penchant for tyrants, at school, at work and in the theatre where, when I was young, they flourished, having come from army backgrounds. I had enjoyed testing myself against them. How many times could they beat you up before they had to come to terms with you? However, now I was shaken by a blast of late-adolescent fury. I'd forgotten how adults talk down to you, when they're not ignoring you, and how they hate to hear your opinion while giving their own. You're at one of your parents' dinner parties and your parents' friends ask you how your exams are going and you tell them you have failed and you are glad, glad, glad. Your parents tell you not to be rude, and you've just been to see *If . . .* Your parents want a gin and tonic but you want a machine gun and the revolution, and you want them now.

Despite this, I guessed that Patricia had an intelligence and intensity my former persona would have enjoyed. I liked the fact that the one thing I wouldn't have said about her, even after only cursory inspection, was that she was serene. Long periods of inner investigation and deep breathing, or whatever therapy she practised, hadn't seemed to have cured her of irritability or incipient fury.

When she did look at me, with what I was afraid was some perception, I felt I would shrivel up. For the first time I felt that someone had seen me as an impostor, a fake, as not being what I seemed. The game was up, the pretence was over.

'What did you say your name was?' she asked.

'Leo Raphael Adams.'

She snorted. 'Arty, bohemian parents, eh?'

'I suppose so.'

'I probably knew them.'

'You didn't.'

'What did they do?'

'Lots of things.'

'Lots of things, eh?'

'They moved around a lot.'

'Good for them,' she said. 'What do you want to do?'

'Work here for a bit,' I replied. 'I'll do anything you want me to.'

'I should hope so. But don't pretend to take what I say literally, Leo, when you know I mean "in life".'

'In life? I don't know,' I said genuinely. 'I've no idea. Why do I have to "do" anything?'

65

She imitated me. 'Don't know. Don't care. Don't give a shit.'

I shaded my eyes, as if from the sun. 'Why do you keep staring at me?'

'Your blank face.'

I said, 'Is it blank? I've looked at it a lot and –'

'I can imagine, dear.'

'I've never thought of it as blank.'

'Is there one intelligent thought in there – something that will make me think, "I haven't heard that before"? I must have forgotten', she went on, 'that conversation isn't a male art.'

There was a lot I did want to say, but if I started on at her I wouldn't know what it was like to be young.

I said, 'You want me to leave.'

'Only if you want to.' She started to giggle. 'We don't usually have men working here, though there's no rule against it. I may be an old-style sixties feminist, and the self-esteem of women in a male world may be of interest, but it wasn't my intention to set up a nunnery. Your porky prick' – she looked directly at my crotch – 'will certainly put the cat among the pigeons. I think that will amuse me. You can stay . . . for a bit.'

'Thank you.'

Patricia went to the window, leaned out and yelled into the square.

'Alicia!' she called. 'Alicia!' Almost immediately, a girl appeared. 'Take him away,' she said. 'He's working here at the moment. Give him something to do!'

As I walked back, I was aware of someone beside me, as insubstantial and insistent as a shadow.

'I think I'll get out of here,' I said.

'Is that what you normally do – run?'

'If I'm feeling sensible.'

'Don't start getting sensible.'

I said, 'Something about me seemed to enrage her.'

'You take it personally?'

'I've decided to.'

'Why?'

'It made me wonder what sort of power I might have over her.'

'You'll never have any power over her.'

Alicia was not a girl, but a young woman from London, a frail poet with a squint and a roll-up in the corner of her mouth. She told me she had been staying at the Centre for three months, at the expense of an American benefactor, writing and teaching. Despite the relentless sunlight and the hunger for it of the other women, Alicia had not tanned. Her skin remained remorselessly 'Camden High Street in the rain', as I thought of it. She was to show me the roof of the Centre, where I would sleep. It was baking during the day and most likely cold at night, but it suited me, being secluded. I like the sky, though until now have lacked the time to 'commune' with it.

While I unpacked my few things, Alicia opened a spiral note-book, coughed her soul out, tore at her nails with her teeth, and asked whether I minded hearing her poetry.

'Why not?' I said. 'I haven't had any contact with poetry since I was at school.'

'Where were you at school?'

'All over the place.'

'Read anything?'

'Toilet walls.'

She warned me: her poetry was mostly about things.

'Things?'

She explained that even here, 'in the cradle of consecutive thought', the language of the New Age and of self-help, now beyond parody, had taken over the vocabulary of emotional feeling and exchange. If the language of the self was poisoned, it was disastrous for a poet. This was yet to happen to objects without souls, on which she had decided to concentrate her powers.

'Give me an example,' I said.

She began with a poem about kettles and toasters. I liked it, so she followed up with another about her Hoover, and with a further one about music systems, which was unfinished. When I asked her to go on, she told me what the others were to be about – carpets, beds, curtains – and requested suggestions for more.

I changed my shirt, a moment I always enjoyed, and said I thought one about windows would be good.

'Windows?' she said. 'What are you talking about?'

'What's wrong with windows?'

She explained that it was 'too poetic' a subject. Quoting John Cage, she said she was interested in the 'white' emotions rather than the 'black' ones. She needed to get past the 'black' ones to the 'white' ones.

'D'you see?'

'Not a word of it. Me, I'm only the cleaner.'

'That's who I'm writing for. Cleaners and crooks – I mean cooks. Some poems open only for the ignorant.'

'I must be your man, then.'

She was looking at me. Her face was pale but unmarked, as though her despair had neglected to invade it. Yet now, one of her eyes was twitching like a trapped butterfly. I wanted to go to her and press my finger against it. But maybe I would have just pulled it off and torn it to pieces. The poor girl must have fallen in love at that moment.

The work I had to do at the Centre was hard. My body was uncomplaining – it liked being stretched and exerted – but my mind kicked up a fuss. In a life devoted to myself, it had been years since I'd been forced to do anything against my will. I'd always been reasonably successful at getting women to look after me. Now I helped with the cooking; it was good to learn to cook. I emptied the bins and carried heavy sacks of food from the vans; I was taught how to build a wall. I swept, cleaned and painted the rooms. I guessed that this was what the world was like for most people, and it didn't harm me to be reminded of it.

I came to appreciate the simplest things. I grew a beard and learned t'ai chi, yoga and how to play a drum. I swam long distances, sunbathed, read, and listened to the women at meal times and at night, just hanging around them, as I had my mother as a child. I cultivated a reputation for shyness and silence. I might have been a beauty, but direct attention was the last thing I craved. Sometimes I would massage the women, singing to myself. One time, I saw one of the group lying under a tree reading my last play, which was produced five years ago. As I walked past her, I said, 'Any good?'

'The play's not as good as the film.'

I had begun to love the beauty of the island and the peace it gave me. I was almost free of the desire to understand. Agitation and passion seemed less necessary as proofs of life. I wondered whether, when I returned to my old body, my values would be different. I had been certain that I wanted to go back, but it was a question that wouldn't leave me alone now. There were decent arguments on both sides. What could have been worse? I would put it off for as long as possible.

Patricia usually appeared at breakfast and made a speech about the purpose and aims of the Centre. Once, she told us one of her dreams; then she interpreted it, to prevent any misunderstanding. There was an impressed silence, before she swept away. She uttered few words in my direction but she always looked hard at me as if we were connected in some way, as if she were about to speak. I supposed she looked at everyone like this, now and again, to make them feel part of her community. I no longer believed she understood me, but did I make her particularly curious? She seemed to say: what do you really want? It agitated me. I kept away from her but she remained in my mind, like a question.

Patricia's workshops were the most popular and intense, and

always full. However, as Alicia told me in confidence, they were known more for the quantity of tears shed than for the quality of wisdom transmitted. But I was only a kitchen skivvy and took no part. Taking my father's advice, I was on a working holiday.

Ten days after I'd started, Patricia came into the kitchen, where I laboured under the regime of an old Greek woman with whom I could barely communicate. I'd never seen Patricia in the kitchen before. Like the obdurate adolescent I wanted her to see me as, I refused to meet her look. She had to tell me to stop peeling potatoes.

'Just stop now.'

'Patricia, I wouldn't feel good about leaving half a potato.'

'To hell with potatoes! I am about to begin my dream workshop with the new group. I've decided that it's time you joined us.'

'Me? Why?'

'I think you should learn something.'

'Oh, I don't want to learn. I had years of it and nothing went in, as you pointed out.' She looked hurt, so I said, 'What kind of thing is it?'

She sighed. 'We free-associate around people's dreams. We might write around them, or paint or draw. Or even dance. I've seen you shake your butt, at the disco. The girls were certainly intrigued, as they are when you parade around the place with your shirt off. But you keep away from the workshop members, don't you?'

'It goes without saying.'

'Even that idiot with the ghost?'

'Ah, yes,' I said. 'That damned ghost.'

The ghost always cheered Patricia up.

One of the women who'd recently come to the Centre and been allocated a room in town, as some people were, had stood up at breakfast and told us her room was haunted. Typically, Patricia imagined this was a ruse for the woman to be moved to a superior room with a sea view – not something Patricia could offer or fall for. Instead of moving her, Patricia had deputed me to sit, all night, in the doorway of the woman's room, keeping an eye out for the revenant.

'Watching for ghosts is one of your duties,' Patricia had said to me, barely containing her delight. 'When the bastard turns up, you deal with it.'

'Such work wasn't in my original job description,' I said. 'And do ghosts use doors?'

'Get lost and do it. Ghosts use all orifices.'

I had told Alicia, 'Wait 'til they hear this back in London – that I've been employed on a ghost-watch.'

That night, I'd stayed awake as long as I could but had, of course, fallen asleep in the chair. The ghosts came. Nothing with a sheet over its head bothered me, but my own internal shades and shadows, by far the most hideous, had become mightily busy. The woman I guarded slept well. By morning, I was in a cold sweat with rings the colour of coal under my eyes. The women at the Centre, when they weren't being solicitous, found they hadn't laughed as much since they'd arrived.

'Particularly not with the ghost-woman,' I said now to Patricia.

'Good. You're not included in the price of the holiday.' She went on, 'Now, come along. People pay hundreds of pounds to participate. I want you to see what goes on here. Tell me. Surely you don't believe that only the rational is real, or that the real is always rational, do you?'

'I haven't thought much about it.'

'Liar!'

'Why say that?'

'There's more to you than you let on! How many kids your age whistle tunes from *Figaro* while they're peeling potatoes?'

She strode out, expecting me to follow her, but I'm not the sort to follow anyone, particularly if they want me to.

I looked at the old Greek woman, washing the kitchen floor. This was the kind of reality I was adjusted to: getting a patch of earth the way you want it while thinking of nothing.

However, I left the kitchen and, outside, went up the steps. In the large, bright room, I could see that Patricia, along with the rest of the class, had been waiting for me.

She pointed at the floor. 'Sit down, then we'll start.'

Around the group she went, soliciting dreams. What a proliferation of imagination, symbolism and word-play there was in such an ordinary group of people! I stayed for over an hour, at which point there was a break. Breathing freely at last, I hurried out into the heat. I kept going and didn't return, but went into town, where I had provisions to buy for the Centre.

When I returned, Alicia was waiting under a tree outside, with her notebook. She stood up and waved in my face.

'Leo, where have you been?'

'Shopping.'

'You've caused a terrible fuss. You can't walk out on Patricia like that,' she said. 'I kind of admire it. I like it when people are driven to leave my lessons. I know there's something pretty powerful going on. I don't like poetry to be helpful. But we masochists are drawn to Patricia. We do what she says. We never, ever leave her sessions.'

'I had work to do,' I said. I wasn't prepared to say that I had left Patricia's workshop because it had upset me. Dreams had always fascinated me; in London, I wrote mine down, and Margot and I often discussed dreams over breakfast.

My dream on the 'ghost-watch' had been this: I was to see my dead parents again, for a final conversation. When I met them – and they had their heads joined together at one ear, making one interrogative head – they failed to recognize me. I tried to explain how I had come to look different, but they were outraged by my claims to be myself. They turned away and walked

72

into eternity before I could convince them – as if I ever could – of who I really was.

The other dream was more of an image: of a man in a white coat with a human brain in his hands, crossing a room between two bodies, each with its skull split open, on little hinges. As he carried the already rotting brain, it dripped. Bits of memory, desire, hope and love, encased in skin-like piping, fell onto the sawdust floor where hungry dogs and cats lapped them up.

Much as I would have liked to, I couldn't even begin to talk about this with the group. My 'transformation' had isolated me. As Ralph could have pointed out, it was the price I had to pay.

I couldn't either, of course, say this to Alicia, who had become my only real friend at the Centre. She came from a bohemian family. Her father had died in her early teens. At fifteen, her mother took her to live in a sex-crazed commune. It had made her 'frigid'. She felt as neglected as a starving child. Now, she overlooked herself, eating little but carrying around a bag of carrots, apples or bananas which she'd chop into little pieces with a penknife and devour piece by piece. She only ever ate her own food, and, I noticed, would only eat alone or in front of me.

In the evenings, she and I had begun to talk. Twice a week there were parties for the Centre participants. The drinking and dancing were furious. The women had the determined energy of the not quite defeated. They liked Tamla Motown and Donna Summer; I liked the ballet of their legs kicking in their long skirts. After, it was my job to clear away the glasses, sweep the floor, empty the ashtrays and get the Centre ready for breakfast. I did it well; cleanliness had become like a poem to me. A cigarette butt was a slap in the face. Alicia liked to help me, on her knees, late at night, as the others sat up, confessing.

Alicia had begun to write stories and the beginning of a novel, which she showed me. I thought about what she was doing and commented on it when I thought I could be helpful. I liked being useful; I could see how her confidence failed at times.

In the late evenings, when I'd finished work, sometimes we went to the beach. We'd walk past couples who'd left the bars and discos to copulate in the darkness: French, German, Scandinavian, Dutch bodies, attempting, it seemed, to strangle the life out of one another. Our business seemed more important, to talk about literature. Sex was everywhere; good words were less ubiquitous.

Since my mid-twenties, I'd taught both literature and writing at various universities and usually had a writing workshop in London. I'd been interested by how people got to speak, and to speak up, for themselves, and by the effect this had on all their relationships. When it came to Alicia, some sort of instruction was something I fell into naturally, and liked.

Nevertheless, I tried to speak in young tones, as if I knew only a little; and I tried not to be pompous, as I must have been in my old body. It was quite an effort. I was used to people listening or even writing down what I said. The pomposity was useful, for emphasis, and my authority could seem liberating to some people. Alicia seemed to like the authority I was able to muster, at times. Being older could be useful.

I had to be wary, too, of this thin, anxious girl. If she was the reason I didn't leave, when she asked me about myself and my education I was evasive, as if I didn't quite believe my own stories, or, in the end, couldn't be bothered with them, which frustrated her. She wanted more of me. I could see she knew I was holding a lot back.

'What have you been writing?' I asked now, as we walked.

'A poem about windows.'

'Everyone knows poems and windows don't go together.'

'They'll have to get along,' she said. 'Like us.' Then she said, 'Hurry, you've got to go and see Patricia.'

'Now? Is she angry with me?'

74

She squeezed my hand. 'I think so.'

Her fear increased mine. I was reminded of all kinds of past transgressions and terrors: of my mother's furies, of being sent to the headmistress to be smacked on the hand with a ruler. In my youth, all sorts of people were allowed to hit you, and were even praised for doing it; they didn't thank you if you returned the compliment. Now, as numerous other fears arose, I went into such a spin it took me several moments to remember I was called Leo Adams. I could choose to behave differently, to revise the past, as it were, and not be the scared boy I was then.

'Come on,' I said. 'Walk with me.'

'Aren't you afraid of her?' Alicia asked.

'Terrified.'

'I am, too. Are you going to leave?'

'Well, I don't see why I shouldn't.'

'Please don't.' She went on, 'But there is something else, too. She heard your joke.'

'She did? She didn't mention it to me.'

'She might now, perhaps.'

'How did it get round?'

She blushed. 'These things just do.'

A few days ago I had made a joke, which is not a good idea in institutions. It was not a great joke, but it was on the spot and had made Alicia suddenly laugh in recognition. I had called the Centre a 'weepeasy'. I used the word several times, as we young people tend to, and that was that. It had entered the bloodstream of the institution.

Now, we walked through the village to Patricia's. The shops were closed; the place was deserted. Most people were having their siestas, as was Patricia at this time, usually.

Outside Patricia's, Alicia said she'd wait for me under a tree across the square.

I knocked on the door, and Patricia's irritable face appeared at the window. I'm glad to say I always annoyed Patricia; by being alive at all, I failed her. On this occasion, to my dismay, she brightened.

She had come to the door wearing only a wrap-around skirt. Her large brown breasts were hanging down.

'My,' I said, and then blushed. I knew she'd heard it as 'mine'. I went on, 'Patricia, there's something I need to talk to you about.'

'I'm glad you've come, Oddjob,' she said. 'I've got some work for you. Why did you leave my workshop?'

'I wanted to think about it.'

'Did you enjoy it, then?' When I nodded, she said, 'If so, how much? Very, very much? Just very much? Quite a lot? Or something else?'

'Let me think about that, Patricia.' She was looking at me. I said, 'I did like it, in fact.'

'If you did really, you can say why – in your own words.'

I said, 'You used the dream, not as a puzzle to be solved, with all the anxiety of that, as if one of us would get it right, but as a felt image, to generate thoughts, or other images. That was useful. I haven't stopped thinking.'

'That's a good thing to say.' She was flattered and pleased. 'You see, you can be almost articulate, if you really want to be. By the way, I heard what you called the Centre. Weepeasy,' she said. 'Right?'

'Sorry,' I said, bowing my head.

'Is that what you think?'

'It's easy to make people cry.' I went on, 'Confession, not irony, is the modern mode. A halting speech at Alcoholics Anonymous is the paradigm. But what concealments and deceptions are there in this exhibition of self-pity? Isn't it tedious for you?'

'There's no rigour here any more, you could be right. Or any progress. It's become the same every day. I can tell you, that's the least of it.' Then she said, 'Please, come here.'

'Sorry?'

'Here!' I shuffled forward. She put her arms around me and pressed her breasts into my body. 'I am feeling tense today. I wanted to run a centre for self-exploration, only to discover I'd started a small business. You can't explore anything if you don't get the figures right – the eighties taught some women that, at least. Now I'm sick of being an accountant and I'm sick of being wise. Sometimes, I only want to be mad.'

'Yeah,' I said. 'Being the wise woman must be a right bore.'

'Who takes care of me? I have to mother everyone! You've been attending the massage class, haven't you? You know how to do it.'

By now, she was pulling at my fingers.

'Patricia –'

'Massage me, Leo, you dear boy. There's the oil.'

'I want to talk about Alicia.'

'Who wants to hear about that funny little thing? Oh, talk, talk about what you want, as long as you smooth out my soul.'

Her skirt dropped to the floor. She walked across the room, located the oil, and lay down on a towel on her low bed.

She was watching me scratch my stomach. There were certain conversations I'd missed in this new life. You might have a new body but if your mind is burdened the differences doesn't count for much.

'Go on,' she said.

I told her how Alicia had got sweet on me and that I was concerned about it. I emphasized that I hadn't deliberately led her on.

Of course, I loved the attention of the women at the Centre – who didn't, admittedly, have much else to look at – and had walked around barefoot, wearing only shorts. Celibacy had increased my desire; I wanted to live less in my mind. I remember Margot telling me, years ago, this thing about certain school phobics. Some boys, of particularly disturbed sexuality, imagined that their bodies had turned into penises. The dreaded school was their mother's forbidden body. I was all sex, a walking prick, a penis with an appended body. I didn't flirt; I was unprovocative. I didn't need to do anything.

In my mad mind, I became a kind of performer. Many of my friends have been actors, singers or dancers, men and women who used their bodies in the service of art, or as art itself; people who were looked at for a living. Those of us who cannot perform, who imagine from the audience only an examination of our faults, can have little idea of the relationship between player and voyeur, of how the audience, like a sea of feeling, might hold you up, if you can use it. What do you see and hear out there in all that blackness? What are the watchers doing to you? What was the stripper or any celebrity doing but increasing and controlling envy and desire? This was a splendidly erotic activity, it seemed to me.

It had been years since I had danced, and now, since I didn't need much sleep, I danced every night in one or other of the town's discos, with women from the Centre. Most of them were older than forty, some were over fifty. They knew the chances of their being loved, caressed, wanted, was diminishing, even as their passion increased, in the sun. I danced with them, but I didn't touch them. If I'd been a 'real' kid, I probably would have gone to bed, or to the beach, with several of them. I was their pornography, a cunt teaser. But at least everyone knew where they stood with me.

Usually, while I danced, Alicia watched me, or sat on a chair drinking and smoking. She never danced herself, but took a lot of pleasure in others' enjoyment. Oddly enough, the music most people preferred originated in my day: 1950s rock 'n' roll, and 1960s soul. I knew every note. It sounded fresher and more lasting than the laboured literary work of me and my contemporaries.

In one of the town's discos, while dancing with my 'coven', as

I called them, several of the local men started to taunt me. They didn't like this spoiled kid dancing with and hugging these happy women night after night, as well as looking after their bags, fetching them drinks and making sure they all got safely back to the Centre. One night, they gathered around me at the bar and said they wanted to see what sort of man I was. They could find this out only on the beach, where we would be able to have 'a good talk'. Alicia and the other women had to escort me out of there in a group. Looking back, I could see the men standing at the door, smoking and sneering.

Why did this happen? How did they see me? I enquired of Alicia. As someone who had everything, and a future, too. There was nothing I couldn't do or be, she seemed to think. They hated it and wanted it. They could have killed and eaten me.

There were other fantasies about me. A woman in her fifties had told Alicia that I made the women feel inadequate. I was a problem-free rich kid bumming around the world before going to work for a bank. 'We're trying to restart our troubled lives here. He's just passing through,' she said.

'Maybe that is what you are,' Alicia continued, after she'd told me, throwing down her roll-up and rubbing out the stub with her sandal. 'You have the confidence, poise and sense of entitlement of a rich kid. Isn't that right?'

I didn't answer; I didn't know what to say. I hadn't anticipated this much envy. I had, though, known actors who'd become movie stars and been made paranoid and withdrawn as much because of the pressure of imagined spite as that of fame.

I laboured over Patricia's crumpled and folded flesh, humming and thinking. I was good at this; at least I'd learned to love giving comfort and pleasure.

I said, 'How can I deal with this? I am beginning to feel like an object. It is not pleasant, it's persecution.'

'You are supremely enviable,' she said, her voice muffled by the towel. 'You're like the woman everyone wants but no one understands. What you require is support and protection.'

'Who from?'

'That is up to you. But you must ask for it.' She went on, 'It doesn't sound as if you've done the wrong thing, Oddjob. You've made her and some of the others love-sick but you haven't misled anyone. You're a good lad. Women of Alicia's age – they'd fall in love with a plank of wood.'

I was working hard at Patricia's body. To my dismay, as I punched and pummelled, she didn't seem to relax, but began breathing harder.

She turned, put out her hands and untied the string which held up my trousers.

'Please, Patricia,' I said. 'Don't –'

She was holding my penis. 'That's a mighty fine thing you've got there. Know how to use it?'

'No, I guess you could show me.'

'You haven't slept with Alicia?'

'That's right.'

'You're a good boy, then. Now, be an even better boy for me.'

Her eyes were glazed with desire.

I said, 'I thought you were supposed to be a wise woman?'

'Even the wise need a prick now and again. You've been fluttering your eyelashes at me for days, don't think I haven't noticed. I'm very intuitive. Now, can you follow through?'

I didn't want to disappoint her; I didn't want her to feel her age or resent me.

Her hands were rough, and at one point I wondered whether she might be wearing gloves. I remembered that for exercise she liked to build stone walls. But, to my surprise, I became excited.

Her noises were honest and forthright. I was sitting facing her. We were rocking. I must have been holding my breath. 'Breathe, breathe,' she ordered. I did what she said. She went on. 'Relax and breathe from your stomach, that way you'll hold out longer.'

It worked, of course. When I'd relaxed, she said, 'Now, continue.'

Patricia howled, 'Adore me, adore me, you little shit!'; she dug her fingers into me, scratched and kicked me, and, when she came, thrust her tongue into my mouth until I almost gagged.

'I needed that,' she said at last. She was lying on the bed, legs apart, almost steaming. 'Dear boy, do fetch me a glass of water.'

I took it to her.

'Thanks, Oddjob. A job well done, eh?'

I sat on the end of the bed and said, 'Now you'll be able to give an orgasm workshop.'

'You know,' she said, 'a lot of the women here think you're a haughty little kid. I don't mind that. I like it. I could humble you, you know.'

'Thank you, Patricia,' I said. 'I think you just have. I'd better go now.'

'One more thing,' she said.

Patricia opened her legs and, from the end of the bed, had me look at her masturbate busily. At times her entire hand seemed to disappear into her body, as if she were about to turn herself inside out.

'Bet you haven't seen that before,' she murmured.

'No,' I said sourly. 'One lives and learns.'

She was about to fall asleep. She waved me away, but not before saying, 'You come back here tonight. Bring your things. Everything will be better if you come and live here.'

'Why would that be?'

'This is the best room in the village. See you tonight!'

I scurried away across the square. Alicia called after me, caught me up and put her arm through mine.

'You're still here?'

'But why not?'

'Alicia, I'm on my way to the beach.'

'Are you okay? Can't I come with you?'

I didn't like to make her run behind me, but I needed to wash myself. I knew she was still there because she was shouting out poems – not her own – as we went, to remind me of the good things.

I stripped off and ran into the sea. I swam and jogged on the beach until I was exhausted. I lay down next to her with the sun on me. Soon, I'd dozed off. When I opened my eyes, she was sitting there wearing just a cigarette, her arms hugging her knees. Unlike the other women at the Centre, she never removed her clothes but always wore a long-sleeved top and ankle-length skirt.

'What is it?'

She said, 'You slept with her.' Her hands shook as she drew on her cigarette. 'Everyone in this hemisphere will have heard.'

'But you didn't cover your ears.'

'I listened to your music. Every note.'

'What will you do with what you heard? Write about it – or is it too human for you?'

'If that was all I was capable of, I'd hate myself!' She took my hand and placed it on her foot. 'Will you look at me? We can't have sex. You don't want to. Perhaps you've had more than enough for today. I have never had an orgasm, and I am a virgin. Touch me, if you feel like it.' She lay back. 'Would you?'

After my earlier experience, I couldn't claim to be erotically absorbed. I did begin to rub her with the palms of my hands; then, when I began to stroke her with my fingers and her eyes closed, my mind began to wander.

'I need to borrow this.'

I took her notebook and pen, and began to make an inventory of what I found on her flesh. I did this, as they say on television, in no particular order. I went to what interested me.

The first thing I noticed was a light brown eyelash on her throat, one of her own. On her forehead there was one hard spot and one pus-filled, with several others under the skin. Her hair looked as though it had been dyed a while ago; parts of it had been bleached by the sun. It was hard to make out its original colour. Her lips were a little ribbed and sore, the bottom more than the top.

I found a purplish bruise, recent, on her side where, perhaps, she had knocked into a table. On her knees there were three little childhood scars. I ran my fingers along the still-livid scar where, I guessed, she'd had her gall-bladder removed. She had five painted toenails, all chipped, and five, on the other foot, unpainted: I guess she must have got bored. There was a lot of sand, mostly dry, between her toes, on the soles of her feet and instep.

She wore cheap silver ear-rings, but I didn't feel she was interested in personal adornment. One ear lobe was slightly inflamed. I also found a leaf on her leg, several insects, dead and alive, in different places, and dirt on her leg. The skin around her fingernails had been pulled and torn. Her cheap watch told the wrong time. Her teeth seemed good; perhaps she had worn a brace as a child, but they were stained, now, from smoking, and one was chipped. There were random and quite deep scratch-marks on one arm (left), which I had noticed before but hadn't attended to. They appeared to have been done with an insufficiently sharp object – a penknife, say, rather than a razor-blade – as if she'd decided to doodle on herself on the spur of the moment, without preparing.

I peered into her ears and mouth, between her legs and then her toes, where I discovered another insect; I looked up her nose – surprisingly hairless, compared to mine. On her chest she had scored what I guessed to be the word 'poet'. On her thigh, there were other words which had been recently bleeding.

I wrote, in the fatuous modern manner, 'This is a Person in the Here and Now Lying Down', and jotted it down, forensically, working in silence for an hour. I kept the dead insects, the leaf, a couple of pubic hairs, an example of the dirt, a smear of blood and vaginal mucus, and a record of the words, inside her note-book. Mostly her eyes were closed, her breaths deep and long.

I awoke her from her 'dream', and showed her what I'd been doing.

'No one's ever done a nicer thing for me,' she said.

'Pleasure.'

'You said to me once, what people want is to be known. Can I ask you: what is that scar you have?'

'What scar? Where?'

She looked at me as though I were stupid, before pointing it out to me. It was under my elbow, in the soft flesh.

'You don't know what it is?'

'I probably do,' I said, irritably. 'I don't even remember where I got it.'

'You don't want to know yourself. You don't know yourself as well as you know me. I don't understand that. If you knew your-self you wouldn't have done what you did with that woman.'

'I don't see why we have to know either ourselves or each other.'

'But what else is there?'

'Enjoying each other.'

'Knowing is enjoying, for me.'

These were the sort of wrangles we liked. After, we walked back in silence.

I noticed, out at sea, a large yacht with little boats carrying pro-visions out to it. I'd forgotten that everyone from the Centre had been invited to a party on it that evening. I hadn't taken much notice at the time, but there were numerous rumours about the owner. He was either a gangster, film producer or computer mag-nate. I wasn't sure which was considered to be worse. I was sur-prised when Patricia announced at breakfast that we were all going. I was intending to miss it; I couldn't see that Patricia would even notice my absence. How things had changed since then!

Hadn't she said to me, a couple of hours ago, 'See you tonight!'

I couldn't defy Patricia and remain at the Centre. If I was going to leave, I'd have to know where I was going.

I said goodbye to Alicia and went to the roof to think. I discovered myself to be even more furious than before about what Patricia had done to me, and furious with myself for having failed to escape untouched. I would insist on sleeping alone tonight, and leave for Athens by the first boat. I packed my bags in readiness. I was young; I could run.

## 5

I went to eat in a taverna in town, reading at the table. After a few pages, I thought 'I can do this.' I pulled some paper from my rucksack and started on a story, which offered itself to me. It was something seen, or apprehended as a whole – almost visual – which I felt forced to find words for. My hands were shaking; without literature I couldn't think, and felt stifled by a swirl of thoughts which took me nowhere new. But writing and the intricacies of its solitude was a habit I needed to break in order to stray from myself. Some artists, in their later life, become so much themselves, they go their own way, that they are no longer open to influence, to being changed or even touched by anyone else, and their work takes on the nature of obsession. Margot once said to me, 'When you think or feel something important, instead of saying it, you write it down. I'd love it to rain on your computer!'

It did. I put away my pen and paper, paid, and left.

At the Centre the voices, usually so quietly fervent, were almost raucous. Everyone, apart from Patricia, who had yet to appear, had gathered in colourful skirts, dresses and wraps. Some wore bells on their ankles; many wore bras. The night air, invariably sweet, vibrated with clashing female perfumes; jewellery flashed and jingled. Excitement about the party on the yacht was so high that some people were already dancing.

I was wearing my usual shorts and white T-shirt. I'd bought this body because I liked it as it was, a pure fashion item which didn't require elaboration.

I laughed when I saw that Alicia had attempted to comb her hair, making it look even more frizzy. With the light behind her, she looked as though she had a halo. She also wore lipstick, which I'd never seen on her. It was as if she were trying out being 'a woman'.

'I was afraid you wouldn't come,' she said.

'Me too,' I replied.

'We're on the trip, then.'

'Looks like it.'

Our singularity made us both seem insubordinate, as if we were refusing to enter into the spirit of the evening, which was how, to my regret, I'd been as a young man – rebellion as affectation. Not that anyone seemed to notice. With the arrival of Princess Patricia in a long tie-dyed skirt and with flowers in her hair, the party became impossible to resist.

At Patricia's entrance, I said to Alicia, 'I didn't realize we were attending a film première!'

After posing in the door until everyone became silent and took her in, she came to me, kissed me on the lips, patted my face, licked her lips, and refused to acknowledge Alicia.

'Are we ready?'

She held my arm and pulled me along, telling the others to follow. It was clear: she wanted to go on the cruise because she wanted to show me off.

Patricia and I led what became a kind of procession through the village to the beach. The old men, sitting at café tables watching us pass, seemed not only to be from another era, but appeared to be another kind of species altogether.

86

On the beach, where other foreigners from the island were gathering, a band greeted us. In the distance, the yacht, the only bright thing in the dark ocean, glittered beneath the emerging stars. Despite Patricia's attention, I was glad to be there.

Small boats carried us to the yacht. Patricia sat beside me, holding my hand. 'I've been walking on air ever since our love-making. You were just what I needed.' She kept leaning across me.

'Patricia . . .' I was going to tell her, coyly, that I didn't want things to 'move along' too quickly. 'I think we –'

She interrupted me. 'You didn't even get changed,' she said. 'Hold still, then. Let me put this in.' She was fiddling with my ear. 'Now we have matching ear-rings.' She patted my face, sat back and looked at me.

I touched my ear. 'Oh, yes,' I said, perplexed. 'I must have forgotten I'd had it pierced.'

'There are several holes. What a funny boy you are,' she said. 'I've watched you dancing. You do it wonderfully. You must have trained somewhere.'

'I did.'

'Where?' She went on, 'Will you dance with me all night?'

'Not all night, Patricia.'

She took my hand and slipped it between her thighs. 'Most of it, then, darling boy.'

We were helped from the boat onto the yacht. The owner, Matte, an excitable young man, greeted us on deck.

'Thank you, Patricia, for bringing your crew! You are all welcome!' he said. He waved at the women following us. 'Come along, girls! Let's get down!'

As we looked around the boat, Strauss's *Also sprach Zarathustra* in the von Karajan version began playing. I adore Richard Strauss, but am ready to admit how much great music has been turned into kitsch. Where is there to turn for something that sounds fresh today, except to the new or weird? You couldn't turn Bartók's quartets or Webern's meditations into easy listening.

Oddly, though, the Strauss didn't seem only sententious. Against the sea and sky, in this place, and taken by surprise – which, it seems to me, is often the best way to hear music; walking into a shop one Saturday morning and hearing Callas; tricked into amazement – it thrilled and uplifted me again.

This was what I, as a young man, would have wanted.

Food, drink and sexual possibility appeared to be limitless. Matte's uniformed staff walked about with trays, some of which held sex toys and condoms. There was a disco and a band. Those people already there appeared to be British, American and European playboys, models, actors, singers, pleasure-seekers, indolent aristocrats. There were also people that even I recognized from the British newspapers, pop stars and their partners, and actors from soap operas. These were people with groovy sunglasses and ideal bodies – I guessed that different parts of their bodies were of different ages and materials – who made it clear they had seen all this before, and liked being looked at.

Alicia nudged me. 'Someone's staring at you.'

A young woman was indeed looking at me. I smiled, and received a timid wave.

'As always, you're popular,' said Alicia. 'Can I ask who it is?'

'I don't know. She looks like a movie star.'

'You know movie stars?'

'Of course not, but they all know me.' I returned the woman's wave. 'Come on.'

We all strolled around. Patricia seemed to be doing a fine impression of Princess Margaret in her heyday. Alicia and I, at least, weren't sure whether to resist or swoon at the sight of so much gold. Alicia said she liked the way English Londoners were sneery and hated to be credulous, whereas I now found that tedious. This time round I wanted to like things.

When, for a moment, Alicia went to fetch a drink, the 'film

star' who'd waved earlier covered herself up and hurried over.

'How funny to meet you here,' she said, kissing me.

I kissed her back; I had to. But I was afraid she'd known me as 'Mark'; perhaps we'd been 'married'. I vowed that when I next saw Ralph I would put an end to his immortality.

'Don't you know me?'

I looked at her until a picture came into my mind. It was of an old woman in a wheelchair wearing a pink flannel night-gown. This woman and I had become Newbodies on the same day. We were, in a sense, the same age.

I said, 'Good to see you. How are you enjoying it?'

'I don't know. Wherever I go, people try to touch or have me. If I don't comply, they're nasty. Still,' she said, 'I wouldn't have men fighting over me if I were a pile of ash.'

'Oh, I don't know. What else will you do?'

'I've got a record contract,' she said. 'And you?'

'It's strange, like being a ghost.'

She glanced around. 'I know. Relax now. There are others here like us. Everyone else is so silly and blind.'

'How many others like us?'

I looked at the faces and bodies behind her. How would I know who was who?

'More than you think. We play tennis and we stay up late at cards, talking about our lives. We have plenty of time, you see. Like pop stars and royalty, we stick together.'

I thought of them, the beauties around a table together, like moving statues, an art work.

I said, 'Soon, everyone in the world will know.'

'Oh, yes, I think so. Does it matter? Come and talk to me later.' She was looking down at her feet. 'Do you love your body now?'

'Why shouldn't I?'

'I'm a little too tall and my waist is too thick. My feet are big. Overall, I'm not comfortable.'

She left when Alicia rejoined me. 'You say you don't know that woman. Will you go with her now?'

'Go where? I don't know what you're talking about.'

'You can if you want,' Alicia said. 'There is time. We've set sail.'

'Set sail for where?'

Alicia was laughing at me. 'I don't know. But I do know that setting sail is what boats tend to do. We're on here until dawn.'

I ran to the side of the boat. We were already in motion. It hadn't occurred to me that I wouldn't be able to escape at any time. I considered jumping into the sea, but wasn't convinced I could swim so far. Anyway, Patricia was beside me straight away. She seemed to be insisting that I stay beside her all night. Not only at her side, in fact, but within touching distance.

She was rubbing my shoulders. 'I've never seen anything like you. I've never wanted anyone so much. I'd never have given myself permission to touch someone like you before.' Her fist was somewhere in my head. 'Where did you get that hair?'

I almost said, 'I saw it in a fridge and bought it, along with everything else you like about me.' I wondered whether that would matter. Now, at least, I knew something. The world is different for the beautiful. They're desired, oh yes; other bodies are all over them. But they don't necessarily like them.

'Come and see this,' Patricia said, without a glance at Alicia. 'A young man will be interested.'

I followed her through the boat to a cabin door. She pushed it. The room within was almost completely dark.

I stepped in. It took a couple of minutes for my eyes to adjust. There must have been about thirty naked people in the room, with a greater proportion of men than women. In a corner, there were Goyaesque mounds of bodies, lost in one another. It was difficult to tell which limb belonged to which body. I wondered whether some of the limbs had become independent of selves, turning into creatures in their own right, arms dancing with legs, perhaps, and torsos alone. There was music, talking, and – a lonely noise – the sound of others' pleasure.

Patricia tugged at my shirt. 'Let's join in.'

'I'm feeling queasy,' I said. 'I'm not used to the . . . motion.'

'Where are you going?'

I hurried through the rooms, corridors and decks of the boat, looking for somewhere she wouldn't find me for a while. For ages I heard her calling my name.

I found a small cabin. Candles were burning; the music was North African. There were oriental cushions, wall hangings, rugs, a lot of velvet. The style amused me, reminding me of the 1960s.

I liked the boat. Why couldn't I get work as a deckhand? But I was annoyed at having to leave the Centre, where I had expected to spend the rest of my time in this body. But I had got in too far with the people there. It was no longer restful. Whatever happened tonight, I would leave the island in the morning, taking the first boat wherever it went. I would go to another island and find a job in a bar or disco.

I heard footsteps. It wasn't Patricia, but Matte, the owner of the yacht, in shorts, bright shirt and flip-flops.

'What the fuck are you doing in here?'

'Am I in the wrong place?' I got up. 'You forgot to set aside a quiet room. It was chaotic and I needed to get away.'

He walked right up to me and stared into my eyes. 'Always ask first.'

I said, 'If I had a room, it'd be like this. The mid-sixties has always been one of my favourite periods.'

'Right. Want a glass of wine now?'

'If that's okay. We were introduced, but in case you've forgotten, the name's Leo.'

He said, 'Matte. Why would someone your age be interested in the sixties?'

'Must be something to do with my parents. And you?'

He was fixing drinks for both of us. 'Those days people knew how to have a laugh. 'Cept I was the wrong age.'

His manner of speaking gave me the impression that English wasn't his first language, but it was impossible to tell where he was from. I'd have been inclined to say, if asked, 'from nowhere'.

'Was this your father's boat?'

His body stiffened. 'Why the hell should it be?'

'I'm asking, is it a family possession?'

He said, 'I hate it when people suggest I haven't worked, that I'm only a rich playboy. I do play at things – I play at being a playboy – but it's a vacation, not a vocation.'

'Sorry,' I said. 'You wouldn't be the first to think of me as a fool. I'll get out.'

He came after me and pulled me back roughly. 'Wait right here. You have to stay now.'

'Why?'

'I recognize you from somewhere.'

'How could we have met? I'm neither a teacher nor student, only a cleaner at the Centre on the island.'

'Ever been a builder?'

'No.'

'Coach driver?'

'Nope.'

'I have seen you,' he continued, screwing up his eyes. 'It's not your face that I particularly recognize.' He walked round me then, as if I were a sculpture. 'It'll come back to me.'

'Are you sure?'

'I might look like a hairy idiot but I've got perfect vision and an excellent memory.'

He was making me nervous, more nervous, even, than Patricia. He chopped out some generous lines of coke and offered me one.

'Thanks,' I said.

He was snorting one himself when there was a knock on the door. It was one of his Thai staff. Matte went to him and then, to my surprise, turned to me.

'I'm being told that someone called Patricia is looking for you.'

'Oh, Christ.'

Matte laughed, and said to the man, 'He can't be found any-where at the moment. He's indisposed.' He shut the door. 'She's after you, eh? Wants your body.'

'Maybe I should appreciate her appreciation more. There'll be a time when no one will want to jump my old bones.'

'The one thing I've never wanted is to get old, to see your own skin blotted and withered.'

'Why is that?'

'I'm from a big family. As a kid, I hated grandmothers, aunts, old men and women kissing me. Their lips, mouths, breath over me – makes me nearly lose me lunch to think of it.'

I said, 'I remember my grandmother's cheeks and hands, her cardigan, her smell, with nothing but love. She had learned things, which made me feel safe. Anyhow, you haven't been old yet. How do you know you won't like it?'

'I haven't died yet. Or visited Northampton. I just know they won't agree with me.'

He kept looking at me as though there was something he wanted to know or ask me.

I said, 'I'll only be here a minute. All I want to do is relax.'

'You do that. I've got a party to run.'

'Right.'

Somewhat self-consciously, I turned to look out at the dark sea, hoping that when I turned back he'd be gone. I heard him lock the door. Before I could speak, I was hit, and lost my bearings.

Instinctively, I imagined Matte had struck me from behind, smashing his fist onto the back of my head with some strength. That was how it felt. But he had encircled my neck with his arm, kicked my legs away and forced me to my knees. I thought: now he's going to shoot me in the back of the head. During this I recalled, incorrectly I hope, a line from Webster: 'Of all the deaths, a violent one is best.'

'What are you doing?'

'Leo, shut it! If you keep still I won't damage you.'

'Keep still for what?'

He was searching in my hair, not unlike the way I would grab my kids and examine their heads for nits. I said, 'I never had you down for a madman.'

''Scuse me,' he said, relaxing his grip. 'I found the mark.'

'Mark?'

'Didn't you know? I guess they like to believe it's all seamless. You can get up now. How old are you really? No need to pretend. I am nearly eighty. A good age in a man, don't you think?'

I murmured, 'You look well.'

'Thanks. So do you.'

# 6

He said, 'Senex bis puer.'

'An old man is twice a boy?'

'That's the one. I've just taken up wrestling, along with the kick boxing.' He put up his hands. 'Wonderful sport. I'll show you a few moves later.'

I wiped my face. 'I think I've got the idea.'

But I pushed him then, a couple of times, quickly, and he fell back. He was flushed with fury. For a moment, I thought we'd be wrestling. We'd have enjoyed that. But before he could react, I'd dropped my hands and was laughing, so the argument was whether he'd lose his temper or not.

He managed not to, distracting himself by opening a cabinet

within which there was a monitor. He switched it on and flicked to a channel showing the orgy room. I spotted Alicia dancing alone, naked. She looked freer than I had seen her before.

'Want this on? Or would you prefer to slip into someone comfortable – when I've finished with you.'

'Neither.'

'Nor me,' he said. 'Nothing's ever new for people like us. It takes a lot to turn us on – if anything does at all.'

'What else is there? Why have we done this?'

'But there is something left. You don't know?'

'Not unless you go to the trouble of telling me,' I said.

'Murder. It is the deepest, loveliest thing. You haven't tried it yet?' I shook my head. 'One must experience everything once, don't you think?'

I said, 'No one's ever hit me like that.'

'Shame.'

'Why did you do it?'

He touched my neck, chest and stomach. 'I considered that body for myself, but wanted something a bit wider and more chunky. I'm surprised it hung around there for so long. Still, they did have an excellent choice of new facilities. It would have looked good on me. It doesn't look bad on you. How does it feel?'

I moved my limbs a bit. 'Fine – until you attacked me.'

'How long have you had it?'

'Not even three months.'

'I didn't hurt you, did I?'

'I'll survive,' I said. 'I'm just a little annoyed. Thanks for the concern.'

'It was your body I was thinking of, rather than you. Hey, what d'you think of my body?' Without waiting for a reply, he removed his shirt. 'Sometimes, all you want is to be able to look in the mirror without disgust.' I nodded approvingly, but, obviously, not approvingly enough. 'What about this?' he said. He was showing me his penis, even slapping it against his leg with obscene pride. 'It just goes on and on.'

'Incomparable.'

'That's what they all say. How are my buns?'

'Jesus. With those you could be your own hotdog.'

'I've been in this body for three years. You get used to bodies, and the person you become in them. As with jeans, Newbodies are better the more they're worn in. You forget you're in them.' He pulled at his stomach. 'Look at that: I'm increasing here, but I don't want to be perfect. I figured out that perfection makes people crazy, or feel inferior.'

'Whereas', I said, 'it's one's weaknesses that people want to know?'

'Maybe,' he said. 'No one ever gets rid of those. I think I'll do another ten years – or even longer, if things go well – in this facility before moving on to something fitter.' He filled his glass once more and held it out. 'To us – pioneers of the new frontier!'

'We have a secret in common,' I said, 'you and me. Do you get to discuss it much with others?'

'They do talk about it, "the newies". But I want to live, not chatter. I love being a funky dirty young man. I love pouting my sexy lips and being outstanding at tennis. My serve could knock your face off! You should have seen me before. I've got the photographs somewhere. What's the point of being rich if you're lopsided and have a harelip? It was a joke, a mistake that I came out alive like that! This is the real me!'

'What I miss,' I said, 'is giving people the pleasure of knowing about me.'

He was unstoppable. 'Soon everyone'll be talking 'bout this. There'll be a new class, an elite, a superclass of superbodies. Then there'll be shops where you go to buy the body you want. I'll open one myself with real bodies rather than mannequins in the window. Bingo! Who d'you want to be today!'

I said, 'If the idea of death itself is dying, all the meanings, the values of Western civilization since the Greeks, have changed. We seem to have replaced ethics with aesthetics.'

'Bring on the new meanings! You're a conservative, then.'

'I didn't think so. I guess I don't know what or who I am. It's always uplifting, though, to meet a hedonist – someone relieved of the tiring standards which hold the rest of us back from the eternal party.'

'You still think I'm just a playboy, do you? Look at those books!' He pointed at a shelf. 'I'm taking those in! Euripides, Goethe, Nietzsche. I'm dealing with the deepest imponderables. You know what happened to me? I was seventy-five years old. My wife leaves me – not for some virile fucker, but to become a Buddhist. She prefers old fat stomach to me! Some other cultures go for different body shapes, you know.' He went on, 'Mostly, my children don't bother with me. They're too busy with drugs! My friends are dead. I can buy women, but they don't desire me. I didn't just work all my life, I fought and scrambled and dug into the rock surface of the world with my fuckin' fingernails! I lost it all and I was dying and I was depressed. You think I wanted to check out in that state?'

'It sounds hard to say it, but that's a life, I guess. It's the failures, the hopeless digressions, the mistakes, the waste, which add up to a lived life.'

If he'd been in a pub, he'd have spat on the floor. 'You're only an intellectual,' he said. 'I deserved a better final curtain. I bought one! I can tell you, I'm doing some other pretty worthwhile things. Let's hear from you now. What are you doing with your new time?'

'Me? I'm only a menial at the Centre.'

He made a face. 'You're going to keep doing that?'

'I'm definitely not doing anything worthwhile. In fact, I can't tell you what a relief it is to have had a career rather than having to make one. Now, I'm going to enjoy my six months.'

'You're really going back into your slack old body suit?'

'This is an experiment. I wanted to find out what this would be like. But I'm still afraid of anything too . . . unnatural.'

He had been pacing about. Now he sat down opposite me. His tone was more than businesslike; he was firm, but not quite threatening, though it seemed he could become so.

He said, 'You can sell that one, then.'

'Sell what?'

'That body.'

'Sell it?'

'Yeah, to me. I'll pay you well. You will make a substantial profit which you and your family can live on for the rest of your God-given life.'

'What about my old body?'

'I'll get that back for you. No problem. An old body sack is about as valuable as a used condom.' He was looking at me passionately. 'It's a good deal. What do you say?'

'I'm puzzled. You've got the money. Go and buy one. I went to a place, a kind of small hospital. I'm sure you did the same.'

'I did. You think those places are easy to find? It's not that simple any more.'

'What d'you mean?'

'You were either well connected or lucky,' he said. He was drumming his fingers. 'Things have changed already.'

'In what way?' He didn't want to say. 'To put it objectively,' I went on, 'if people want bodies so badly, they could eliminate someone. Unlike you, I'm not recommending it, only suggesting what seems obvious. This isn't the only desirable body around.'

'Bodies have to be adapted. The 'mark' on the head tells you that's been achieved. The body you are in now isn't valuable in itself, but the work that's been done on it is. The people who do it are like gods, extending life. There are only three or four doctors in the world today who can do this operation, and they're like the men who made the atomic bomb – hated, admired and feared, having changed the nature of human life.'

'Do you know these body artists?'

'I can get to at least one of them,' he said. 'And I have ill acquaintances who will pay a great deal to be moved into another body facility.'

'People who will give everything rather than die. I can understand that. Wow, I'm in big demand,' I said. 'But I'll wait for my six months to be up. What's the rush?'

'Someone might be dying in awful pain with only weeks to live. They might not be able to wait for your little "try-out" to come to an end.'

'That, as they say, is life.'

'What the fuck are you talking about?'

I said, 'Is it someone you know? A friend or a lover?'

'Shut up!'

I said, 'Fine. But that's what I've decided to do. I'm not handing my body over to anyone. I'm just settling in. We're getting attached.'

'But you don't even want it! How can a few months matter when you're going back? I would advise you most strongly to sell it now.'

'Strongly, eh?'

'If I were you, I wouldn't want to put myself in unnecessary danger. You're not the sort to be able to look after yourself.'

'Matte, it's my decision. I don't want your money, and I don't want my "body holiday" interrupted.'

He was having difficulty controlling himself. Some anxiety or fury was flooding him. He walked about the cabin, with his face turned away from me.

'The demand is there,' he said. 'The bodies of young women, on which there has always been a premium, are in big demand in the United States. These women are disappearing from the streets, not to be robbed or raped but to be painlessly murdered. There are machines for doing it, which I am hoping to be involved in the manufacture of. It's a beautiful procedure, Leo. The sacked bodies are kept in fridges, waiting for the time when the operation will have been simplified. When it'll be like slotting an engine into a car, rather than having to redesign the car itself each time. People might even start to share bodies to go out in, the way girls share clothes now. They'll say to one another, "Who'll wear the body tonight?" There's no going back. Immortality is where some of us are heading, like it or not. But there will be some people for whom it will be too late.'

I was interested to meet someone in my situation and I would have liked to have spent at least one evening with a group of Newbodies – we waxen immortals – sitting around a card table, discussing the past, of which there would have been plenty, no doubt. His tone concerned me, however. I was afraid and wanted to get out of there but he had locked the door. I didn't want to provoke him; he seemed capable of anything. So when he said, 'Come, look at this – it might interest you,' I went with him.

I followed him through narrow, twisting corridors. We passed a door outside of which stood two big men in white short-sleeved shirts. Matte nodded at the men and exchanged a few words with one of them in Greek. I was going to ask Matte what they were guarding, but I had been too curious already.

We went down another corridor. At last, Matte knocked on the door of another cabin. An upper-class English voice said, 'Come.'

The room was dark, apart from the light shed by a table-lamp. At a desk sat a woman in her thirties, writing and listening to gentle big-band music. Her clothes appeared to be from another time, my mother's, perhaps, though I could see her hair and teeth were not. If there was something palpably strange about her, I'd have said she resembled an actress in a period film whose contemporary health and look belied the period she appeared to be representing.

Matte went to her. They spoke, and she continued her work.

He stood beside me at the door and whispered, 'That woman is a child psychologist, a genius in her field. Years ago, as a man, she looked after one of my children who was seriously disturbed. She knows almost everything about human beings. When he was ill, not long ago, I paid for him to become a Newbody. He had arthritis and was bent double. He needed to finish his book and to continue to help others, as a woman. Don't you think that's a pretty charitable thing?' He gave me a look that was supposed to shame me. 'She's not sweeping the floor somewhere and chasing sex.' He shut the door. 'What would you ask her?'

'How to die, I guess.'

'Death is dead.'

'Oh, no, everyone'll miss it so, and there would be other psychologists', I said, 'to build on his or her work.'

'She can do that herself. Life renewing itself.'

'How's her book?'

'Looks like she'll need several lifetimes. She's . . . thorough.'

'Read it?'

'A boxful of notes? Most of the time she lies on deck, "thinking". She has too much sex for my liking. I'll accept one of your points: she'd go faster if she thought she was going to snuff it. Wish she'd update her taste, too. She insists on listening to that old-time music, which reminds me of days I want to forget.'

'I guess you can't force anyone to like speed garage,' I said. 'Do your kids know you now?'

'They don't know where I am. They're not speaking to me. When they get older, if they behave themselves, I'll get them new bodies as birthday presents.'

'They'll want that?'

'Those crazy kids'll totally love it. They've been in bands and clinics and stuff. They get exhausted – you know, the lifestyle. This way they can carry on. I'm holding off telling them because I know they're gonna want to get off to a new start right away.'

'What's wrong with that?'

'If they haven't suffered enough, they're not gonna appreciate it. This isn't for everybody.'

I didn't want to listen to him, or argue any more. As with Ralph Hamlet, I found the encounter disturbing. Matte and I were both mutants, freaks, human unhumans – a fact I could at least forget when I was with real people, those with death in them.

I said, 'I need to see where Patricia is.'

For a moment I thought he wouldn't let me go. But what could he do? He was thinking hard though. Then we shook hands. 'There's plenty of women here who would be attracted to you,' he said. 'Take who you want.'

'Thanks.'

'You must think more seriously about the body sale.' He gave me his card and looked me up and down once more. 'I'm your man – first in line with a bag of cash. Look after yourself.'

I knew he was watching me walk away.

I went outside. The moon and stars were bright; the air was warm. On the deck, most of the guests had gathered and were dancing wildly, yelling and whistling. The female Newbody I'd met earlier was performing: kicking out, swaying and singing in front of a guitarist and keyboard player, encouraging us to worship her as she worshipped herself.

I asked someone, 'What's she called?'

'Miss Reborn,' I was told.

When I touched Patricia on the shoulder, she took me in her arms. 'I looked for you everywhere.'

'Matte and I were talking.'

'He wanted your opinion on things, eh?' she said with unnecessary sarcasm.

'I can't say I learned a lot about him.'

'Why not?' she said. 'Up here, I've been following the rumours and fantasies. His family are wealthy, that's for sure.'

'Is that all?'

'Kiss me.' I did so. She said, 'His beloved brother, who is much older than him, is dying, apparently, from an incurable disease.'

'His brother?'

'Dying painfully – on this boat, in a sealed cabin, they say.'

'Really?'

'He is yards from us, as we frolic here.' I recalled the two men guarding a door. 'That's made you think.'

'Why don't we dance while there's time? I can't believe that singer. Look at her move.'

'Oh, yes,' she said. 'Why didn't you suggest we dance earlier?'

'It's not too late.'

'You little liar, you weren't talking to Matte at all,' she said. 'You were fucking. You're all cock. How many were there?'

'Too many to mention.'

'I know that if you and I are to be together it's something I'm going to have to live with.'

'That's right.'

Her head was on my shoulder. While we danced, I could think over what Matte had said. It wasn't difficult to see why he wanted my body for his brother. But why didn't he go and buy one, as I had? That was what I didn't understand – why he was so keen on me.

I tried to forget about it. I began to enjoy dancing with Patricia, holding and kissing her, examining the folds and creases of her old neck and full arms, the excess flesh of her living body, and holding her mottled hands. I thought about something he'd said, 'Who wants a lot of Oldbodies hanging about the world? They're ugly and expensive to maintain. Soon, they'll be irrelevant.'

Yet there was something in her I didn't want to let go of. Her body and soul were one, she was 'real', but how could such a notion count against immortality?

Matte had filled me with anxiety and foreboding. I wasn't aware of how long Patricia and I danced, but I guessed the night was gone. We must have been around the islands and back to where we'd started. I'd been on that boat far too long.

Patricia had her hands inside my shirt. 'You make me feel all slippy. I want you again. I can't wait to have you.'

Much as I was glad to be with her, I didn't think I could go through all that.

'You might have to wait a bit,' I said.

'Why?'

'Oh, I don't know. I'm tired. Look,' I said. 'There's plenty of men about. Young men on their own, too.'

I could see at least three or four well-built guys standing around the edge of the dance floor.

'Tell me something,' she said. I noticed a new clarity in her eyes. 'You won't tell me the truth, I know that. But I'll know anyway. Does touching me, kissing me, licking me . . . is it something you'd rather not do? Does my body disgust you?'

Her physical presence, her body, didn't repel me, in fact. My sister had been a nurse. She'd taught me not to find bodies repellent, only the people inside them. It was Patricia's proprietorial attitude I found difficult. While I was thinking about this, she watched me.

'Now I know,' she said. 'I thought that was it. It took me a while to figure it out.'

'Yes,' I said. 'What you do to me is a description of what you say men do to women, lower and humiliate them. It's fascistic. Patricia, whatever happened to the revolution?'

She stepped back from me, as if something had exploded inside her body.

I slipped away, moving quickly now. It wasn't her I wanted to get away from. Out of the corner of my eye I had seen Matte pointing me out to another man, who was looking to see where I was. Other men were moving towards him.

I went round to the other side of the yacht and stripped off to my pants. I tied my shoes together and stuck them down the back. I could see a few lights on the shore in the distance. Preparations were being made for disembarkation, but it would take some time. I couldn't wait. I climbed onto the rail and dived into the sea.

I had surfaced and been swimming a few minutes when I heard voices. There were splashes behind me. Others were joining in. Why? I stopped for a moment and looked behind. By the light of the ship, I could tell that the swimmers following me didn't resemble women from the Centre, but men from the boat. They were not stoned or drunk revellers either. They were swimming with purpose, without churning up the water. They must have been Matte's men. They were quick and strong. So was I; and I had the advantage, just.

I ran out of the water, put on my shoes and sprinted up the beach into the village. A few bars and discos were still open. The square was full of noise and people. I could have disappeared into the crowd somewhere, but what then? Soon everyone would start to disperse. Anyhow, I didn't want to risk running into any of my other enemies.

I hurried through the narrow alleys towards the Centre. When I got there, it was deserted, to my relief. I relaxed a little and made myself a cup of tea. I would hide out in the place until the morning. But the more I thought about it, the less safe I felt. The men following me had seemed determined. It wouldn't have been difficult for Matte to find out where I was staying, and he was ruthless.

As I was collecting my washbag and a few other things from the roof, I thought I heard someone rattling the handle of the door in the wall. I didn't hear any raised female voices either.

Hurrying now, I picked up several items of women's clothing, spread out on the roof to dry, and shoved them in my rucksack.

When I heard voices within the building and saw a torchlight flash, I leapt from the roof of the accommodation block to the roof of the kitchen. I jumped down the side of the building to a narrow concrete ledge below. I knew the only way out now was down the side of the hill. I wasn't sure how steep it was exactly, but I was in no doubt that it was a stiff gradient.

Not only that, the terrain was rough. As I teetered there, trying to decide what to do, I was aware of how strong the desire to live was. Had it come to it, I could have stood on that ledge for days. I'd been depressed in my life, at times; suicidal, even. But I wasn't ready to give up my mind or my body. I wanted to live.

I jumped. It must have been twenty feet down. After hitting the earth, every staggering step was perilous. It seemed to be rocky and sandy at the same time. I couldn't stop to think. I slipped and fell most of the way; it was impossible for me to stay on my feet. My body got cut all over. What was the foliage made of? Tin? Razors? It was like rolling through broken glass. However, to my knowledge I wasn't being followed.

At the bottom of the hill, I halted. I couldn't hear anyone following me. I waited for more of the night to pass. Cautiously, I made my way towards the beach. By now, even the copulators had gone.

I broke into the bathroom of a deserted restaurant where I washed and shaved off my beard. Then I lay down on some benches, pulling a damp tarpaulin on top of me. There were slithery creatures, insects and dogs around, and men who wanted my body. I didn't sleep.

I was at the harbour before it was light, waiting for the first boat to take me back to Piraeus. I'd get to Athens and decide my next move. I had covered my head in a long, light scarf; I wore a wrap-around skirt and dark glasses. I wouldn't get on the boat until the last moment.

I was sitting at the back of a café facing the harbour when someone whispered the name I'd so foolishly given myself in my arrogance. Even as I thought of running once more, I began to shiver with terror.

Alicia, of course, had come looking for me.

'How did you find me?' I said. I indicated my outfit. 'Do these colours suit me?'

'Yes, but not all at once.'

'Some of the men on the island have been threatening me again. I know they work down here.'

She said, 'I thought: what would I do here? Where would I hide? And there you were.'

'Right,' I said. 'Do I look conspicuous?'

'Only to me. Anyone try to pick you up yet?'

'I'm too much of a tragic figure.'

'A tragic figure with most unladylike hairy ears,' she said. We had coffee together. She said, 'You're running.'

'Time to move on. Did you enjoy it last night?'

'Something strange happened. I'll tell you about it another time.' Then she said, 'I won't be staying at the Centre much longer. Patricia will be after me, when she finds you've gone. I'm disappointed you're fleeing like this.'

'I'm sorry if I have made things difficult for you, but she'll never leave me alone.'

'It's the price the beautiful have to pay. Aren't you used to it yet?'

Watching the boat being loaded up, I was getting nervous; I asked if she minded getting me a ticket from the harbour office. I could see several likely candidates for Matte's men.

On the ship, I hid in the women's toilet. After, when people started to bang on the door, I had to come out. I thought I was done for. I made my way to the car deck and hid under a blanket on the back seat of an old Mercedes. The boat docked and the driver got in without noticing me. Outside, as the traffic queued to leave, I hopped out of the car and ran for it. I sprinted out of there and into the crowd, and got a taxi.

# 7

I'm not sure why, but I returned to the part of London I knew. I felt safer, and more at ease in my mind, in a familiar place. In your own city, you don't have to think about where you are. Being pursued had frightened me; I was scared all the time now. I had no idea whether Matte would still be following me. I must have convinced myself that he'd lost interest in me. Perhaps his brother had died; maybe he'd found another body. I am, however, old enough to know how few of our thoughts bear any relation to the way things are.

I checked into the same dismal hotel as before. When I needed money I worked in a factory packing Christmas toys. Perhaps Matte was right, and it had been a mistake to 'hire' a body for six months. I didn't have time to begin a new life as a new person, and, expecting to go back, I missed my old life. I was in limbo, a waiting room in which there was no reality but plenty of anxiety.

One morning at eight, there was a knock on my door.

In this hotel, there were always knocks on the door – refugees, thieves, prostitutes, drug dealers; people who would never be able to afford new bodies or even to feed adequately the one they already had; people looking for other people and no one wanting to do you a favour, if it wasn't in exchange for another one. Usually, though, they would declare themselves. This time there was no reply.

Maybe Matte had come for my body. I'd seen the movie. Men in dark suits were outside. While they were kicking the door in, I'd hide in the shower with my gun, or climb out of the bathroom window and down the fire-escape. That was the young man's route, and I wouldn't be a young man in my mind, however lithe my body. For there was another part of me, my older mind, if you like, which was, by now, outraged by the violation, the cheek of it. My body wasn't for sale, though I had, of course, purchased it myself.

'How did you find me?'

Alicia was sitting on the bed; I stood looking at her. She had shaved her head and put on weight. She wore a top with a bow at the front.

'Why have you grown a full beard?'

'Alicia, I am hoping to be taken seriously.'

I'd forgotten how nervous she was. 'Leo, it's good to see you. How much do you mind me coming to see you?'

'Not as much as you might think. I do need to know how you tracked me down.'

'I haven't told Patricia – she isn't downstairs, if that's what's bothering you. I looked through your things one time . . . trying to . . . I wanted to know who you were. You do know, I guess, that you're as elusive as a spy. It turned me into a spy. I found a receipt for this hotel and wrote the address into one of my poems. Still,' she said, 'if you want to be private, why shouldn't you be? Do you want me to go?'

'I'll come with you. Let's get out of here. I never stay in this room during the day.'

I was putting on my coat.

She said, 'You're writing.'

In the corner of the room, on a small table, were some papers.

'Please don't look at that,' I said.

'Why not?'

'Leave it! I'm trying . . . to do something about an old man in a young man's body.'

'You've done a lot. Is it a film?' She was turning the pages. 'There's dialogue. It's professionally laid out. Have you written before?'

'You encouraged me, Alicia.'

'It was the other way around. Will you try to sell it?'

'You never know. Give it here now.'

'What a strange boy you are!'

I took the papers from her and put them under the bed.

In the café, I asked, 'How is my friend Patricia?'

'What a trouble-maker you are. People had paid to attend her classes but she refused to get out of bed. You showed her something was possible, some intensity of feeling with a man, and you took it away again. She would send for me and we'd talk about you for hours, wondering who you were. She would rage and weep. The only relief was when that man from the boat came to see her.'

'Man?'

'The playboy. Matte.'

'Alicia, what happened?'

'I was sent out of the room. I heard everything from outside the window.'

'And?'

'You owed him something, he said. He wouldn't say what it was. You didn't borrow money from him?' I shook my head. 'He wanted to find you, wanted to know whether there was anyone who knew you.'

'Did he threaten Patricia?'

'He didn't need to. She was delighted to talk about the intricacies of your character, insofar as she understood it, for hours. Not that this interested Matte. Of course, she doesn't know where you are. I left the island a few days later and went to Athens.'

'Were you followed?'

'Why would I be? What's going on?' Alicia said. 'You know what Patricia wanted? For you to run the place with her.'

'I'd have liked to do that,' I said. 'For a while. It would have been fun. Impossible too, of course, with her attitude towards me.'

'You'd have done it?' she said. 'Don't you have any doubts?'

'What?'

'About yourself. About what you are capable of? That makes you different to a lot of people. Different to most people, in fact.'

'Yes,' I said, 'I do have doubts. I just don't want them getting in the way of my mistakes.'

She said, 'Something else happened. I haven't told you the whole story. When you disappeared from the boat that last night –'

'Yes, sorry. I couldn't stand it –'

'Some people went back to the Centre. But I was hanging around to see whether you might return. A lot of our group stayed on the boat until after breakfast. The dawn was lovely. Matte came to me. He realized I was from the Centre. I don't look like the other people he knows, with their perfect bodies. He took me to his room. He wanted information about you.'

'What did you say?'

'He was sitting there opposite me, opening and shutting his legs like a trap. He looked almost as handsome as you. I promised to tell him everything I knew about you if he fucked me. I told him I was an unorgasmic virgin. It was time, you see. He was amused, and seems to have looked into these things. "Apparently, the use of virgins", he told me, "prolongs life. The headmaster of a Roman school for girls lived to one hundred and fifty. Rather that than ingesting the dried cells of foetal pigs, or drinking snake oil." He seemed to think it was a decent exchange. He fucked me hard, right there on the floor. It was wonderful. Is it always like that? I'm pregnant.'

'By him? Matte?'

She patted her stomach. 'Don't ask me if I'll keep it.'

'The world is full of single mothers. It's the only way, these days. What use are men? But he's not a good man.'

'I don't need to tell you, a good man is hard to find. Ask Patricia!'

'Alicia, that was a mad thing to do! You don't know him!'

'One day, I'll present him with a bill.'

'But why him?'

'You'd turned me on and I couldn't wait any longer. No one else on that boat seemed much interested in having me. I know I'm not beautiful, and as a girl all I wanted was to be beautiful. Matte was looking at me like a hungry wolf I couldn't keep from the door.'

'It's like having a kid with the devil.'

'If he's really bad, you'd better tell me the details. I can only consider my position if I know the facts. Otherwise . . . I'm going ahead with it.'

She was waiting; she seemed to be aware that there was more I knew.

'I only met him once,' I said. I kissed and cuddled her. 'Congratulations.'

'Thanks.'

'What will you do now?'

'I'm back living with Mother. Things are dark. I need to tell you, I don't know how to go on.'

I was looking at her. 'People either want eternal life or they want out right now.'

'Can you think of reasons to continue?'

'Lots. Pleasure.'

'Only that?'

'Children,' I added, 'if you like them. They always gave me more pleasure than anything else.'

'Good, good,' she said.

With her, I always felt I had to justify the most basic things, which discomforted me. Still, I liked her; I'd always liked her. I wanted to help her. Then I had an idea. I told her I had something to sort out; we agreed to meet later.

When we parted, I went to an Internet café and sent an email in my given name, to a friend who was the editor of a literary magazine which published fiction, some journalism and photographs. I urged him to see Alicia as soon as possible. I told him I didn't want my name mentioned. Then I rang Alicia and told her she had to go and see this man after lunch. After some argument she agreed to go to his office, read him a couple of poems and talk about herself.

Later that day, when we met again in a local pub, she told me he'd given her a job reading manuscripts and sorting out the office three days a week.

'That's great,' I said. 'Are you pleased?'

She kissed me. 'I knew that somehow this had happened through you, Leo. But the odd thing was, he didn't know your name.'

'No,' I said. 'He wouldn't remember me. But my father was well connected.'

'Who was your father? Or is that your privacy, right?'

We were sitting in a bar by the window where I could monitor the street for murderers. I recognized a few local people. They all looked like murderers. However, there was one person in particular I had been looking out for during the last few days, without properly admitting it to myself, someone I couldn't search out, but had to wait for.

It had to be now. There she was, my wife, across the road. The wheel of her shopping cart had come off. She was fiddling with it, but it would have to be fixed properly. At a loss, she stood there, looking around. The cart was heavy, full of provisions. She couldn't leave it and she couldn't carry it home.

I asked Alicia to excuse me. I crossed the road to my wife and asked if she were okay.

'I'm rather stuck, dear.'

'These small accidents can be devastating. Can I?'

I hauled the cart into a doorway and took a look at it. I'm not mechanical, but I could see the wheel had sheared off.

'Do you live far?'

'Ten minutes' walk.'

I said, 'I'll be a good Samaritan. Wait one minute.'

I went back to Alicia.

'This is my good deed for the week, perhaps for the century. Meet me in three hours at the pub on the corner.'

She was looking at me. 'You'd go home with any woman, apart from me.'

'It must seem like that.'

'Can't we bring up the kid together?'

I kissed her. 'Later.'

I recrossed the road and picked up the cart in my arms.

'Which way?'

It was heavy and awkward. I walked slowly, with exaggerated complaints, in order to spend more time with my wife.

'Don't you have anyone to help you?' I said.

'Not at the moment.'

We were approaching my house. I noticed the front gate was wonky and needed repairing.

She opened the front door. 'Would you like to come in?' I hesitated. 'Just for a minute,' she said.

'If it's all right with you. I wouldn't mind a glass of water.'

Inside, she said, 'Can I ask . . . what do you do?'

'I've been travelling. Gap year.'

She went into the kitchen and I looked around. Nothing had changed, but everything was slightly different.

My son, now the same age as me, came downstairs and put his head round the door. I almost gave way. It was him I wanted to touch, his hands and face. In the last few years it had become more difficult for us to touch each other. He was embarrassed, or he didn't like my body. I loved, still, to kiss his cheeks, even if I had to grab him and pull him towards me.

'All right, Mum?' Mike said. 'Hello,' he said to me.

I must have been staring.

'My cart broke,' she said.

'Your heart?' he said.

'Cart, you big idiot!'

He came into the room. He looked alert, happy and healthy. I could see my old self in the way he held himself. I missed me. I missed, too, my pleasure in him, in living close to his life, in knowing what he did and where he went.

I was dismayed to see he was carrying my new laptop, a gorgeous little sliver of light I'd bought just before deciding to become someone else. I had been intending to use it in bed. I had always been attracted to the instruments of my trade. Sometimes, merely buying a new pen or computer was enough to get me back to work.

'That looks good,' I said.

'Yes.' He said to his mother, 'I'm borrowing this for a while. I'll return it before Dad gets back. Have you heard from him?'

'He sent his love,' she called.

'Is that all?' he said. 'He won't mind me borrowing this, then. By the way, happy anniversary. Shame to be on your own.'

'I'll raise a glass later,' she said.

I said, 'Can I ask what anniversary it is?'

'Not my wedding anniversary,' she said, 'but the anniversary of the day I met my husband. He's away on business at the moment, the fool.'

'Why fool?'

'His breathing was painful. He couldn't walk far. I could see it in his face, but I don't think he knew how ill he had become. Before he started out on his jaunt across the continent, I had decided we should enjoy the time we had left together. Still, I didn't want to put him off his pleasures.'

Mike said, 'Mum, are you okay? Can I go?'

'Please do.'

He shut the front door.

I asked, 'Would you like me to get going, too?'

'But I must offer you some tea. I'd feel bad if I didn't, after you helped me.'

'You're very trusting.'

'I noticed you looking at the books just now. No burglar or lunatic would do that.'

'Your boy is a great-looking kid.'

'He's doing well. His girlfriend's pregnant.'

'Really? How wonderful. Congratulations.'

'Adam will be back for the birth, I know he will.'

I went upstairs to the bathroom. Coming out, I noticed my study door was open. The books I'd been using before I left were piled on the coffee table, next to the CDs I'd bought but not yet played. I couldn't resist sitting down at my desk. I looked at the photographs of my children at various ages. I knew where everything was, though my hands were bigger and my arms longer than before. The ink in my favourite fountain pen still flowed. I wrote a few words and shoved the paper in my pocket. I had to tear myself away.

When I returned, I sat beside Margot and poured the tea. I glanced at the wedding ring I'd bought her and said, 'Where are you from?'

'Me? You're asking me?' she said. 'Do you want to know?'

'Why not?'

'No one's much interested in women of my age.'

When she told me where she was born, and a little about her parents, I asked other questions about her early life and upbringing. I followed what occurred to me, listening and prompting.

I had heard some of this before, in the years when we were getting to know each other. I had not, though, asked her about it for a long time. How many times can you have the 'same' conversation? But the past was no more inert than the present: there were different tones, angles, details. She mentioned people I'd never heard of; she talked about a lover she'd cared for more than she'd previously admitted.

Her story made more sense to me now, or I was able to let more of it in. We drank tea and wine. She was stimulated by my interest, and amazed by how much there was to tell. She wanted to speak; I wanted to listen.

I asked only about her life before she met me. When my name arose and she did speak about me a little, I didn't follow it up. I wish I'd had the guts to listen to every word – my life judged by my wife, a summing up. But it would have disturbed me too much.

How she moved me! Listening to her didn't tell me why I loved her, only that I did love her. I wanted to offer her all that I'd neglected to give in the past few years. How withdrawn and insulated I'd been! It would be different when I returned as myself.

Two hours passed. At last, I said, 'Now, I really must get going. I should let you get on.'

'What about you?' she said. She was shaking her head. 'I feel as though I'm coming round from a dream. What have we been doing together?'

I went over to the table on which sat a music system and a pile of CDs.

'Can I play a tune?'

She said, 'Oh, tell me, why did you ask me all those questions?'

'Did they bother you?'

'No, the opposite. They stimulated me . . . they made me think . . .'

'I'm interested in the past. I am thinking of becoming a medieval historian.'

'Oh. Very good.' She added, 'But what you asked was personal, not historical. You are a curious young man, indeed.'

'Something happened to me,' I said. 'I was changed by something. I . . .'

She waited for me to continue, but I stopped myself. Sometimes there's nothing worse than a secret, sometimes there's nothing worse than the truth.

She said, 'What happened?'

'No. My girlfriend is waiting for me down the street.'

I put on my wife's favourite record. I kissed her hands and felt her body against mine as we danced. I knew where to put my hands. In my mind, her shape fitted mine. I didn't want it to end. Her face was eternity enough for me. Her lips brushed mine and her breath went into my body. For a second, I kissed her. Her eyes followed mine, but I could not look at her. If I was surprised by the seducibility of my wife, I was also shocked by how forgettable, or how disposable, I seemed to be. For years, as children, our parents have us believe they could not live without us. This necessity, however, never applies in the same way again, though perhaps we cannot stop looking for it.

At the door, my wife said, 'Will you come for tea again?'

'I know where you are,' I replied. 'I don't see why not.'

'We could go to an exhibition.'

'Yes.'

I said goodbye, and reluctantly left my own house. Margot had placed a bag of rubbish outside the front door, ready to be taken to the dustbins. I was annoyed my boy hadn't done it; he must have had his hands full, carrying my laptop.

I took the rubbish round to the side of the house. From where I stood, through a hole in the fence, I could see the street. There was a car double-parked on the other side of the road, with two men in it. It was a narrow street and irritable drivers were backed up behind the car. Why didn't they move on? Because the men in the car were watching the house.

I slipped out of the front gate and headed up the road, away from them. It was true: they were following me. I went into my usual paper shop. Outside, the men were waiting in the car.

When I continued on my way, they followed me. Who were these men who followed other men?

I knew the streets. Under the railway line, beside the bus garage, was a narrow alleyway through which, years ago, I'd walked the children to school. I turned into it and ran; they couldn't follow me in the car.

Of course, they wanted me badly and were waiting at the top of the alley. This wasn't the death I wanted. I walked quickly. Further down the street the three of them got out of the car and stood around me. Their faces were close; I could smell their after-shave. There were a lot of people on the street.

'Where are you taking me?'

'You'll find out.'

Another of them murmured, 'I've got a gun.'

One of them had put his hand on my arm. It riled me; I don't like being held against my will. Yet I gained confidence; the gun, if it was really a gun, had helped me. I didn't believe they'd shoot me. The last thing they'd want to do was blow up my body.

I started to shout, 'Help me! Help me!'

As people turned to look, the men tried to pull me into the car, but I kicked and hit out. I heard a police siren. One of the men panicked. People were looking. I was away, and running through the closely packed market stalls. The three of them weren't going to chase me with guns through the crowd on market day.

As soon as I could, I rang Ralph's mobile from a phone box.

It was impossible for us to meet. He was 'up to his neck in lit-erature'. Unfortunately, the fool had already told me where he was.

Half an hour later, I pushed open the pub door and entered. I'm a sentimentalist and want always for there to be the quiet interminability of a London pub in the afternoon, rough men playing pool, others just sitting in near silence, smoking. I couldn't see Ralph, but did notice a sign which said 'Theatre and Toilets'.

I tripped down some narrow stairs into an oppressive, dank-smelling room, painted black. There were old cinema seats and, in one corner, a box-office the size of a cupboard. Pillars seemed to obstruct every clear view of the tiny stage. I saw from the posters that they were doing productions of *The Glass Menagerie* and *Dorian Gray*.

A woman hurried over, introducing herself as Florence O'Hara. She wanted to know how many tickets I wanted for *The Glass Menagerie*, in which she played the mother. Or did I want tickets for *Hamlet*, in which she played Gertrude? If I wanted to see them both, there was a special offer.

As she said this, I was surprised to see, sitting in the gloom, unshaven and in a big overcoat, a well-known actor, Robert Miles, who'd been in a film I'd written seven years ago. Before it began shooting, he and I had had tea together several times.

I looked at Florence more closely. I could recall Robert trying to get her a small part in the film. They'd been lovers, and were still connected in some way.

Had I not been inhabiting this wretched frame, Robert and I could, no doubt, have exchanged greetings and gossip. Instead, when he saw me looking at him, being both nervous and arrogant, he got up and walked out.

At the same time, Ralph emerged, in the costume of a Victorian gentleman or dandy, with a top hat in his hand. We shook hands, and I sat behind him in the theatre seats.

'I haven't got long,' he said.

'Nor me.'

'There's a show later. During the day, I'm working on a new play with Robert Miles. He's trying his hand at directing. I'm working with the best now.'

Ralph was looking tired; his face seemed a little more lined than before.

He said, 'I'm playing Dorian Gray as well. Florence is Sybil.

I'm having the time of my life here.' He glanced at me. 'What's wrong? What can I do for you now?'

I told Ralph that Matte had 'recognized' me, was a Newbody himself, required a body for his brother, and was in pursuit of mine. How could this not bother Ralph? After all, wasn't he, theoretically, in a similar position?

'You come to me with these problems, but what can I do about any of them?'

'Ralph, anyone would recognize that, as with anything uniquely valuable – gold, a Picasso – bad people will be scrambling and killing for it. How could they not? But I can't just remove this body as I could a necklace.'

'At least, not yet,' he said. Ralph was looking around agitatedly. 'You stupid fool. Why have you come here? You might have led them to me. They could kidnap me while I'm on stage and strip me down to my brain.'

'How would they know you're a freak like me?'

'Don't fucking call me a freak! Only if you bloody well tell them. And I'm always afraid my maturity is going to give me away. What have you done to alert these people?'

By now, I was yelling, and I had big lungs.

'If you think this isn't going to be something that a lot of people aren't going to know about, you're a fool.'

He leaned closer to me. 'You get full-on, full-time security. Big guys around you all the time. That's the price of a big new dick and fresh liver.'

'How am I going to afford it?'

'You'll have to work.'

'At what?'

'What d'you think? You used to be a writer. You can start again, in another style. You could become . . . let's say, a magical realist!' I could see Florence in the dressing-room doorway, waving at him. 'Imagine where I'll be in ten years' time, in fifteen, in twenty! How do you know I won't be running one of the great theatres or opera houses of the world?' I was sitting there with my head in my hands. 'I didn't tell you. I will now. Ophelia and I – the girl playing that part, of course – are getting married. I didn't tell you this either: we have a child together. A few days old, and perfect. I was afraid for a while that it would be some kind of oddity.'

'Well done.'

'Are you going to see the show? Maybe it's better you don't hang around here, if you're being chased.'

I indicated my body. 'All I want', I said, 'is to be rid of this, to get out of this meat. I want to do it tonight, if possible.' He was looking at me pityingly. 'I guess I could find the hospital myself, but I'm in a hurry. What's the address of the place you took me to?'

'Up to you,' he said, sceptically.

He told me the address. I wouldn't forget it. He was glad to be rid of me.

I said, 'Good luck with the show. I'll come and see it in a few days' time, with my wife. She and I are planning to spend a lot of time together.'

At the top of the stairs, I heard Florence's voice behind me.

'What name?' she called.

'What?'

'What name for the tickets to the show?'

'I'll let you know.'

'Don't you even know your own name?'

Coming into the pub was a young woman with a baby in a sling. Ralph's kid, I guessed. But I was in too much of a hurry to stop. There was a miserable cab office at the end of the street where, in my old frame, I had known the drivers and listened to their stories.

I told the cabbie to drive fast. As we went, I looked around continuously, staring into every car and face for potential murderers, thinking hard, convinced I was still being followed. Where I was going wasn't far, but I had to be careful.

Not long after we'd left the city, I said, suddenly, to the driver, 'Drop me off here.'

'I thought you wanted –'

'No, this is fine.' We were approaching an area of low, recently built industrial buildings. 'Listen,' I said, holding up the last of my money, 'give me the petrol can you keep in the back of the car. I've broken down near by, and I'm in a hurry.'

He agreed, and we went round to the boot of the car. He gave me the can and I wrapped it in a black plastic bag. I picked it up and headed for a pub I'd noticed. There, I had a couple of drinks and went into the toilet. I locked the cubicle door and stripped.

It took some time and I was careful and thorough. When I'd finished, and got back into my clothes, I left the pub and ran through the bleak streets towards the building, or 'hospital', I remembered. Soon, I was disoriented, but the address was right. The layout of the streets and the other buildings was the same. Then I saw it. The place had changed. It could have been years ago that I was there. The building I believed to be the 'hospital' was encircled by barbed wire; grass was poking up through the concrete. In the front, an abandoned filing cabinet was lying on its side. What sort of elaborate disguise was this?

I climbed the fence and pushed my way through the wire, which had been severed in several places. Nobody seemed bothered about security. The front door of the 'hospital' wasn't even locked. However, it was getting dark. I tried the lights, but the electricity had been turned off. Bums had probably been sleeping there on rotten mattresses. The place also seemed to have been vandalized by local kids. I guessed that everything important had been taken away long before that. There were no bodies around, neither new nor old. I didn't know what to do now but there was no reason to stay.

I heard a voice.

# 8

'We weren't too bothered about capturing you earlier. We guessed you'd end up here.'

Matte emerged from the gloom. A torch was shining in my face. I covered my eyes.

I asked, 'You always knew about this place?'

'I knew the caravan would have moved on, but figured out you'd be less well connected than me. I still need that body.'

'Looks like I'm going to need it myself.'

'You've argued yourself out of it. Someone else's need is greater.'

'Your brother?'

'What? Let me worry about him.'

I said, 'You can take the body. There's a lot of life still in it. All I want is the old one back.'

'Come through here.' He pointed to the door, and added, 'This place smells bad, or is it just you?'

'It's the place, too.'

He said, 'Jesus, what the fuck have they been doing, burning bodies?'

I followed him, surrounded by his three men, into another room. I noticed there were no windows; the floors were concrete and covered with broken glass and other debris. The tiles had been pulled up and smashed. Long, bright neon lights were positioned precariously. A man in blue doctor's scrubs was standing there with two assistants, all of them masked. In the middle of the room stood the sort of temporary operating table they use on battlefields, along with medical instruments on steel trays. I was looking around for my old body. Maybe it was being kept in another room and they'd wheel it in. I couldn't wait to see it again, however crumpled or corpse-like it might seem.

'Where's my old body?' I said to the man I assumed to be the doctor. 'I won't get far without it.'

He looked at Matte, but neither of them said anything.

'I see,' I said. 'There's no body. It's gone.' I sighed. 'What a waste.'

'Tough luck,' he said. 'You're going to eternity. When I've sorted this out, my brother and I are off to Honolulu for a family reunion. The only shame is, he'll remind me of you.'

I noticed, on the floor, what looked like a long freezer on its side. It was large enough for a body the size of mine. There was a wooden box, too, big enough for a dead brain. Brains didn't take up much room, I guessed, and were not difficult to dispose of.

'Can I have a cigarette?' I said.

'That's what did for my brother.'

'My last,' I said. 'Then I'll give up. Promise.'

'Glad to hear it,' said Matte. 'Okay. Get on with it.'

One of the men handed me a cigarette. 'Arsehole.'

'You too,' I said.

The man made a move towards me. Matte said, 'Don't damage him! No bruises, and don't cut him up.'

I said, 'I'm going to undress now, have a smoke, and then I'll be ready for you.'

'Good boy,' said Matte. 'You wanted a death and now you're going to get one.' When I removed my jacket and shirt, Matte looked at me approvingly. 'You look good. You've kept yourself in shape.'

'Look at my dick, guys.' I was waving it at them. 'Wouldn't you like to have one of these?'

Matte said, 'What the fuck's that aftershave you're wearing?'

I lit my lighter, and moved backwards.

125

'It's petrol,' I said. 'I'm soaked in it. Never had petrol in my hair before. You come near me, pal, and this body you want goes up in flames like a Christmas pudding. And you too, of course.'

I held the lighter close to my chest. I didn't know how much closer I could get it without turning into a bonfire. Still, rather self-immolation than the degradation which would otherwise be my fate. I'd go out with a bang, burning like a torch, screaming down the road.

Apart from Matte, everyone retreated. The doctors shrank back. Matte wanted to grab me. There was a moment when, to be honest, he could have done it. But the others' fear seemed to affect him. He didn't know what to do; all he could do was play for time.

There was nothing behind me but the door, which was open. I picked up my shirt and trousers, before turning and fleeing. I ran, and I guess they ran, but I ran faster and I knew my way out of there.

I climbed the fence, got dressed and continued to run. It was dark, but I was fit and had some idea where I was going. They'd get in their cars and pursue me, but I was being canny now. I was away. They would never find me.

It didn't occur to me for a long time to consider my destination. When I felt safe I rested in someone's garden. I needed a drink, but sweat and petrol don't smell good together. The last thing I needed was suspicious looks. I was carrying my credit cards, but I realized there was nowhere I could go now; not back to my wife, to my hotel, or to stay with friends. I wouldn't be safe until Matte's brother died, or Matte turned his attention elsewhere. Even then there could be other criminals pursuing me. It was as though I were wearing the *Mona Lisa*.

I was a stranger on the earth, a nobody with nothing, belonging nowhere, a body alone, condemned to begin again, in the nightmare of eternal life.

# HULLABALOO IN THE TREE

'Come along now!'

The father, having had enough, decided it was time they all left the playground.

A week ago, in this park, they had run into an Indian friend, a doctor, who'd been shocked by the disrespect and indiscipline of the father's children. The second seven-year-old twin, the one in the Indiana Jones hat, had said to the doctor friend, 'What are you – an idiot?'

The father had had to apologize.

'They are speaking to everyone like this?' the friend had said to the father. 'I know we live here now, but you have let them become Western, in the worst way!'

No English friend would have presumed to say such a thing, the father had commented, later at home.

'The problem is,' the kid had replied, 'he's a brown face.'

The father, furious and agitated ever since, thought he should start being more authoritative.

'We're going!' he said now, in what he considered to be almost his 'sharpest' voice.

He picked up the blue plastic ball and strode out of the enclosed playground and into the park. The seven-year-old twins had been hitting each other with sticks and the two-year-old had been flung from the roundabout, scraping his leg.

Still, they would walk across Primrose Hill to a café on the other side. The children had been asking for drinks; he wanted a coffee. What better way was there to spend a Sunday morning in the adult world?

To his surprise, his three sons followed him without complaint. His friend should have been there to witness such impressive obedience. His wife-to-be had run into an acquaintance and he could see her still chatting, beside the swings. He had already interrupted her once. Why was it that the time he most wanted to talk to her was when she was engaged with someone else?

Outside the playground, in the open park, with the hill rising up in front of him and the sky beyond it, he felt like walking forwards for a long time with his eyes closed, leaving everyone behind, in order, for a bit, to have no thoughts. For years, before his children were born, he seemed to have forfeited Sundays altogether. Now the poses, the attitude, the addictions and, worst of all, the sense of unlimited time had been replaced by a kind of exhausting chaos and a struggle, in his mind, to work out what he should be doing, and who he had to be to satisfy others.

He didn't walk towards the hill, however, but stood there and held the ball out in front of him.

'Watch, you guys! Pay attention!' he said.

What were fathers for if not to kick balls high into the air while their sons leaned back, exclaiming, 'Wow, you've nearly broken through the clouds! How do you do that, Daddy?'

He enjoyed it when, after this display, they grabbed the ball and tried to kick it as he had done. The seven-year-olds, who lived a few streets away with their mother but were staying for the weekend, had begun to imitate many of the things he did, some of which he was proud of, some of which were ridiculous or irrelevant, like wearing dark glasses in the evening. When they went out together they resembled the Blues Brothers. Even the two-year-old had begun to copy the languid way he spoke and the way he lay on the couch, reading the paper. It was like being surrounded by a crowd of venomous cartoonists.

Now, the father dropped the ball towards his foot but mis-kicked it.

'Higher, Daddy!' called the two-year-old. 'Up, up, sky!'

The two-year-old had long blond hair, jaggedly cut by his mother, who leaned over his cot with a torch and scissors while he was asleep. The boy was wearing a nappy, socks, T-shirt and shoes, but had refused to put his trousers on. The father had lacked the heart to force him.

The father jogged across and fetched the ball. Making the most of their attention while he still had it, he screamed, 'Giggs, Scholes, Beckham, Daddy, Daddy, Daddy – it's gone in!' and drove the ball as hard and far as he could, before slipping over in the mud.

Some shared silences, particularly those of confusion and dis-belief, you never want to end, so rare and involving are they.

The oldest twin set down and opened the small suitcase in which he kept his guns, the books he'd written and a photograph of the Empire State Building. He peered into the tree through the wrong end of his new binoculars.

'It's far, far away, nearly in heaven,' he said. 'Here, you see.'

The father got to his feet. Removing his sunglasses, he was already looking up to where the ball, like an errant crown, was resting on a nest of smallish twigs, at the top of a tree not far from the entrance to the playground.

The two-year-old said, 'Stuck.'

'Bloody hell,' said the father.

'Bloody bloody,' repeated the two-year-old.

The father glanced towards the playground. His wife-to-be still hadn't emerged.

'Throw things!' he said. One of the older boys picked up a leaf and tossed it backwards over his head. The father said, 'Hard things, men! Come on! Together we can do this!'

The twins, who welcomed the pure concentration of a crisis,

began to run about gathering stones and conkers. The father did the same. The youngest boy jumped up and down, flinging bits of bark. Soon, the air was filled with a hail of firm objects, one of which struck a dog and another the leg of a kid passing on a bicycle. The father picked up one of the twins' metal guns and hurled it wildly into the tree.

'You'll break it!' said the son reproachfully. 'I only got it yesterday.' The father began to march away. 'Where are you going?' called the boy.

'I'm not going to hang around here all day!' replied the father. 'I need coffee – right now!'

He would leave the cheap plastic ball and, if necessary, buy another one on the way home.

Did he, though, want his sons to see him as the sort of man to kick balls into trees and stroll away? What would he be doing next – dropping twenty-pound notes and leaving them on the street because he couldn't be bothered to bend down?

'What are you up to?' His wife-to-be had come out of the playground. She picked up the youngest child and kissed his eyes. 'What has Daddy done now?'

The twins were still throwing things, mostly at each other's heads.

'Stop that!' ordered the father, coming back. 'Let's have some discipline here!'

'You told us to do it!' said the elder twin.

The second twin said, 'Don't worry, I'm going up.'

Probably the most intrepid of the two, he ran to the base of the tree. As well as his Indiana Jones hat, the second twin was wearing a rope at his belt 'for lassoing', though the only thing he seemed to catch was the neck of the two-year-old, whom otherwise, most of the time, he liked. At six o'clock that morning the father had found him showing the little one his penis, explaining that if he tugged at the end and thought, as he put it, about something 'really horrible, like Catwoman', it would feel 'sweet and sour' and 'quite relaxed'.

The boy was saying, 'Push me up, Daddy. Push, push, push!'

The father bundled him into the fork of the tree, where he clung on enthusiastically but precariously, like someone who'd been dumped on the back of a horse for the first time.

'Put me up there too,' said a girl of about nine, who'd been watching and was now jumping up and down beside him. 'I can climb trees!'

The two-year-old, who had a tooth coming through and whose face was red and constantly wet, said, 'Me in tree.'

'I can't put the whole lot of you up there,' said the father.

The youngest said, 'Daddy go in tree.'

'Good idea,' said his wife-to-be.

'I'd be up there like a shot,' said the father. 'But not in this new shirt.'

His wife-to-be was laughing. 'And not in any month with an "r" in it.'

Unlike most of his male antecedents, the father had never fought in a war, nor had he been called upon for any act of physical bravery. He had often wondered what sort of man he'd be in such circumstances.

'Right,' he said. 'You'll see!'

They were all watching as the father helped the boy down and clambered into the tree himself. His wife-to-be, who was ten years younger, shoved him with unnecessary roughness from behind, until he was out of reach.

Feeling unusually high up, the father waved grandly like a president in the door of an aeroplane. His family waved back. He extended a foot onto another branch and put his weight onto it. It cracked immediately and gave way; he stepped back to safety, hoping no one had noticed the blood drain from his face.

He might, this Sunday morning, be standing on tip-toe in the fork of a tree, a slip away from hospital and years of pain, but he did notice that he had the quiet attention of his family, without the usual maelstrom of their demands. He thought that however much he missed the peace and irresponsibility of his extended bachelorhood, he had at least learned that life was no good on your own. Next week, though, he was going to America for five months, to do research. He would ring the kids, but knew they were likely to say, in the middle of a conversation, 'Goodbye, we have to watch *The Flintstones*,' and replace the receiver. When he returned, how different would they be?

Now he could hear his wife-to-be's voice calling, 'Shake it!'

'Wiggle it!' shouted one of the boys.

'Go, go, go!' yelled the girl.

'Okay, okay,' he muttered.

At their instigation, he leaned against a fat branch in front of him, grasped it, gritted his teeth, and agitated it. To his surprise and relief there was some commotion in the leaves above him. But he could also see that there was no relation between this activity and the position of the ball, far away.

The nine-year-old girl was now climbing into the tree with him, reaching out and grasping the belt of his trousers as she levered herself up. It was getting a little cramped on this junction, but she immediately started up into the higher branches, stamping on his fingers as she disappeared.

Soon, there was a tremendous shaking, far greater than his own, which brought leaves, twigs, small branches and bark raining down onto the joggers, numerous children and an old woman on sticks who were now staring at the hullabaloo in the tree.

This was a good time, he figured, to abandon his position. He would pick up the ball when the girl knocked it down. In fifteen minutes' time he would be eating a buttered croissant and sipping a semi-skimmed decaf latte. He might even be able to look at his newspaper.

'What's going on?'

A man had joined them, holding the hands of two little girls.

The youngest twin said, 'Stupid Daddy was showing off and –'

'All right,' said the father.

The man was already removing his jacket and handing it to one of the girls, saying, 'Don't worry, I'm here.'

The father looked at the man, who was in his late thirties, ruddy faced and unfit looking, wearing thick glasses. He had on a pink ironed shirt and the sort of shoes people wore to the office.

'It's only a cheap ball,' said the father.

'We were just leaving,' said the wife-to-be.

The man spat in his palms and rubbed them together. 'It's been a long time!'

He hurried towards the tree and climbed into it. He didn't stop at the fork, but kept moving up, greeting the girl, who was a little ahead of him, and then, on his hands and knees, scrambling beyond her, into the flimsier branches.

'I'm coming to get you, ball . . . just you wait, ball . . .' he said as he went.

Like the father and the girl, he continually shook the tree. He was surprisingly strong, and this time the tree seemed to be exploding.

Below, the crowd shielded their faces or stepped back from the storm of detritus, but they didn't stop looking and voicing their encouragement.

'What if he breaks his neck?' said the wife-to-be.

'I'll try to catch him,' said the father, moving to another position.

The father remembered his own father, Papa, in the street outside their house in the evening, after tea, when they'd first bought a car. Like a lot of men then, particularly those who fancied themselves as intellectuals, Papa was proud of his practical uselessness. Nevertheless, Papa could, at least, open the bonnet of his car, secure it and stare into it, looking mystified. He knew that this act would be enough to draw out numerous men from neighbouring houses, some just finishing their 'tea'. Papa, an immigrant, the subject of curiosity, comment and, sometimes, abuse, would soon have these men – civil servants, clerks, shop owners, printers or milkmen – united in rolling up their sleeves, grumbling, lighting cigarettes and offering technical opinions. They would remain out in the street long after dark, fetching tools and lying on their backs in patches of grease, Papa's immigrant helplessness drawing their assistance. The father had loved being out on the street with Papa who was from a large Indian family. Papa had never thought of children as an obstacle, or a nuisance. They were everywhere, part of life.

The three pale boys, Papa's grandchildren, born after he'd died, were looking up at the helpful man in the tree and at the ball, which still sat in its familiar position. Had the ball had a face, it would have been smiling, for, as the man agitated the tree, it rose and fell like a small boat settled on a lilting wave.

The man, by now straddling a swaying bough, twisted and broke off a long thin branch. At full stretch, he used it to jab at the ball, which began to bob a little. At last, after a final poke, it was out and falling.

The children ran towards it.

'Ball, ball!' cried the youngest.

The wife-to-be started to gather the children's things.

The man jumped down out of the tree with his arms raised in triumph. His shirt, which was hanging out, was covered in thick black marks; his hands were filthy and his shoes were scuffed, but he looked ecstatic.

One of his daughters handed him his jacket. The father's wife-to-be tried to wipe him down.

'I loved that,' he said. 'Thanks.'

The two men shook hands.

The father picked up the ball and threw it to the youngest child.

Soon, the family caravan was making its way across the park with their bikes, guns, hats, the youngest's sit-in car, a bag of nappies, a pair of binoculars (in the suitcase), and the unharmed plastic ball. The children, laughing and shoving one another, were discussing their 'adventure'.

The father looked around, afraid but also hoping his Indian friend had come to the park today. By now, *he* had something to say. If children, like desire, broke up that which seemed settled, it was a virtue. Much as he might want to, he couldn't bring up his kids by strict rules or a system. He could only do it, as people seemed to do most things in the end, according to the way he was, the way he lived in the world, as an example and guide. This was harder than pretending to be an authority, but more true.

Now, at the far side of the park, as the children went out through the gate, the father turned to look back at the dishevelled tree in the distance. How small it seemed now! It had been agitated, but not broken. He would think of it each time he returned to the park; he would think about something good that had happened on the way to somewhere else.

# FACE TO FACE WITH YOU

Ann was cooking breakfast when Ed shouted from the window.

– Come and look! New people are moving in!

Ann hurried over to stand beside Ed. Together, they looked down from their window on the first floor; there was a good view of the street and the entrance to their block.

A small van was parked outside. Ed and Ann watched as two men carried furniture inside, supervised by a man and a woman of around thirty, the same age as Ed and Ann.

– They look okay, said Ed. – What a relief. Don't you think? Decent, ordinary people.

– We'll see. Ann returned to the tiny kitchen at the other end of the living room. – They'll bring a whole life with them, won't they, which we'll get to learn something about whether we like it or not.

The flat upstairs had been empty for a month. Ed and Ann had enjoyed the silence. Going to bed had become a pleasure again. The previous occupant, a musician, had not only returned home from work at three or four in the morning and played music, but had seemed to enjoy moving furniture at midnight, slaughtering animals and making various other unidentified sounds which tormented the couple from the day they moved in. They were considering renting another place when he left. It would have been a shame, as they liked the flat, the neighbourhood, the look of the people in the street.

– Ed, your breakfast's ready, said Ann.

They ate quickly in order to return to their position. It wouldn't take long to empty the van.

– Two well-used armchairs, said Ann.

– A jug now, said Ed, craning to look over her shoulder. – A cracked old thing with flowers on it!

– Perhaps, like me, she loves to see things being poured. Milk, water, apple juice!

– Now a guitar!'

– A rug. Nice colour. Bit scruffy, like everything else.

– Student things, really. But that new toaster must have cost them a bit, as well as the music system. Like us, they've been buying better things recently. Look.

Some of the cardboard boxes had come open; other objects the men and the couple carried in unpacked. It seemed to Ed and Ann that the couple had similar tastes to them in music, books and pictures.

– Eventually we'll have to go and say hello, said Ann.

– I suppose so.

– You never like meeting new people.

– Do you?

Ann said – I used to. You never know what interest you will find, or what life-journey they will help you begin.

He said, – What life-journey? We'll have to be careful, otherwise they'll be in and out of our place the whole time.

– Do they look like that to you? she said. – Like the sort of people who'd be in and out? What an assumption to make about strangers!

– So far they haven't taken any interest in their surroundings, said Ed. – Even I would look up at the building I was moving into.

– They're busy right now. They must be incredibly stressed. Actually, I don't believe you would look up.

Ed and Ann had been living together for three years. She was thirty and he was thirty-two. She was an assistant to a TV producer; he worked for a computer firm.

Ed and Ann had intended to go shopping, but this event was more compelling. The couple made coffee, fetched chairs and ate chocolate biscuits beside the window. When nothing much was happening, each of them in turn showered and dressed.

The van was empty. After paying the removal men, the new tenants disappeared into their flat. Ed and Ann had never been into the upstairs apartment, or into any of the other three apartments in the building. But it could only have been the same size as theirs, with a similar layout: bedroom, living room with a narrow kitchen at the end, and a bathroom.

Ed and Ann stood there, listening to the couple moving about.

Ann said, – I can tell they're trying to decide what to do with everything. When things are in place they tend to stay where they are. Nothing changes without a real effort. That happened to us.

– Perhaps we should change something now, said Ed. – What d'you think?

– Don't be silly. Listen, she said, looking up at the ceiling as though it were really transparent. – What they're doing is trying to find a way to merge their things, their lives, in other words.

– I want to know why we've wasted so much time doing this, he said. – I feel cheated. Let's go and see that Wong Kai-Wei film.

– Oh, no, she said. – I need something lighter.

Just as Ann and Ed were getting ready to go to the cinema, still trying to decide which film to see, the couple upstairs seemed to race out of their flat. Ed and Ann heard their feet on the uncarpeted stairs and the crash of the heavy front door.

– Look! called Ann, who had run back to the window.

Ed joined her immediately. – They're standing there in the street. They don't know where to go.

– Either they don't know the area or they can't make up their minds what to do.

– Weren't we like that?

– They've decided. At last! There they go.

– What's he reading? Can you see the book he's carrying?

– He's going to read! she said. – Aren't they going to talk? You're like that. He only opens books!

– He doesn't know anything except there's a hole in the centre of him! He's hungry for information!

– Doesn't he want information about her?

– That's not enough.

Ed and Ann watched the couple walk away, until they turned the corner.

A few hours later, when Ed and Ann returned from the cinema, they looked at each other as if to say, where are they? Almost at that moment the couple from upstairs returned too. Ed and Ann heard the door to the flat upstairs slam; after a while they played a record.

– Ah, said Ed. – That's what he likes.

It was a modern jazz record, known to people who liked 'fusion' but not, he guessed, to the general public. It made Ed want to hear it again, as if for the first time. He felt embarrassed to put his copy on, for fear the couple upstairs thought he was imitating them. Yet why should he have his life dictated by theirs? He played the record with the sound low, lying on the floor with his ear against the speaker.

– What do you think you're doing? said Ann.

When the record stopped, Ed heard the woman upstairs yawn, then the man laughed and seemed to throw his shoes across the floor.

The following week, Ed and Ann were aware of the upstairs couple going to work, to the pub, to the supermarket, and to the second-hand furniture shop to buy a bedside table. The couple left for work at a similar time to Ed and Ann. The man walked to the same tube station as Ed, on the other side of the street. Ann said she'd seen the woman in the bus queue. But they had not actually run into each other face to face yet. They had had no reason to say hello.

– But, as Ann said, – it's inevitable. Aren't you looking forward to it? I don't know anyone who has too many friends.

On Sunday Ed and Ann went to their local coffee shop for breakfast. It was a small café with only eight tables. They had just sat down when Ed noticed something in the Travel section of the newspaper, written by someone his age. 'Bastard,' he murmured, folding the page and tearing it out, to read later.

He looked up to see the couple from upstairs walking towards them. They came into the coffee shop, chose the table in the other alcove and ordered. They ate croissants and, just like Ed and Ann, the woman read the Culture pages and the man looked over the Travel section. He made a face, tore out an article, folded it up and put it in his jacket pocket.

Ed was about to comment on this when Ann said, – Is she attractive? Do you like her legs? You were looking at them.

– All I want is to see her cross them. Then I'll get on with my life. Her hair's all over the place. If she cut it and it was spiky, sort of punky, we could see what she was like.

Ann pulled back her own hair. – What d'you think? Look at me, Ed. What do you see?

– It's as if the sun's come out on a cloudy day, he replied, returning to his newspaper. Then he said in a low voice, – I guess we should go and say hello. Would you mind . . . going over?

– Me? I'm shocked. Why not you?

– You wanted to meet them. And it's always me, he said.

Nevertheless, Ed got to his feet. The man, too, in the other alcove was already getting up. Ed went to him.

The two men shook hands and introduced themselves.

– I'm Ed from the flat downstairs, Ed said. – This is Ann, my wife. Here she is.

Ann had joined them. – I'm sorry, I didn't catch your names, she said.

Ed said, – Ann, these are our new upstairs neighbours, Ed and Ann.

– Hello, Ann, said Ann. – Pleased to meet you. Do you want to hear about the neighbourhood?

– We thought you looked a little lost, said Ed.

– We'd love to hear about it, said Ann from upstairs.

Later the four of them walked back together, parting at the door of Ed and Ann's flat.

Inside, Ed and Ann didn't speak for a while. Ed watched Ann walking about; she seemed to be shaking her head as if she had water in her ears. Ann watched Ed glancing at the ceiling. They sat at the table, close together.

Ed whispered, – What time did they invite us for?

– Seven-thirty.

– Right. Are you looking forward to it?

– I'm wondering what they'll cook and whether they'll do it together.

He said, – We'll see. It'll be useful to get a look at their apartment, too. We've been talking about it for a while.

– What shall we wear?

– What? Normal clothes, he said. – It's a casual, neighbourly thing, isn't it?

– Maybe so, said Ann. – But I don't feel casual at this moment. Do you?

– No, he said. – I don't feel casual. I feel tense. I don't even know what we should do now.

When Ed and Ann first met, they developed the habit, on Sunday afternoons, of going to bed to make love. They still did this sometimes; or they lay down and he read while she wrote in her journal of self-discovery. Now they took off their clothes and got into bed as if they were being observed. They had never before been self-conscious about any noise they might make. They had never lain there without touching at all. When Ed glanced at Ann's unmoving body he knew she was listening for footsteps on the wooden floor above. It wasn't until they heard the sound of Ed and Ann making love upstairs that they felt obliged to get down to it themselves, finishing around the same time.

Slowly, they climbed the stairs to Ed and Ann's apartment for supper.

At around eleven-thirty they returned home, watched each other drink a glass of water – it was part of their new health regime – and went to bed. Upstairs, Ann and Ed were in bed, too.

Ed and Ann felt it was a tragedy that they knew the layout of Ed and Ann's flat upstairs. It was the same as theirs. But Ed and Ann had also placed their chairs, shelves, table, bed and other furniture in the same position. By the banging of doors, even the flushing of the toilet, the use of the shower, the scraping of chairs on the wooden floor, the selection of music, and the location of their voices and then the silence when they went to bed, they would know where Ed and Ann were in the flat and what they were doing.

After work the following day, Ed and Ann went to a local pub to eat and talk. Ed and Ann upstairs were already home. The TV was on and they'd changed out of their work clothes. Ed and Ann guessed the couple upstairs would be making supper.

But when Ed and Ann left the pub to walk home, they turned a corner and bumped into Ed and Ann who said, – We're off to that place you said served good food.

– Thank you for supper last night, they said. – We enjoyed it.

– We enjoyed having you, said Ed and Ann. – We must do something else together.

– Yes, said Ann, staring at Ann. – We must! We'll come round to you! We'll wait for you to set a date.

– We'll do that, said the other Ann.

Ed and Ann watched the other couple go into the pub.

When they got home, knowing Ed and Ann upstairs were out, Ed and Ann were able to talk in their normal voices.

– We will have to invite them back.

– Yes, said Ann. – We had better do that. Otherwise we will appear impolite.

– Maybe we should invite someone else, too, said Ed. – Another couple, perhaps.

– It'll make it less of a strain.

– Why should it be such a strain anyway? he asked.

– I don't know.

But neither of them thought it a good idea to invite another couple. For some reason they didn't want anyone else to see them with Ed and Ann upstairs. It might mean they had to discuss it.

At work, one lunchtime that week, Ed brought up the subject of his neighbours with a friendly colleague. Ed hadn't told Ann that he was intending to talk about this with anyone else, but he had to: the situation seemed to be making him preternaturally tired and paranoid. Sitting on the tube, where he could see the other Ed at the other end of the carriage reading the same book, what could he do but wonder whether anyone else was similarly shadowed?

– Suppose, he told the friend, – that a couple moved in upstairs who were very similar to you.

Once he'd relieved himself of this, Ed awaited his friend's reply. Of course the friend didn't see how this could be a problem. Ed tried to put it more clearly.

– Suppose they were not only quite similar, but were – how shall I put it? – exactly the same. It's as if they're the originals and you're only acting out their lives. Not only that, you thought they were petty, and a bit dim, and that their lives were dull, and that they were not generous enough with each other – they didn't see how much they would benefit from more giving all round – and they had nothing much to say for themselves . . . You know the sort of thing.

The friend said, – Naturally, they'd have the same ideas about you, too.

– I guess that's right, said Ed, nervously. – Let me put it like this: what if you met yourself and were horrified?

– I wouldn't be horrified but so amused I'd laugh my head off, said the friend. – Am I such a bad person? Is that what this important conversation is about?

Of course what Ed had described was not something of which this friend had had any experience. How could he possibly appreciate how terrible and oppressive such a thing could be? The only people Ed and Ann knew who had had this experience were Ed and Ann upstairs.

Ed and Ann tried to forget about their upstairs neighbours. They wanted to go about their lives as normally as possible. But the night following Ed's conversation with his friend, there was a knock on the door of the flat. When Ed opened it, he saw it was Ed. It turned out that both Anns were at evening classes and should be back soon. Ed wanted to borrow a CD he had heard Ed mention at supper. He had lost his own copy and wanted to tape Ed's.

– Come in, said Ed. 'Make yourself at home. I wasn't doing anything important.'

Ed offered him a drink. Then Ann phoned to say she was having a drink with a friend. The other Ann did the same. Ed stayed until the bottle was finished. He poured it himself and even asked if Ed minded turning off the TV – it was 'distracting' him. He talked about himself and didn't leave off until both Anns returned, around the same time.

When Ed and Ann were under the bedsheets, Ed said, – How could he do it? Just turn up and put me under that kind of pressure? I could have been . . .

– What? said Ann.

– Writing a piece about that journey I made to Nepal two years ago.

– Which I bet you weren't doing, said Ann. – Were you?

– Maybe I was about to start washing out my best fountain

pens. Ann, you know I've been intending to.

– I'm afraid you'll never begin that other journey, the deepest one, inside!

– I don't want to hear that! You make me feel awful!

She said, – What do we do in the evenings but watch TV and bicker? Tell me, what did Ed say?

– I learned a lot. He's in the wrong job. Can't get along with the people he works with. He has ambition, but it is unfocused. You go out of your house, people always say – it's the first thing – what do you do? They judge you by what you're achieving and by your importance. Yet to him everyone else seems cleverer and with a much better idea of what's going on. He realizes that whether he feels grown up or not, from the world's point of view he is now an adult.

– He knows he's not going to be rich!

– Rich! Nothing is moving forward for him. His fantasy is to be a travel writer. As if! Doesn't know if he'll ever make a living at it. Doesn't even know if he'll ever begin. His friends are making a name for themselves. He gets up in the morning, contemplates his life and can't begin to see how to fix it.

– Do they discuss it? Do they talk?

– Talk! He complains that she doesn't know whether to stay with him. She doesn't know whether this is the best of what a life can offer. She really wants to be a teacher, but he won't encourage her. He thinks she's a flake, interested only in her body, wasting their money on fake therapies and incapable of saying anything with any pith in it. There's a man at work who's older, who guides her, who will guide her away from him. I expect he's fucked her already.

– Oh, she wants to be inspired!

– Is that what she calls it?

– Wait a minute, she said. – Can you please stop? I have to get a drink of water.

– Go on then, drink! he said. – The couple's sex life has tailed off but they don't know if this is a natural fluctuation. If they have children they'll be stuck with each other in some way or other for good. Neither of them has the resources to make a decision! It's trivial in many ways, but in others it's the most important thing in their lives. All in all, they're going crazy inside.

– Some people's lives! said Ann.

For the next two weeks Ann and Ed went out after work, together sometimes, but mostly separately, not returning until late. Ed even took to walking around the streets, or sitting in bars, in order not to go home. He kept thinking there was something he had to do, that there was something significant which had to be changed, but he didn't know what it was. Once, in a pub in which there were many mirrors, Ed thought he saw Ed from upstairs sitting behind him. Thinking he'd seen the devil, he stood up and rushed out, gasping and gesticulating at nothing. He took to spreading out his newspaper and sitting on it beside the pond in a small park near by, wondering what ills could be cured by silence. Except that one evening, under the still surface of the pond, he saw pieces of his own face swimming in the darkness, like bits of a puzzle being assembled by God, and he had to close his eyes.

However compelling the silence by the pond, it didn't follow that they could not hear Ed and Ann upstairs in the morning, and it didn't obviate the problem of the weekends, or the fact that they had promised to invite Ed and Ann for supper, something they had to get past, unless it was to remain a troublesome, undischarged obligation.

Meanwhile, Ed and Ann bought new clothes and shoes; Ann had her hair cut. Ed started to exercise, in order to change the shape of his body. One night, Ann decided she wanted to get a cat but decided a tattoo would be less trouble. A badger, say, on her thigh, would be unique, a distinguishing mark.

Ed said, – That would be going too far, Ann!

– You won't let me be different! screamed Ann.

– They're driving you crazy! This is really getting to you.

– And it's not to you?

– That's it! he said, staring up at the ceiling. – They will have heard everything now!

– I don't care! she said. – I'm inviting them in here, then we'll know the truth!

She took a sheet of paper from the drawer, wrote on it, and took it upstairs, pushing it under the door. A few minutes later, it was returned with thanks.

– They can't wait to see us, said Ann, holding up the piece of paper.

The following weekend, Ed and Ann moved the table into the living room and put out glasses and cutlery; they shopped, cooked and talked things over. They both agreed that this event was the hardest thing they'd had to get through.

At a quarter to eight they opened the champagne and drank a glass each. At eight o'clock there was a knock on the door.

The two Anns and the two Eds kissed and embraced. Ed was looking healthy – he'd been swimming a lot. His Ann was wearing a long white dress which clung to her. She had nothing on underneath. It was so tight that to sit down she had to pull it up to her knees. She showed them her new tattoo.

It was late, almost morning, when the party broke up. Ed and Ann had left, and Ed and Ann were blowing out the candles and clearing a few things away when they fell upon each other and had sex on the rug, which they pulled under the table.

– We did it. I enjoyed the evening, said Ann, as they lay there.

– It wasn't so bad, said Ed.

– What was the best bit, for you?

– I'm thinking of it now, he said.

– I'll stroke your face, then, she said, – while you go over it in your mind.

The two Anns had been talking about their careers. Ed from upstairs, seated near the window and leaning back, had been looking out over the dark street, enjoying the small cigar Ed had given him. Ed had asked him a question, which the other Ed had chosen to answer at length, but only in his mind, though his lips smacked occasionally. Ed had watched his upstairs neighbour smoke, his impatience subsiding, trying to see what he liked and disliked about this familiar stranger. He had thought, 'I know I can't take all of him in now. All I have to do is look at him, face him, without turning away. If I turn away now, everything will be worse and I could be done for.'

As he had continued to look, with pity, with affection, with curiosity, until the two of them had seemed alone together, Ed had found himself thinking, – He's not so bad. He's lost hope, that's all. He has everything else, he's alive, and there's nothing wrong with him or her, or any of us here now. We only have to see this to grasp something valuable.

– And did you like her tonight? Ann said.

– I did, he said. – Very much so.

– What did you like?

– Her kindness, her intelligence, her energy and her soul. The fact she listens to others. She looks for good things about others to pick up on.

– Wonderful, she said. – What else?

He told her more; she told him what she had thought.

A fortnight later, on a Saturday morning, Ann went to the window.

– Ed, the van is here, she said.

– Good, said Ed, joining her. – There's the guitar, the rug, everything.

The van was parked outside. The familiar objects were being

carried in the opposite direction by the same two men. Ed and Ann from upstairs had given up their flat; they were going to Rio for six months and would leave their things with their parents. While they were away, they would think about what to do on their return.

When the van was packed, Ed and Ann went downstairs to wish their neighbours good luck. On the pavement, the couples said goodbye, wished each other well and exchanged phone numbers, sincerely hoping they would never have to see each other again.

The apartment upstairs was empty once more. Ed and Ann went back into their own flat. The silence seemed sublime.

– What shall we do now? said Ann.

– I don't know yet. Then he said, – Oh, but now I do.

– What?

He offered her his hand. In the bathroom, she undressed and stood there with her foot up on the side of the bath, to let him look at her, before she sat down. He filled the jug from the sink taps and went to her and let water fall over her hair, body and legs. Her face was upturned and her eyes were eager and bright, looking at him and into the water, cascading.

# GOODBYE, MOTHER

If you think the living are difficult to deal with, the dead can be worse.

This is what Harry's friend Gerald had said. The remark returned repeatedly to Harry, particularly that morning when he had so wearily and reluctantly got out of bed. It was the anniversary of his father's death. Whether it was seven or eight years, Harry didn't want to worry. He was to take Mother to visit Father's grave.

Harry wondered if his children, accompanied perhaps by his wife Alexandra, would visit his grave. What would they do with him in their minds; what would he become for them? He would never leave them alone, he had learned that. Unlike the living, the dead you couldn't get rid of.

Harry's mother was not dead, but she haunted him in two ways: from the past, and in the present. He talked to her several times a day, in his mind. This morning it was as a living creature that he had to deal with her.

He had been at home on his own for a week. Alexandra, his wife, was in Thailand attending 'workshops'. When they weren't running away, the two children, a boy and a girl, were at boarding school.

The previous night had been strange.

Now Mother was waiting for him in her overcoat at the door of the house he had been brought up in.

'You're late,' she almost shouted, in a humorous voice.

He knew she would say this.

He tapped his watch. 'I'm on time.'

'Late, late!'

He thrust his watch under her face. 'No, look.'

For Mother, he was always late. He was never there at the right time, and he never brought her what she wanted, and so he brought her nothing.

He didn't like to touch her, but he made himself bend down to kiss her. What a small woman she was. For years she had been bigger than him, of course; bigger than everything else. She had remained big in his mind, pushing too many other things aside.

If she had a musty, slightly foul, bitter smell, it was not only that of an old woman, but a general notification, perhaps, of inner dereliction.

'Shall we set off?' he said.

'Wait.'

She whispered something. She wanted to go to the toilet.

She trailed up the hall, exclaiming, grunting and wheezing. One of her legs was bandaged. The noises, he noticed, were not unlike those he made getting into bed.

The small house seemed tidy, but he remembered Mother as a dirty woman. The cupboards, cups and cutlery were smeared and encrusted with old food.

Mother hadn't bathed them often. He had changed his underwear and other clothes only once a week. He had thought it normal to feel soiled. He wondered if this was why other children had disliked and bullied him.

In the living room the television was on, as it was all the time. She would watch one soap opera while videoing another, catching up with them late at night or early in the morning. Mother had always watched television from the late afternoon until she went to bed. She hadn't wanted Harry or his brother or father to speak. If they opened their mouths, she told them to shut up. She hadn't wanted them in the room at all. She preferred the faces on television to the faces of her family.

She was an addict.

It gave him pleasure to turn off the TV.

Alexandra had recently started, among what he considered to be other eccentricities, a 'life journal'. Before Harry left for work, she sat in the kitchen overlooking the fields, blinking rapidly. She would write furiously across the page in a crooked slope, picking out different coloured children's markers from a plastic wallet and throwing down other markers, flinging them right onto the floor where they could easily upend him.

'Why are you doing this writing?'

He walked around the table, kicking away the lethal markers. It was like saying, why don't you do something more useful?

'I've decided I want to speak,' she said. 'To tell my story –'

'What story?'

'The story of my life – for what it is worth, if only to myself.'

'Can I read it?'

'I don't think so.' A pause. 'No.'

He said, 'What do you mean, people want to speak?'

'They want to say what happiness is for them. And the other thing. They want to be known to themselves and to others.'

'Yes, yes . . . I see.'

'Harry, you would understand that,' she said. 'As a journalist.'

'We keep to the facts,' he said, heading for the door.

'Is that right?' she said. 'The facts of life and death?'

Perhaps Mother was ready to speak. That might have been why she had invited him on this journey.

If she'd let little in or out for most of her life, what she had to say might be powerful.

He was afraid.

This was the worst day he'd had for a long time.

He didn't go upstairs to the two small bedrooms, but waited for her at the door.

He knew every inch of the house, but he'd forgotten it existed as a real place rather than as a sunken ship in the depths of his memory.

It was the only house in the street which hadn't been torn through or extended. Mother hadn't wanted noise or 'bother'. There was still an air-raid shelter at the end of the garden, which had been his 'camp' as a child. There was a disused outside toilet which hadn't been knocked down. The kitchen was tiny. He wondered how they'd all fitted in. They'd been too close to one another. Perhaps that was why he'd insisted that he and Alexandra buy a large house in the country, even though it was quite far from London.

He would, he supposed, inherit the house, sharing it with his brother. They would have to clear it out, selling certain things and burning others, before disposing of the property. They would have to touch their parents' possessions and their own memories again, for the last time.

Somewhere in a cupboard were photographs of him as a boy wearing short trousers and Wellington boots, his face contorted with anguish and fear.

Harry was glad to be going to Father's grave. He saw it as reparation for the 'stupid' remark he'd made not long before Father died, a remark he still thought about.

He led Mother up the path to the car.

'Hasn't it been cold?' she said. 'And raining non-stop. Luckily, it cleared up for us. I looked out of the window this morning and thought God is giving us a good day out. It's been raining solid here – haven't you noticed? Good for the garden! Doesn't make us grow any taller! We're the same size! Pity!'

'That's right.'

'Hasn't it been raining out where you are?' She pointed at the ragged front lawn. 'My garden needs doing. Can't get anyone to do it. The old lady up the road had her money stolen. Boys came to the door, saying they were collecting for the blind. You don't have to worry about these things . . .'

Harry said, 'I worry about other things.'

'There's always something. It never ends! Except where we're going!'

He helped Mother into the car and leaned over her to fasten the seat belt.

'I feel all trapped in, dear,' she said, 'with this rope round me.'

'You have to wear it.'

He opened the window.

'Oooh, I'll get a draught,' she said. 'It'll cut me in two.'

'It'll go right through you?'

'Right through me, yes, like a knife.'

He closed the window and touched the dashboard.

'What's that wind?' she said.

'The heater.'

'It's like a hair-dryer blowing all over me.'

'I'll turn it off, but you might get cold.'

'I'm always cold. My old bones are frozen. Don't get old!'

He started the engine.

With a startlingly quick motion, she threw back her head and braced herself. Her fingers dug into the sides of the seat. Her short legs and swollen feet were rigid.

When he was young, there were only certain times of the day when she would leave the house in a car, for fear they would be killed by drunken lunatics. He remembered the family sitting in their coats in the front room, looking at the clock and then at

Mother, waiting for the moment when she would say it was all right for them to set off, the moment when they were least likely to be punished for wanting to go out.

To him, now, the engine sounded monstrous. He had begun to catch her fears.

'Don't go too fast,' she said.

'The legal speed.'

'Oh, oh, oh,' she moaned as the car moved away.

Awake for most of the previous night, Harry had thought that she was, really, mad, or disturbed. This realization brought him relief.

'She's off her head,' he repeated to himself, walking about the house.

He fell on his knees, put his hands together and uttered the thought aloud to all gods and humans interested and uninterested.

If she was 'ill', it wasn't his fault. He didn't have to fit around her, or try to make sense of what she did.

If he saw this only now, it was because people were like photographs which took years to develop.

Harry's smart, grand friend Gerald had recently become Sir Gerald. Fifteen years ago they'd briefly worked together. For a long time they'd played cricket at the weekends.

Gerald had become a distinguished man, a television executive who sat on boards and made himself essential around town. He liked power and politics. You could say he traded in secrets, receiving them, hoarding them and passing them on like gold coins.

Harry considered himself too unimportant for Gerald, but Gerald had always rung every six months, saying it was time they met.

Gerald took him to his regular place where there were others like him. He was always seated in a booth in the corner where

they could be seen but not overheard. Gerald liked to say whatever was on his mind, however disconnected. Harry didn't
imagine that Gerald would do this with anyone else.

Last time, Gerald had said, 'Harry, I'm older than you and I've
been alive for sixty years. If you requested any wisdom I'd have
fuck-all to pass on, except to say: you can't blame other people
for your misfortunes. More champagne? Now, old chap, what's
on your mind?'

Harry had told Gerald that Alexandra had taken up with a
female hypnotist; a hypnotherapist.

'She's done what?' said Gerald.

'It's true.'

Gerald was chuckling.

Harry noticed that Mother was trembling.

On the way to see her, Harry had worried about her liking the
new Mercedes, which he called 'God's chariot'.

The car and what it meant had no interest for her. Her eyes
were closed.

He was trying to control himself.

A year ago, a friend had given him and Alexandra tickets for a
'hypnotic' show in the West End. They had gone along sceptically.
She preferred serious drama, he none at all. He couldn't count
the Ibsens he had slept through. However, he did often recall one
Ibsen which had kept his attention – the one in which the protag-
onist tells the truth to those closest to him, and destroys their
lives.

The hypnotist was young, his patter amusing, reassuring and
confident. Members of the audience rushed to the stage to have
his hands on them. Under the compère's spell they danced like
Elvis, using broom handles as microphone stands. Others put on
big ridiculous glasses through which they 'saw' people naked.

After, he and Alexandra went to an Italian restaurant in Covent Garden for supper. She liked being taken out.

'What did you think of the show?' she asked.

'It was more entertaining than a play. Luckily, I wasn't taken in.'

'Taken in?' she said. 'You thought it was fake? Everyone was paid to pretend?'

'Of course.'

'Oh, I didn't think that at all.'

She couldn't stop talking about it, about the 'depths' of the mind, about what was 'underneath' and could be 'unleashed'.

The next day, she went into town and bought books on hypnotism.

She hypnotized him to sleep in the evenings. It wasn't difficult. He liked her voice.

Harry was thirteen when Father crashed the car. They were going to the seaside to stay in a caravan. All summer he had been looking forward to the holiday. But not only had Mother been screeching from the moment the car left their house, but, a non-driver herself, she had clutched at Father's arm continually, and even dragged at the driving wheel itself.

She was successful at last. They ran into the front of an oncoming van, spent two nights in hospital and had to go home without seeing the sea. Harry's face looked as though it had been dug up with a trowel.

He looked across at Mother's formidable bosom, covered by a white polo-neck sweater. Down it, between her breasts, dangled a jewel-covered object, like half a salt pot.

At last, she opened her eyes and loudly began to read out the words on advertising hoardings; she read the traffic signs and the instructions written on the road; she read the names on shops. She was also making terrible noises from inside her body, groaning, he thought, like Glenn Gould playing Bach.

Visiting Father's grave had been her idea. 'It's time we went back again,' she had said. 'So he knows he hasn't been forgotten. He'll hear his name being called.'

But it was as if she were being dragged to her death.

If he said nothing, she might calm down. The child he once was would have been alarmed by her terrors, but why shouldn't she make her noises? Except that her babbling drove out everything else. She ensured there was no room in the car for any other words.

He realized what was happening. If she couldn't actually take the television with her in the car, she would become the television herself.

Alexandra was interested in the history of food, the garden, the children, novels. She sang in the local choir. Recently, she had started to take photographs and learn the cello. She was a governor of the local school and helped the children with their reading and writing. She talked of how, inexplicably, they suffered from low self-esteem. It was partly caused by 'class', but she suspected there were other, 'inner' reasons.

Her curiosity about hypnotism didn't diminish.

A friend introduced Alexandra to a local woman, a hypnotherapist. 'Amazing Olga', Harry called her.

'What does she do?' he asked, imagining Alexandra walking about with her eyes closed, her arms extended in front of her.

'She hypnotizes me. Suddenly, I'm five years old and my father is holding me. Harry, we talk of the strangest things. She listens to my dreams.'

'What is this for?'

For Harry, telling someone your dreams was like going to bed with them.

'To know myself,' she said.

Amazing Olga must have told Alexandra that Harry would believe they were conspiring against him.

She touched his arm and said, 'Your worst thoughts and criticisms about yourself – that's what you think we're saying about you in that room.'

'Something like that,' he said.

'It's not true,' she said.

'Thank you. You don't talk about me at all?'

'I didn't say that.'

'Nobody likes to be talked about,' he said.

'As if it weren't inevitable.'

In the train to work, and in the evenings when he fed the animals, he thought about this. He would discuss it with Gerald next time.

Faith healers, astrologers, tea-leaf examiners, palm readers, aura photographers – there were all manner of weirdo eccentrics with their hands in the pockets of weak people who wanted to know what was going on, who wanted certainty. Uncertainty was the one thing you couldn't sell as a creed, and it was, probably, the only worthwhile thing.

What would he say about this?

He did believe there was such a thing as a rational world view. It was based on logic and science. These days, 'enlightenment values' were much discredited. It didn't follow they were worthless. It was all they had.

'If you or one of the children fell sick, Alexandra . . .' he put to her one night.

It was dark, but he had switched on the garden lights. They were sitting out, eating their favourite ice-cream and drinking champagne. His trees shaded the house; the two young labradors, one black, one white, sat at their feet. He could see his wood in the distance, carpeted with bluebells in the spring, and the treehouse he would restore for his grandchildren. The pond, stifled by duckweed, had to be cleaned. He was saving up for a tennis court.

This was what he had lived for and made with his labour. He wasn't old and he wasn't young, but at the age when he was curious about, and could see, the shape of his whole life, his beginning and his end.

'You'd go to a doctor, wouldn't you? Not to a faith healer.'

'That's right,' she said. 'First to a doctor.'

'Then?'

'And then, perhaps to a therapist.'

'A therapist? For what?'

'To grasp the logic –'

'What logic?'

'The inner logic . . . of the illness.'

'Why?'

'Because I am one person,' she said. 'A whole.'

'And you are in control?'

'Something in me is making my life – my relationships, I mean – the way they are, yes.'

He was opposed to this, but he didn't know what to say.

She went on, 'There are archaic unknown sources which I want to locate.' Then she quoted her therapist, knowing that at university he had studied the history of ideas. 'If Whitehead said that all philosophy is footnotes to Plato, Freud taught us that maturity is merely a footnote to childhood.'

He said, 'If it's all been decided years ago, if there's no free will but only the determinism of childhood, then it's pointless to think we can make any difference.'

'Freedom is possible.'

'How?'

'The freedom that comes from understanding.'

He was thinking about this.

\*

His car had left the narrow suburban streets for bigger roads. Suddenly, he was in a maze of new one-way systems bounded by glittering office blocks. He drove through the same deep highway several times, to the same accompaniments from Mother.

Setting off from home that morning, he had been convinced that he knew how to get to the cemetery, but now, although he recognized some things, it was only a glancing, bewildered familiarity. He hadn't driven around this area for more than twenty-five years.

Mother seemed to take it for granted that he knew where he was. This might have been the only confidence she had in him. She loved 'safe' drivers. She liked coaches; for some reason, coach drivers, like some doctors, were trustworthy. Being safe mattered more than anything else because, in an inhospitable world, they were always in danger.

He didn't want to stop to ask the way, and he couldn't ask Mother for fear his uncertainty would turn her more feverish.

Cars driven by tattooed south London semi-criminals with shaven heads seemed to be pursuing them; vans flew at them from unexpected angles. His feet were cold, but his hands were sweating.

If he didn't keep himself together, he would turn into her.

He hadn't spoken to Mother for almost three months. He had had an argument with his brother – there had almost been a fist fight in the little house – and Mother, instead of making the authoritative intervention he had wished for, had collapsed weeping.

'I want to die,' she'd wailed. 'I'm ready!'

The forced pain she gave off had made him throw up in the gutter outside the house.

He had looked up from his sick to see the faces of the neighbours at their windows – the same neighbours, now thirty years older, he'd known as a child.

They would have heard from Mother that he was well paid.

Sometimes he was proud of his success. He had earned the things that other people wanted.

He worked in television news. He helped decide what the news was. Millions watched it. Many people believed that the news was the most important thing that had happened in the world that day. To be connected, they needed the news in the way they needed bread and water.

He remembered how smug he had been, self-righteous even, as a young man at university. Some went to radical politics or Mexico; others sought a creative life. The women became intense, quirkily intelligent and self-obsessed. Being lower middle class, he worked hard, preparing his way. The alternative, for him, he knew, was relative poverty and boredom. He had learned how to do his job well; for years he had earned a good salary. He had shut his mouth and pleased the bosses. He had become a boss himself; people were afraid of him, and tried to guess what he was thinking.

He worried there was nothing to him, that under his thinning hair he was a 'hollow man', a phrase from the poetry he'd studied at school. Being 'found out', Gerald called it, laughing, like someone who had perpetrated a con.

Harry's daughter Heather talked of wanting confidence. He understood that. But where could confidence originate, except from a parent who believed in you?

There she was next to him, vertiginous, drivelling, scratching in fear at the seat she sat on, waving, in her other hand, the disconnected seat-belt buckle.

It wasn't long before Alexandra started to call it 'work'.

The 'work' she was doing on herself.

The 'work' with the different coloured pens.

The 'work' of throwing them on the floor, of being the sort of person who threw things about if she felt like it.

'Work,' he said, with a slight sneer. 'The "work" of imagining an apple and talking to it.'

'The most important work I've done.'

'It won't pay for the barn to be cleared and rebuilt.'

'Why does that bother you so much?'

Money was a way of measuring good things. The worth of a man had to be related to what he was able to earn. She would never be convinced by this.

Her 'work' was equivalent to his work. No; it was more important. She had started to say his work was out of date, like prisons, schools, banks and politics.

She said, 'The cost and waste of transporting thousands of people from one part of the country to another for a few hours. These things continue because they have always happened, like bad habits. These are nineteenth-century institutions and we are a few months from the end of the twentieth century. People haven't yet found more creative ways of doing things.'

He thought of the trains on the bridges over the Thames, transporting trainloads of slaves to futility.

In the suburbs, where Mother still lived, the idea was to think of nothing; to puzzle over your own experience was to gratuitously unsettle yourself. How you felt wasn't important, only what you did, and what others saw.

Yet he knew that if he wasn't looking at himself directly, he was looking at himself in the world. The world had his face in it! If you weren't present to yourself, you'd find yourself elsewhere!

Almost all the men in the street had lighted sheds at the end of the garden, or on their allotments, to which they retreated in the evenings. These men were too careful for the pub. The sheds were where the men went to get away from the women. The women who weren't employed and had the time, therefore, to be disturbed. It was a division of labour: they carried the madness for the men.

'All right, Mother?' he said at last. 'We aren't doing so badly now.'

They had escaped the highway and regained the narrow, clogged suburban roads.

'Not too bad, dear,' she sighed, passing the back of her hand across her forehead. 'Oh, watch out! Can't you look where you're going? There's traffic everywhere!'

'That means we go slower.'

'They're so near!'

'Mother, everyone has an interest in not getting killed.'

'That's what you think!'

If Mother had kept on repeating the same thing and squealing at high volume, he would have lost his temper; he would have turned the car round, taken her home and dumped her. That would have suited him. Alexandra was coming back tomorrow; he had plenty to do.

But after a few minutes Mother calmed down, and even gave him directions.

They were on their way to the cemetery.

It was easy to be snobbish and uncharitable about the suburbs, but what he saw around him was ugly, dull and depressing. He had, at least, got away.

But, like Mother continuing to live here when there was no reason for it, he had put up with things unnecessarily. He had never rebelled, least of all against himself. He had striven, up to a point – before the universe, like his mother, had shut like a door in his face.

*

He was afraid Alexandra would fall in love with some exotic idea, or with Thailand, and never want to return. Mother's irritability and indifference had taught him that women wanted to escape. If they couldn't get away, they hated you for making them stay.

There was a couple he and Alexandra had known for a long time. The woman had laboured for years to make their house perfect. One afternoon, as he often did, Harry drove over for tea in their garden. The woman cultivated wild flowers; there was a summerhouse.

Harry sighed, and said to the man, 'You have everything you could want here. If I were you, I'd never go out.'

'I don't,' the man replied. He added casually, 'If I had my way, of course, we wouldn't live here but in France. They have a much higher standard of living.'

The man did not notice, but at this the woman crumpled, as if she'd been shot. She went inside, shut the windows and became ill. She could not satisfy her husband, couldn't quell his yearnings. It was impossible, and, without him asking her to do it, she had worn herself out trying.

If Alexandra was seeking cures, it was because she didn't have everything and he had failed her.

Yet their conflicts, of which there was at least one a week – some continued for days – weren't entirely terrible. Their disagreements uncovered misunderstandings. Sometimes they wanted different things, but only in the context of each other. She was close to his wishes, to the inner stream of him. They always returned to each other. There was never a permanent withdrawal, as there had been with Mother.

It was a little paradise at times.

In the newspapers, he learned of actors and sportsmen having affairs. Women wanted these people. It seemed easy.

There were attractive women in the office, but they were claimed immediately. They didn't want him. It wasn't only that he looked older than his years, as his wife had informed him. He looked unhealthy.

Plastic, anonymous, idealized sex was everywhere; the participants were only young and beautiful, as if desire was the exclusive domain of the thin.

He didn't think it was sex he wanted. He liked to believe he could get by without excessive pleasure, just as he could get by without drugs. He kept thinking that the uses of sex in the modern world were a distraction. It didn't seem to be the important thing.

What was important? He knew what it was – impermanence, decay, death and the way it informed the present – but couldn't bring himself to look straight at it.


'Where is Alexandra today?' Mother asked. 'I thought she might come with us. She never wants to see me.'

Mother's 'madness' had no magnetism for Alexandra; her complaints bored her; Alexandra had never needed her.

He said, 'She's gone to Thailand. But she sends beautiful letters to me, by fax, every day.'

He explained that Alexandra had gone to a centre in Thailand for a fortnight to take various courses. There were dream, healing, and 'imaging' workshops.

Mother said, 'What is she doing there?'

'She said on the phone that she is with other middle-aged women in sandals and bright dresses with a penchant for Joni Mitchell. The last I heard she was hugging these women and taking part in rituals on the beach.'

'Rituals?'

He had said to Alexandra when she rang, 'But you can't dance, Alexandra. You hate it.'

'I can dance badly,' she'd replied. 'And that's what I do, night after night.'

Dancing badly.

Harry said to Mother, 'She told me she looked up and the moon was smiling.'

'At her in particular?' said Mother.

'She didn't itemize,' said Harry.

'This is at your expense?'

Alexandra, somewhat patronizingly, had felt she had to explain it wasn't an infidelity.

'There's no other man involved,' she'd said before she left, packing a few things into their son's rucksack. 'I hope there aren't even any men there.'

He had looked at her clothes.

'Is that all you're taking?'

'I will rely on the kindness of strangers,' she had replied.

'You'll be wearing their clothes?'

'I don't see why not.'

It was an infidelity if she was 'coming alive', as she had put it. What could be a more disturbing betrayal than 'more life' even as he felt himself to be fading!

He was a conventional man, and he lived a conventional life in order for her, and the children presumably, one day, to live unconventional ones. Was he, to her, a dead weight? He feared losing sight of her, as she accelerated, dancing, into the distance.

'Anyway,' Mother said, 'thank you, Harry, dear.'

'For what?'

'For taking me to Dad's ... Dad's ...'

He knew she couldn't say 'grave'.

'That's okay.'

'The other sons are good to their mothers.'

'Better than me?'

'Some of them visit their mums every week. They sit with

them for hours, playing board games. One boy sent her on a cruise.'

'On the *Titanic*?'

'Little beast, you are! Still, without you I'd have to take three buses to see Dad.'

'Shame you didn't learn to drive.'

'I wish I had.'

He was surprised. 'Do you really?'

'Then I would have got around.'

'Why didn't you?'

'Oh, I don't know now. Too much to do, with the washing and the cleaning.'

He asked, 'Is there anything else that you would like me to do for you?'

'Thank you for asking,' she said. 'Yes.'

'What is it?'

'Harry, I want to go on a journey.'

One morning, when Alexandra was scribbling, he said, 'I'll say goodbye.'

She came to the door to wave, as she always did if she wasn't driving him to the station. She said she was sorry he had to go into the office – 'such a place' – every day.

'What the hell is wrong with it?' he asked.

The building was a scribble of pipes and wires, inhabited by dark suits with human beings inside. The harsh glow of the computer and TV screens reflected nothing back. Nothing reflected into eternity.

Something changed after she said this.

He travelled on the train with the other commuters. The idea they shared was a reasonable though stifling one: to live without, or to banish, inner and outer disorder.

He was attempting to read a book about Harold Wilson, Prime

Minister when Harry was young. There was a lot about the 'balance of payments'. Harry kept wondering what he had been wearing on his way to school the day Wilson made a particular speech. He wished he had his school exercise books, and the novels he had read then. This was a very particular way of doing history.

He had to put his face by the train window but tried not to breathe out for fear his soul would fly from his body and he would lose everything that had meaning for him.

At work, he would feel better.

He believed in work. It was important to sustain ceaseless effort. Making; building – this integrated the world. It was called civilization. Otherwise, the mind, like an errant child, ran away. It wanted only pleasure, and nothing would get done.

The news was essential information. Without it, you were uninformed, uneducated even. You couldn't see the way the world was moving. The news reminded you of other people's lives, of human possibility and destructiveness. It was part of his work to glance at the French, German, American and Italian papers every day.

However, an image haunted him. He was taking his university finals and a kid in his class – a hippy or punk, a strange, straggly peacock – turned over the exam paper, glanced at the question and said, 'Oh, I don't think there's anything here for me today,' and left the room, singing 'School's Out'.

Beautiful defiance.

Couldn't Harry walk into the office and say, 'There's nothing here for me today!' or 'Nothing of interest has happened in the world today!'?

He remembered his last years at school, and then at university. The other mothers helped their student kids into their new rooms, unpacking their bags and making the beds. Mother had disappeared into herself, neither speaking nor asking questions. As the size of her body increased, her self shrank, the one defending the other. He doubted she even knew what courses he was taking, whether he had graduated or not, or even what 'graduation' was.

She didn't speak, she didn't write to him, she hardly phoned. She was staring into the bright light, minute after minute, hour after hour, day after day, week after week, year after year. Television was her drug and anaesthetic, her sex her conversation her friends her family her heaven her . . .

Television did her dreaming for her.

It couldn't hear her.

After the television had 'closed down', and Father was listening to music in bed, she walked about the house in her dressing gown and slippers. He had no idea what she could be thinking, unless it was the same thing repeatedly.

It was difficult to be attached to someone who could only be attached to something else. A sleeping princess who wouldn't wake up.

He wondered if he'd gone into television so that he would be in front of her face, at least some of the time.

At this, he laughed.

'Don't shake like that,' she said. 'Look where you're going.'

'What journey?' he said.

'Oh, yes,' she said. 'I haven't told you.'


On the way to work, he had started to feel that if he talked with anyone they would get inside him; parts of the conversation would haunt him; words, thoughts, bits of their clothing would return like undigested food and he would be inhabited by worms, gnats, mosquitoes. Going to a meeting or to lunch, if human beings approached, his skin prickled and itched. If he thought, 'Well, it's only a minor irritation', his mind became unendurable, as if a landscape of little flames had been ignited not only on the surface of his skin, but within his head.

The smell, the internal workings of every human being, the shit, blood, mucus swilling in a bag of flesh, made him mad. He felt he was wearing the glasses the stage hypnotist had given people, but instead of seeing them naked, he saw their inner physiology, their turbulence, their death.

At meetings, he would walk up and down, constantly going out of the room and then out of the building, to breathe. From behind pillars in the foyer, strangers started to whisper the 'stupid' remark at him, the one he had made to Father.

His boss said, 'Harry, you're coming apart. Go and see the doctor.'

The doctor informed him there were drugs to remove this kind of radical human pain in no time.

Harry showed the prescription to Alexandra. She was against the drugs. She wouldn't even drink milk because of the 'chemicals' in it.

He told her, 'I'm in pain.'

She replied, 'That pain . . . it's your pain. It's you – your unfolding life.'

They went to a garden party. The blessed hypnotherapist would be there. It would be like meeting someone's best friend for the first time. He would see who Alexandra wanted to be, who she thought she was like.

He spotted Amazing Olga on the lawn. She wore glasses. If she had a slightly hippy aspect it was because her hair hung down her back like a girl's, and was streaked with grey.

Alexandra had copied this, he realized. Her hair was long now, making her look slightly wild – different, certainly, to the well-kempt wives of Harry's colleagues.

The hypnotherapist looked formidable and self-possessed.

Harry wanted to confront her, to ask where she was leading his wife, but he feared she would either say something humiliating or look into his eyes and see what he was like. It would be like being regarded by a policeman. All one's crimes of shame and desire would be known.

He didn't like Alexandra going away because he knew he didn't exist in the mind of a woman as a permanent object. The moment he left the room they forgot him. They would think of other things, and of other men, better at everything than he. He was rendered a blank. This wasn't what the women's magazines, which his daughter Heather read, called low self-esteem. It was being rubbed out, annihilated, turned into nothing by a woman he was too much for.

Sometimes, he and Alexandra had to attend dull dinners with work colleagues.

'I always have to sit next to the wives,' he complained, resting on the bed to put on his heavy black shoes. 'They never say anything I haven't heard before.'

Alexandra said, 'If you bother to talk and listen, it's the wives who are interesting. There's always more to them than there is to the husbands.'

He said, 'That attitude makes me angry. It sounds smart, but it's prejudice.'

'There's more to the women's lives.'

'More what?'

'More emotion, variety, feeling. They're closer to the heart of things – to children, to themselves, to their husbands and to the way the world really works.'

'Money and politics are the engine.'

'They're a cover story,' she said. 'It's on top, surface.'

He was boring. He bored himself.

She was making him think of why she would want to be with him; of what he had to offer.

When he came home from school with news spilling from him, Mother never wanted to know. 'Quiet, quiet,' she'd say. 'I'm watching something.'

Gerald had said, 'Even when we're fifty we expect our mummy and daddy to be perfect, but they are only ever going to be just what they are.'

It would be childish to blame Mother for what he was now. But if he didn't understand what had happened, he wouldn't be free of his resentment and couldn't move on.

Understand it? He couldn't even see it! He lived within it, but like primitive man almost entirely ignorant of his environment, and trying to influence it with magic, in the darkness he couldn't make anything out!

Gerald had said, 'Children expect too much!'

Too much! Affection, attention, love – to be liked! How could it be too much?

On their wedding day, he had not anticipated that his marriage to Alexandra would become more complicated and interesting as time passed. It hadn't become tedious or exhausted; it hadn't even settled into a routine. He lived the life his university friends would have despised for its unadventurousness. Yet, every day it was strange, unusual, terrifying.

He had wanted a woman to be devoted to him, and, when, for years, she had been, he had refused to notice. Now, she wasn't; things had got more lively, or 'kicked up', as his son liked to say.

Alexandra blazed in his face, day after day.

Mother, though, hadn't changed. She was too preoccupied to be imaginative. He wasn't, therefore, used to alteration in a woman.

Last night . . .

He had found himself searching through Alexandra's clothes, letters, books, make-up. He didn't read anything, and barely touched her belongings.

He had read in a newspaper about a public figure who had travelled on trains with a camera concealed in the bottom of his suitcase in order to look up women's skirts, at their legs and underwear. The man said, 'I wanted to feel close to the women.'

When it comes to love, we are all stalkers.

Last night, Harry checked the house, the garden and the land. He fed the dogs, Heather's horse, the pig and the chickens.

Alexandra kept a tape deck in one of the collapsing barns. He had seen her, dancing on her toes, her skirt flying, singing to herself. He'd recalled a line from a song: 'I saw you dancing in the gym, you both kicked off your shoes . . .'

On an old table she kept pages of writing; spread out beside them were photographs she had been taking to illustrate the stories.

She'd said, 'If there's a telephone in the story, I'll take a picture of a phone and place it next to the paragraph.'

In the collapsing barn, he put on a tape and danced, if dancing was the word for his odd arthritic jig, in his pyjamas and Wellington boots.

That was why he felt stiff this morning.

'There is a real world,' said Richard Dawkins the scientist.

Harry had repeated this to himself, and then passed it on to Alexandra as an antidote to her vaporous dreaming.

She had laughed and said, 'Maybe there is a real world. But there is no one living in it.'

It was inevitable: they were nearing the churchyard and a feeling of dread came over him.

Mother turned to him. 'I've never seen you so agitated.'

'Me? I'm agitated?'

'Yes. You're twitching like a St Vitus's dance person. Who d'you think I'm talking about?'

Harry said, 'No, no – I've got a lot to think about.'

'Is something bothering you?'

Alexandra had begged him not to take medication. She'd promised to support him. She'd gone away. The 'strange' had never come this close to him before.

But it was too late for confidences with Mother.

He had made up his mind about her years ago.

Mother hated cooking, housework and gardening. She hated having children. They asked too much of her. She didn't realize how little children required.

He thought of her shopping on Saturday, dragging the heavy shopping home, and cooking the roast on Sunday. The awfulness of the food didn't bother him; the joylessness which accompanied the futile ritual did. It wasn't a lunch that started out hopefully, but one which failed from the start. The pity she made him feel for her was, at that age, too much for him.

She couldn't let herself enjoy anything, and she couldn't flee.

If he had made a decent family himself it was because Alexandra had always believed in it; any happiness he experienced was with her and the children. She had run their lives, the house and the garden, with forethought, energy and precision. Life and meaning had been created because she had never doubted the value of what they were doing. It was love.

If there was anguish about 'the family', it was because people knew it was where the good things were. He understood that happiness didn't happen by itself; making a family work was as hard as running a successful business, or being an artist. To him, it was doubly worthwhile because he had had to discover this for himself. Sensibly, somehow, he had wanted what Alexandra wanted.

She had kept them together and pushed them forward.

He loved her for it.

Now, it wasn't enough for her.


He said, 'Would it be a good idea to get some flowers?'

'Lovely,' said Mother. 'Let's do that.'

They stopped at a garage and chose some.

'He would have loved these colours,' she said.

'He was a good man,' murmured Harry.

'Oh yes, yes! D'you miss him?'

'I wish I could talk to him.'

She said, 'I talk to him all the time.'

Harry parked the car. They walked through the gates.

The cemetery was busy, a thoroughfare, more of a park than a burial ground. Women pushed prams, school kids smoked on benches, dogs peed on gravestones.

Father had a prime spot in which to rot, at the back, by the fence.

Mother put down her flowers.

Harry said, 'Would you like to get down, Mother? You can use my jacket.'

'Thank you, dear, but I'd never get up again.'

She bent her head and prayed and wept, her tears falling on the grave.

Harry walked about, weeping and muttering his own prayer: 'At least let me be alive when I die!'

Father would have been pleased by their attendance.

He thought, 'Dying isn't something you can leave to the last moment.'

He was like the old man, too. He had to remember that. Being pulled in two directions had saved him.

He walked away from Mother and had a cigarette.

His boss had told him unequivocally 'to rest'. He had said, 'To be frank, you're creating a bad atmosphere in the office.'

Harry's fourteen-year-old daughter Heather had run away from boarding school. Returning from the shops two days after Alexandra had left for Thailand, he found her sitting in the kitchen.

'Hello there, Dad,' she said.

'Heather. This is a surprise.'

'Is it okay?' She looked apprehensive.

He said, 'It's fine.'

They spent the day together. He didn't ask why she was there.

He got on well with the boy, who seemed, at the moment, to worship him. He would, Gerald said, understand him for another couple of years, when the boy would be fourteen, and then never again.

Over Heather, he felt sorry and guilty about a lot of things. If he thought about it, he could see that her sulks, fears and unhappinesses, called 'adolescence', were an extended mourning for a lost childhood.

After lunch, when she continued to sit there, looking at him, he did say, 'Is there anything you want to ask me?'

'Yes,' she said. 'What is a man?'

'Sorry?'

'What is a man?'

'Is that it?'

She nodded.

What is a man?

She hadn't said, 'What is sex?' Not, 'Who am I?' Not even, 'What am I doing here in this kitchen and on earth?' But, 'What is a man?'

She cooked for him. They sat down together in the living room and listened to a symphony.

He wanted to know her.

It had taken him a while to see – the screechings of the feminists had made him resistant – that the fathers had been separated from their children by work, though provided with the consolations of power. The women, too, had been separated from important things. It was a division he had had in the back of his mind, had taken for granted, most of his life.

They were lower middle class; his father had had a furniture shop. He had worked all day his entire life and had done well. By the end he had two furniture shops. They did carpeting, too.

Harry and his brother had helped in the shops.

It was the university holidays when Harry accompanied his father on the train to Harley Street. Father had retired. He was seeking help for depression.

'I'm feeling too down all the time,' he said. 'I'm not right.'

As they sat in the waiting room, Father said of the doctor, 'He's the top man.'

'How d'you know?'

'There's his certificate. I can't make out the curly writing from here, but I hope it's signed.'

'It is signed.'

'You've got good eyes, then,' Father said. 'This guy will turn me into Fred Astaire.'

Father was smiling, full of hope for the first time in weeks.

'What's wrong, sir?' said the doctor, a man qualified to make others better.

He listened to Father's terse, urgent account of inner darkness and spiritual collapse before murmuring, 'Life has no meaning, eh?'

'The wrong meaning,' said Father, carefully.

'The wrong meaning,' repeated the doctor.

He scribbled a prescription for tranquillizers. They'd hardly been in there for half an hour.

As they went away, Harry didn't want to point out that the last thing tranquillizers did was make you happy.

Harry was puzzled and amused by Father striking out for happiness. It seemed a little late. What did he expect? Why couldn't he sink into benign, accepting old age? Isn't that what he, Harry, would have done?

He was taking Mother's side. This was the deep, wise view. Happiness was impossible, undesirable even, an unnecessary distraction from the hard, long, serious business of unhappiness. Mother would not be separated from the sorrow which covered her like a shroud.

In life, Harry chose the dullest things – deliberately at first, as if wanting to see what it felt like to be Mother. Then it became a habit. Why did he choose this way rather than his father's?

His daughter Heather had always been fussy about her food. By the time she was thirteen, at every meal she sat at the table with her head bent, her fork held limply between her fingers, watched by her mother, brother and father. Could she eat or not?

Harry was unable to bear her 'domination of the table' as she picked at her food, shoved it around the plate and made ugly faces before announcing that she couldn't eat today. It disgusted him. If he pressurized her to eat, Heather would weep.

He saw that it isn't the most terrible people that we hate, but those who confuse us the most. His power was gone; his compassion broke down. He mocked and humiliated her. He could have murdered this little girl who would not put bread in her mouth.

He had, to his shame, refused to let Heather eat with them. He ordered her to eat earlier than the family, or later, but not with him, her mother or brother.

Alexandra had said that if Heather wasn't allowed to eat with them, she wouldn't sit at the table either.

Harry started taking his meals alone in another room, with a newspaper in front of him.

Alexandra had been indefatigable with Heather, cooking innumerable dishes until Heather swallowed something. This made him jealous. If Mother had never been patient with him, he wanted Alexandra to tell him whether he was warm enough, what time he should go to bed, what he should read on the train.

Perhaps this was why Heather had wanted to go to boarding school.

His resentment of her had gone deep. He had come to consider her warily. It was easier to keep away from someone; easier not to tangle with them. If she needed him, she could come to him.

A distance had been established. He understood that a life could pass like this.


Father, always an active, practical man, had taken the tranquillizers for a few days, sitting on the sofa near Mother, waiting to feel better, looking as though he'd been hit on the head with a mallet. At last, he threw away the pills, and resumed his pilgrimage around Harley Street. If you were sick, you went to a doctor. Where else could you go, in a secular age, to find a liberating knowledge?

It was then that Harry made the stupid remark.

They were leaving another solemn surgery, morbid with dark wood, creaky leather and gothic certificates. After many tellings, Father had made a nice story of his despair and wrong meanings. Harry turned to the doctor and said, 'There's no cure for living!'

'That's about right,' replied the doctor, shaking his pen.

Then, with Father looking, the doctor winked.

No cure for living!

As Father wrote the cheque, Harry could see he was electric with fury.

'Shut your big mouth in future!' he said, in the street. 'Who's asking for your stupid opinion? There's no cure! You're saying I'm incurable?'

'No, no –'

'What do you know? You don't know anything!'

'I'm only saying –'

Father was holding him by the lapels. 'Why did we stay in that small house?'

'Why did you? What are you talking about?'

'The money went on sending you to a good school! I wanted you to be educated, but you've turned into a sarcastic, smart-arsed idiot!'

The next time Father visited the doctor, Harry's brother was deputed to accompany him.

Harry had a colleague who spent every lunchtime in the pub, with whom Harry would discuss the 'problem' of how to get along with women. One day, this man announced he had discovered the 'solution'.

Submission was the answer. What you had to do was go along with what the woman wanted. How, then, could there be conflict?

To Harry, this sounded like a recipe for fury and murder, but he didn't dismiss it. Hadn't he, in a sense – not unlike all children – submitted to his mother's view of things? And hadn't this half-killed his spirit and left him frustrated? He wasn't acting from his own spirit, but like a slave; his inner spirit, alive still, hated it.

'Harry, Harry!' Mother called. 'I'm ready to go.'

He walked across the grass to her. She put her handkerchief in her bag.

'All right, Mother.' He added, 'Hardly worth going home now.'

'Yes, dear. It is a lovely place. Perhaps you'd be good enough to put me here. Not that I'll care.'

'Right,' he said.

Father, the day he went to see the doctor, remembered how he had once loved. He wanted that loving back. Without it, living was a cold banishment.

Mother couldn't let herself remember what she loved. It was not only the unpleasant things that Mother wanted to forget, but anything that might remind her she was alive. One good thing might be linked to others. There might be a flood of disturbing happiness.

Before Father refused to have Harry accompany him on his doctor visits, Harry became aware, for the first time, that Father thought for himself. He thought about men and women, about politics and the transport system in London, about horse racing and cricket, and about how someone should live.

Yet his father never read anything but newspapers. Harry recalled the ignorant, despised father in *Sons and Lovers*.

Harry had believed too much in people who were better educated. He had thought that the truth was in certain books, or in the thinkers who were current. It had never occurred to Harry that one could – should – work these things out for oneself.

Who was he to do this? Father had paid for his education, yet it gave Harry no sustenance; there was nothing there he could use now, to help him grasp what was going on.

He was a journalist, he followed others – critically, of course. But he served them; he put them first.

Television and newspapers bored Alexandra. 'Noise', she called it. She had said, 'You'd rather read a newspaper than think your own thoughts.'

He and Mother made their way back to the car.

She had never touched, held or bent down to kiss him; her

body was as inaccessible to him as it probably was to her. He had never slept in her bed. Now, she took his arm. He thought she wanted him to support her, but she was steady. Affection, it might have been.

One afternoon, when Alexandra had returned from the hypnotherapist and was unpacking the shopping on the kitchen table, Harry asked her, 'What did Amazing Olga say today?'

Alexandra said, 'She told me something about what makes us do things, about what motivates us.'

'What did Mrs Amazing say? Self-interest?'

'Falling in love with things,' she said. 'What impels us to act is love.'

'Shit,' said Harry.

The day she ran away, after the two of them had eaten and listened to music, Heather wanted to watch a film that someone at school had lent her. She sat on the floor in her pyjamas, sucking her thumb, wearing her Bugs Bunny slippers. She wanted her father to sit with her, as she had as a kid, when she would grasp his chin, turning it in the direction she required.

The film was *The Piano*, which, it seemed to him, grew no clearer as it progressed. When they paused the film to fetch drinks and food, she said that understanding it didn't matter, adding, 'particularly if you haven't been feeling well lately'.

'Who's not feeling well?' he said. 'Me, you mean?'

'Maybe,' she said. 'Anyone. But perhaps you.'

She was worried about him; she had come to watch over him.

He knew she had got up later to watch the film another couple of times. He wondered whether she had stayed up all night.

In the morning, when he saw how nervous she looked, he said, 'I don't mind if you don't want to go back to school.'

'But you've always emphasized the "importance of education".'

Here she imitated him, quite well. They did it, the three of them, showing him how foolish he was.

He went on, feebly he thought, but on nevertheless: 'There's so much miseducation.'

'What?' She seemed shocked.

'Not the information, which is mostly harmless,' he said, 'but the ideas behind it, which come with so much force – the force that is called "common sense".'

She was listening, and she never listened.

She could make of it what she wanted. His uncertainty was important. Why pretend he had considered, final views on these matters? He knew politicians: what couldn't be revealed by them was ignorance, puzzlement, the process of intellectual vacillation. His doubt was a kind of gift, then.

He said, 'About culture, about marriage, about education, death . . . You receive all sorts of assumptions that it takes years to correct. The less the better, I say. It's taken me years to correct some of the things I was made to believe early on.'

He was impressed by how impressed she had been.

'I will go back to school,' she said. 'I think I should, for Mum.'

Before he took her to the station, she sat where her mother sat, at the table, writing in a notebook.

He had to admit that lately he had become frustrated and aggressive with Alexandra, angry that he couldn't control or understand her. By changing, she was letting him down; she was leaving him.

Alexandra rarely mentioned his mother and he never talked seriously about her for fear, perhaps, of his rage, or the memory of rage, it would evoke. But after a row over Olga, Alexandra said, 'Remember this. Other people aren't your mother. You don't have to yell at them to ensure they're paying attention. They're not half-dead and they're not deaf. You're wearing yourself out, Harry, trying to get us to do things we're doing already.'

Alexandra had the attributes that Mother never had. He hadn't, at least, made the mistake of choosing someone like his mother, of living with the same person for ever without even knowing it.

Oddly, it was the ways in which she wasn't like Mother which disturbed him the most.

He thought: a man was someone who should know, who was supposed to know. Someone who knew what was going on, who had a vision of where they were all heading, separately and as a family. Sanity was a great responsibility.

'Why did you run away from school?' he asked Heather at last.

Placing her hands over her ears, she said there were certain songs she couldn't get out of her head. Words and tunes circulated on an endless loop. This had driven her home to Father.

He said, 'Are the noises less painful here?'

'Yes.'

He would have dismissed it as a minor madness if he hadn't, only that afternoon . . .

He had been instructed to rest, and rest he would, after years of work. He had gone into the garden to lie on the grass beneath the trees. There, at the end of the cool orchard, with a glass of wine beside him, his mind had become possessed by brutal images of violent crime, of people fighting and devouring one another's bodies, of destruction and the police; of impaling, burning, cutting.

Childhood had sometimes been like this: hatred and the desire to bite, kill, kick.

He had been able to lie there for only twenty minutes. He had walked, then, thrashing his head as if to drive away the insanity.

A better way of presenting the news might be this: a screaming woman, dripping blood and guts, holding the corpse of a flayed animal. A ripped child; armfuls of eviscerated infants; pieces of chewed body.

This would be an image, if they kept it on screen for an hour or so, that would not only shock but compel consideration of the nature of humankind.

He had run inside and turned on the television.

If he seemed to know as much about his own mind as he did about the governance of Zambia, how could his daughter's mind not be strange to her?

There was no day of judgement, when a person's life would be evaluated, the good and the bad, in separate piles. No day but every day.

Alexandra was educating him: a pedagogy of adjustment and strength. These were the challenges of a man's life. It was pulling him all over the place. The alternative wasn't just to die feebly, but to self-destruct in fury because the questions being asked were too difficult.

If he and Alexandra stayed together, he would have to change. If he couldn't follow her, he would have to change more.

A better life was only possible if he forsook familiar experiences for seduction by the unfamiliar. Certainty would be a catastrophe.

The previous evening, Alexandra had rung from her mobile phone. He'd thought the background noise was the phone's crackle, but it was the sea. She had left the taverna and was walking along the beach behind a group of other women.

'I've decided,' she said straight away, sounding ecstatic.

'What is it, Alexandra?'

'It has become clear to me, Harry! My reason, let's say. I will work with the unconscious.'

'In Thailand?'

'In Kent. At home.'

'I guess you can find the unconscious everywhere.'

'How we know others. What sense we can make of their minds. That is what interests me. When I'm fully trained, people will come –'

'Where? Where?' He couldn't hear her.

'To the house. We will need a room built, I think. Will that be all right?'

'Whatever you want.'

'I will earn it back.'

He asked, 'What will the work involve?'

'Working with people, individually and in groups, in the afternoons and evenings, helping them understand their imaginations. It is a training, therefore, in possibility.'

'Excellent.'

'Do you mean that? This work is alien to you, I know. Today, today – a bunch of grown-ups – we were talking to imaginary apples!'

'Somehow it wouldn't be the same', he said, 'with bananas! But I am with you, at your side, always . . . wherever you are!'


He had had intimations of this. There had been an argument.

He had asked her, 'Why do you want to help other people?'

'I can't think of anything else as interesting.'

'Day after day you will listen to people droning on.'

'After a bit, the self-knowledge will make them change.'

'I've never seen such a change in anyone.'

'Haven't you?'

'I don't believe I have,' he'd said.

'Haven't you?'

He'd said agitatedly, 'Why d'you keep repeating that like a parrot?' She'd looked at him levelly. He'd gone on, 'Tell me when and where you've seen this!'

'You're very interested.'

'It would be remarkable,' he'd said. 'That's why I'm interested.'

'People are remarkable,' she'd said. 'They find all sorts of resources within themselves that were unused, that might be wasted.'

'Is it from that "Amazing" woman that you get such ideas?'

'She and I talk, of course. Are you saying I don't have a mind of my own?'

He'd said, 'Are you talking about a dramatic change?'

'Yes.'

'Well,' he'd said. 'I don't know. But I'm not ruling it out.'

'That's something.' She had smiled. 'It's a lot.'

He had wanted to tell Heather that clarity was not illuminating; it kept the world away. A person needed confusion and muddle – good difficult knots and useful frustrations. Someone could roll up their sleeves and work, then.

He got Mother into the car and started it.

She said, 'Usually I lie down and shut the tops of me eyes at this time. You're not going to keep me up, are you?'

'Only if you want to eat. D'you want to do that?'

'That's an idea. I'm starving. Tummy's rumbling. Rumblin'!'

'Come on.'

In the car, he murmured, 'You were rotten to me.'

'Oh, was I so terrible?' she cried. 'I only gave you life and fed and clothed you and brought you up all right, didn't I? You were never late for school!'

'Sorry? You couldn't wait for us to get out of the house!'

'Haven't you done better than the other boys? They're plumbers! People would give their legs to have your life!'

'It wasn't enough.'

'It's never enough, is it? It never was! It never is!'

He went on, 'If I were you, looking back on your life now, I'd be ashamed.'

'Oh, would you?' she said. 'You've been so marvellous, have you, you miserable little git!'

'Fuck you,' he told his mother. 'Fuck off.'

'You're terrible,' she said. 'Picking an old woman to pieces the day she visits her husband's grave. I've always loved you,' she said.

'It was no use to me. You never listened and you never talked to me.'

'No, no,' she said. 'I spoke to you, but I couldn't say it. I cared, but I couldn't show it. I've forgotten why. Can't you forget all that?'

'No. It won't leave me alone.'

'Just forget it,' she said, her face creasing in anguish. 'Forget everything!'

'Oh, Mother, that's no good. Nothing is forgotten, even you know that.'

'Father took me to Venice, and now I want to go again. Before it's too late – before they have to carry me wheelchair over the Wotsit of Cries.'

'You'll go alone?'

'You won't take me –'

'I wouldn't walk across the road with you', he said, 'if I could help it. I can't stand the sight of you.'

She closed her eyes. 'No, well . . . I'll go with the other old girls.'

He said, 'You want me to pay for you?'

'I thought you wouldn't mind,' she said. 'I might meet a nice chap! A young man! I could get off! I'm a game old bird in me old age!'

She started to cackle.

*

'Like what?' Heather asked. 'What educational ideas are no good?'

'I think I have believed that if I waited, if I sat quietly at the table, without making a noise or movement – being good – the dish of life would be presented to me.'

He should have added: people want to believe in unconditional love, that once someone has fallen in love with you, their devotion will continue, whether you spend the rest of your life lying on the sofa drinking beer or not. But why should they? If love was not something that could be worked up, it had to be kept alive.

Mother said, 'Children are selfish creatures. Only interested in themselves. You get sick of them. You bloody hate them, screaming, whining, no gratitude. And that's about it!'

'I know,' he said. 'That's true. But it's not the whole story!'

The restaurant was almost empty, with a wide window overlooking the street.

Mother drank wine and ate spare ribs with her fingers. The wine reddened her face; her lips, chin and hands became greasy.

'It's so lovely, the two of us,' she said. 'You were such an affectionate little boy, following me around everywhere. You became quite rough, playing football in the garden and smashing the plants and bushes.'

'All children are affectionate,' he said. 'I'm fed up with it, Mother.'

'What are you fed up with now?' she said, as if his complaints would never cease.

'My job. I feel I'm in a cult there.'

'A cult? What are you talking about?'

'The bosses have made themselves into little gods. I am a little god, to some people. Can you believe it? I walk in, people tremble. I could ruin their lives in a moment –'

'A cult?' she said, wiping her mouth and dipping her fingers in a bowl of water. 'Those things they have in America?'

'It's like that, but not exactly. It is a cheerleader culture. There are cynics about, but they are all alcoholics. What the bosses want is to display ridiculous little statuettes on their shelves. They want to be written about by other journalists – the little praise of nobodies. Mother, I'm telling you, it's Nazi and it's a slave ideology.'

He was shaking; he had become over-enthusiastic.

He said, more mildly, 'Still, work – it's the same for everyone. Even the Prime Minister must sometimes think, first thing in the morning –'

'Oh, don't do it,' she said. 'Just don't.'

'I knew you wouldn't understand. Alexandra and the kids wouldn't like it if I suddenly decided to leave for Thailand. I have four people to support.'

'You don't support me,' she said.

'Certainly not.'

'That's your revenge, is it?'

'Yes.'

'Excuse me for saying so, dear. We're both getting on now. You could drop dead any minute. You've been sweating all day. Your face is damp. Is your heart all right?'

She touched his forehead with her napkin.

'My friend Gerald had a heart attack last month,' he said.

'No. Your dad, bless him, retired, and then he was gone. What would your wife and the kids do then?'

'Thank you, Mother. What I'm afraid of is that I will just walk out of my job or insult someone or go crazy like those gunmen who blaze away at strangers.'

'You'd be on the news instead of behind it.' She was enjoying herself. 'You'd be better off on your own, like me. I've got no one bothering me. Peace! I can do what I want.'

'I want to be bothered by others. It's called living.' He went on,

'Maybe I feel like this because I've been away for a week. I'll go in on Monday and find I don't have these worries.'

'You will,' she said. 'Once a worry starts –'

'You'd know about that. But what can I do?'

'Talk to Alexandra about it. If she's getting all free and confident about herself, why can't you?'

'Yes, perhaps she can support me now.'


They were about to order pudding when a motorcyclist buzzed down the street in front of them, turned left into a side street, hit a car, and flew into the air.

The waiters ran to the window. A crowd gathered; a doctor forced his way through. An ambulance arrived. The motorcyclist lay on the ground a long time. At last, he was strapped onto a stretcher and carried to the ambulance, which only travelled a few yards before turning off its blue light and klaxon.

'That's his life done,' said Mother. 'Cheerio.'

The ruined motorcycle was pushed onto the pavement. The debris was swept up. The traffic resumed.

Harry and Mother put down their knives and forks.

'Even I can't eat any more,' she said.

'Nor me.'

He asked for the bill.


He parked outside the house and walked her to the door.

She made her milky tea. With a plate of chocolate biscuits beside her, she took her seat in front of the television.

The television was talking at her. She would sit there until bedtime.

He kissed her.

'Goodbye, dear.' She dipped her biscuit in her tea. 'Thank you for a lovely day.'

'What are you going to do now? Nothing?'

'Have a little rest. It's not much of a life, is it?'

He noticed a travel agent's brochure on the table.

He said, 'I'll send you a cheque, shall I, for the Venice trip?'

'That would be lovely.'

'When will you be going?'

'As soon as possible. There's nothing to keep me here.'

While Heather was at home, Alexandra rang, but Harry didn't say she was there. It was part of what a man sometimes did, he thought, to be a buffer between the children and their mother.

In the morning, before she left, Heather said she wanted him to listen to a poem she had written.

He listened, trying not to weep. He could hear the love in it.

Heather had come to cheer him up, to make him feel that his love worked, that it could make her feel better.

After Alexandra had rung from the beach, Harry rang Gerald and told him about the 'imaging', about the 'visualization', the 'healing', the whole thing. Gerald, convalescing, took his call.

'I used to know a psychoanalyst,' he said cheerfully. 'I've always fancied talking about myself for a long time to someone. But it's not what the chaps do. It's good business, though, people buying into their own pasts – if Alexandra can think like that. Before, women wanted to be nurses. Now, they want to be therapists.'

'It's harmless, you're saying.'

Gerald said, 'And sometimes useful.' He laughed. 'Turning dreams into money for all of you, almost literally.'

Gerald imagined it was almost the only way that Harry could grasp what Alexandra was doing.

But it wasn't true.

Harry drove around the old places after leaving Mother. He wanted to buy a notebook and return to write down the thoughts his memories inspired. Maybe he would do it tonight, his last evening alone, using different coloured markers.

It started to rain. He thought of himself on the street in the rain as a teenager, hanging around outside chip shops and pubs – not bored, that would underestimate what he felt, but unable to spit out or swallow the amount of experience coming at him.

It had been a good day.

Walking along a row of shops he remembered from forty years ago, he recalled a remark of some philosopher that he had never let go. The gist of it was: happiness is wanting one thing. The thing was love, if that was not too pallid a word. Passion, or wanting someone, might be better. In the end, all that would remain of one's years would be the quality of one's link with others, of how far one had gone with them.

Harry turned the car and headed away from his childhood. He had to go to the supermarket. He would buy flowers, cakes, champagne and whatever attracted his attention. He would attempt to tidy the house; he would work in the garden, clearing the leaves. He would do the thing he dreaded: sit down alone and think.

The next morning, he would pick up Alexandra at the airport, and if the weather was good they would eat and talk in the garden. She would be healthy, tanned and full of ideas.

He had to phone Heather to check whether she was all right. It occurred to him to write to her. If he knew little of her day-to-day life, she knew practically nothing of him, his past and what he did most of the time. Parents wanted to know everything of their children, but withheld themselves.

He thought of Father under the earth, and of Mother watching television; he thought of Alexandra and his children. He was happy.

# STRAIGHT

For days he had been fearful of this night but wanted to believe he was ready.

However, when he arrived at the party, bearing a bottle of champagne, he started to feel afraid that people would notice, that they would be able to tell right away what had happened to him, and how he had changed. He wondered whether his friends would think badly of him. He considered who would be hostile, who envious and who sympathetic.

His friends were modernizing the house. The floorboards were still bare and some walls unpainted. Wires hung from their sockets; tinsel hung from the wires. The hostess hurried past, wearing antlers. The host, bearing a tray of mince pies, either didn't recognize Brett or took him for granted.

Brett sidled in, shocked that his paranoia hadn't diminished with age, even as his reasonable side told him how unlikely it was that anyone would be in any state to take a close interest in him.

'Brett, Brett!' someone shouted.

'Hallo there!' he replied. 'Whoever you are!'

He had deliberately left it late; the room was crowded. He knew most of the revellers, who were of his age. Now he was able to think about it, he had known some of them for more than twenty years.

He kissed and greeted those near by and went into the kitchen. These were well-off people; they would give a good party. The trestle table was bent with the weight of bottles, cans and food. He added the champagne to the load and looked around.

He wasn't about to drink lemonade. Someone put a glass of wine in his hand. It was a good idea, the perfect cover.

Recently he had been going to the theatre and cinema, and had stayed to the end; he had read at least three books all the way through. This was the first party he'd been to since the incident by the river, as he called it. He had made up his mind to stay a while. There were things it would do him good to look straight at.

He returned to the living room. To his relief, a sombre male friend joined him and began to talk. From where Brett sat, occasionally asking a question, he could observe the other people.

He watched a man trying to zip up his top. The zip stuck; it wouldn't budge. The man pulled it apart and began again. He couldn't get the serrated edges together, and when they did click, they wouldn't move. This went on for some time. Finally the man took the thing off, joined the parts together on his lap and tried to pull it over his head, where it lodged. Others joined in then, tugging the garment and the man in different directions.

Brett was distracted from this by a wet-eyed acquaintance who was dribbling already; his head was bent. Walking like an old man, he looked as though he might collapse. Another friend pulled Brett up, stood close to him, and shouted in first one ear and then the other. When it was obvious that Brett didn't understand, the friend brought a companion over and together they yelled at Brett, or, it seemed, yelled into him, laughing at one another.

Brett was nodding his head. 'I see, I see now.'

'That's it!' said the first friend. 'Brett is with us! Hello, Brett!'

Brett didn't know why they had to stand so near, or why they kept plucking at him. The only thing to do was to have a drink. That was the key to things here; then he would understand. But he couldn't have a drink.

Luckily, Francine fell into the sofa on the other side of him.

'There you are, Brett darling. Thank God you're here. Some of these bloody people are boring fuckers!'

'Are they?'

'You know they are!'

She had made the effort: her lips were bright, her black clothes expensive, her hair colouring and cut the best. She wore high-heeled black suede boots. He noticed, though, when talking to her, that her eyes kept closing, even as she told a story about getting stuck in a lift with her boss. During this narcoleptic monologue, she spilled her drink over him.

He stood up.

'Oh God, God, God! So sorry!' she said. 'I've made you wet.' She was pulling at his wrist. 'Sit down!' She wiped his leg with her hand; she dried her hand on the sofa. 'Don't look so grumpy. You did the same to me once. Except it went over my breasts.'

He looked at her breasts.

'I didn't.'

'You won't remember. You don't remember anything, remember?'

'No,' he said. 'I don't think I do.'

If he'd forgotten, it wasn't only that dissipation had wiped his memory: he hadn't properly been there in the first place.

'You are out of your mind.' Francine shifted closer to him and stroked his hair. 'Your face is smooth. You've shaved, for a change. But you really are gone, this time.'

'Perhaps I am,' he said, and chuckled. 'Please tell me what you're talking about.'

'First, you can give me some of that. Brett, you owe me.'

Her hands were in his crotch, searching for his pockets.

She said, 'Your face is white, dear! I've never seen you so tense or wide-eyed. Is it that pure stuff people are talking about? You shouldn't be taking it, with your blood pressure. Give it to me and get to the rehab!'

'Is there really something wrong with me, Francine? Tell me if you think there is.'

'What's right with you? You haven't laughed at anything I've said.'

'You haven't said anything funny.'

'Don't be a fool, Brett.'

'Stop that fiddling!' he said. 'There's absolutely nothing for you in my pocket.'

It didn't discourage her.

'You banged your head when you fell in the river. That's what did you in. Isn't that right?' She was laughing with her mouth open. 'What were you doing down there, by the river?'

People loved this story; they rang to ask about it, and it was repeated around town. He couldn't deny her.

He said, 'I got Carol to stop the cab after that party because I needed a pee and didn't want people to see me.'

'Is that why you climbed over the wall and slipped?'

'With my cock out, actually, all the way down the ramp. Right into the cold river, I feared. But into the cold mud, luckily.'

'Didn't Rowena and Carol haul you out?'

'Haul me out?' he said. 'They were tottering around hysterically at the top. I could hear them screeching like a zoo. I was told Rowena rang her agent who was having dinner at Gaga and asked him what to do.'

'What did the agent say? I told her to get rid of that fish. I can fix her up with Morton. He did that deal for Ronnie. Maybe I should arrange –'

Brett said, 'If you really want to know about it, the taxi driver pulled me out. Otherwise, I would have gone down for good, and that, as they say, would have been that. He had blankets in the boot which he wrapped me in. He took me home. I guess I messed up his car. D'you think it's too late to call him and apologize?'

'Where did Carol and Rowena go afterwards?'

'Don't know.'

The taxi driver had been tall and dark-skinned, a North African of some sort, wearing worn-out shoes. At home, Brett invited him in and made tea. The man sat there with Brett's mud on him and said he was a law student with two children. He studied half the time and drove the rest; sometimes he slept; occasionally he played with his children.

Brett offered him dry clothes. When the man refused, Brett tried to give him money for his dry-cleaning bill. At this, the man raised his hands in protest.

'What's wrong?' Brett had asked.

'You don't understand!'

'Please tell me –'

'Anyone would have done this thing!'

'Yes, of course!' said Brett. The man seemed relieved. 'I see, I do see,' said Brett.

He shook the man's hand.

Drinking tea only, Brett had thought about this for the rest of the night and went over it again the next day.

Probably the man was religious. But you didn't need religion to save someone. It had not been a sentimental gesture but what you did when someone fell.

Now Brett watched people shouting at one another. They would laugh inexplicably, their mouths almost touching. No one was listening, but what was there to hear? People's words were not in any recognizable order and their gestures were unrelated to anything they said. A couple dancing looked as though they were wrestling.

Brett kissed Francine's cheek. 'It's time I made a move.'

'Already? That's the best suggestion I've heard in minutes.'

They went out into the hall, where she started talking to someone. She and the other person went into the bathroom and Brett left the house.

Outside, he lit a cigarette and looked for his car keys. It was frosty and still. From the house opposite, he could hear voices singing, and a piano.

He had reached the gate when she caught up with him, one arm in her coat.

'You tried to sneak off without me. Would I leave you here alone? Have I ever done that to you? Here are the keys I took from your pocket.'

He helped her on with the coat and said, 'You live way across town.'

'We're going on to Gaga! Please, just for a bit. Then you can take me home.'

'I don't want to go to Gaga, but I'll drop you off there.'

'How will I get home?'

'How have you got home every night for the last fifteen years?'

'What nonsense you talk, Brett. Come on, you've got to sober up for the drive.'

In the car, she was smoking. Her skirt was up.

'You behave so badly, Brett. But somehow I always forgive you.'

'Thank you,' he said. 'Jesus. Have you seen what's going on tonight?'

He drove slowly. The high street was more than busy. Crowds gathered outside bars and clubs. People ran into the road; they shouted and a man threw a punch; there were ambulances and police cars about. He slowed to a stop and waved at the cars behind him. Someone was lying face-down in the road. Others were trying to pull the person to the pavement but couldn't decide which side of the road was best.

He said, 'What you just said sounded strange but intriguing. What do I have to be forgiven for?'

'Brett, where is the light in this wretched car?'

She had managed to empty her bag on to the floor and was

bent double, trying to reclaim her credit cards, cocaine, numerous pills and keys.

He thought he was bleeding. He reached up and realized it was snowing on his head. Slush ran down the back of his neck. Looking for the light, she had released the sun roof. He left it open.

She was saying, 'Forget all that. Brett, the thing is, I think we both need to go away. It's that time of the year. How about Rio?'

'Now?'

'Tomorrow morning.'

'It's too far.'

'Paris? It's only up the road now.'

'What would we do?'

'Eat, drink, go out.'

'I don't want to do that any more.'

'What else is there?'

He said, 'Where am I going to park?'

She had already opened the car door and was heading towards the members' club, plumping her hair and squirting perfume at her throat.

'See you inside!' she called.

They knew him at Gaga. At the end of the night, they often called cabs for him and lent him money to pay for them.

When he pushed the familiar glass door and stepped across the carpet which he remembered, on occasion, feeling against his cheek, he saw a former business partner with mistletoe attached to his forehead by bands of Sellotape.

He pulled Brett to him and started kissing him. 'It's you – you, you bastard! The one who let me down! Now we're both bankrupt!'

'Yes, yes,' said Brett. 'That's right!'

'Been swimming in the river, I hear! How are you doing now?' It took his friend a while to find the words. He was so pleased he repeated them. 'You doing . . . you doing swimmingly . . .' he went, laughing to himself. 'Won't sit down! Busy with something!'

Brett bought Francine a drink and one for himself. How expensive it was! How much money he had spent on it over the years, not to mention energy!

In the bathroom, he threw the drink away and filled his glass with water. What a beautiful drink water was.

He took a seat at the bar and watched the man with the mistletoe weave about until he dropped on to a sofa. There, he went to some trouble to relocate the mistletoe in his open fly. Then he leaned back with his knees apart and began the business – giggling the while – of attracting the waitress's attention.

Over the years, Brett must have sat on all the bar stools and armchairs in the place. He could see a group of his friends settling down to play cards. Johnny, Chris, Carol and Mike. They would be there for a long time; later, they'd go somewhere else. On any other night, he'd have joined them.

The aggression in Gaga seemed high. People wanted help and attention, but they were asking the wrong folks, others just like them. Some of them were wired, with their eyes popping. Others were exhausted, with failing heads. Odd it was, the taking of substances that made you feel worse, that made everything worse in the end. Dissipation was gruelling work, a full-time job. Yet things did get done; these men and women had professions. Brett had to be grateful: at least he had kept his flat and job. He'd only lost his wife.

If he didn't sit with his friends – and he wouldn't; he was cold, while they were hot with enthusiasm – where else was there? How did you get to others? After all, it wasn't only him, or his circle, who was like this. It was his ex-wife's father, his own sister and her boyfriend, who sat around with cans and bottles, fighting and weeping. Or they had been cured but had become addicted to the cure, as tedious off the stuff as they had been on it.

Francine had taken her drink and gone to join a group. He

noticed she continued to watch him, knowing he might shrug her off and leave. He didn't see why this would matter to her.

Brett was content to think of the North African, wondering whether something about the man had influenced him. Like the taxi driver, Brett seemed to be in a world where everyone resembled him but spoke in a foreign language. If the man stayed in England, he would always struggle to understand it, never quite connecting.

He had helped Brett; why shouldn't Brett help him? Brett imagined himself turning up at the man's house, offering to do anything. But what might he do? Wash up, or read to the children? Take them all to the cinema? Why shouldn't he do it, now he felt better? The man might be too shy or suspicious for such things, yet surely he had to stop work for lunch or supper? Brett could listen to him. It would be a way of starting again, or returning to a state of teenage curiosity, when you might take any path that presented itself, seeing where it led.

Brett got down from the stool.

'No you don't.' Francine came over and put her tongue in his mouth. 'You take me home. You've been coming on to me all night.'

He didn't mind taking her home. He had come to dislike his own street and thought he should move to another district. Apart from the fact a change would do him good, living near by was a woman he passed often, an ex-barmaid. If she recognized him, which he doubted, she never acknowledged him. She had four children by different fathers and the youngest was his, he knew it. He had stayed with her one night after a party, four years ago. When he made the calculation, it added up. A drinking acquaintance pointed it out. 'Look at that kid. If I didn't know better, I'd say you were the father.'

He had gone to the playground to watch the child. It was true; she had his own mother's hair and eyes. He had seen the woman shout at the girl. He didn't like passing his only daughter on the street.

In the car, Francine was drinking from a bottle of wine.

'Haven't you had enough yet?' he said. 'Can't you just stop?'

'Tonight I'm going the whole way.'

'Why?'

'That's a fatuous question.'

'But I would like to know, really.'

She started to cry, talking all the while. She didn't think to spare him her misery; perhaps it didn't occur to her that he would be concerned.

The North African man drove strangers night after night, despised or invisible amongst abhorrent fools who had so much of everything, they could afford to piss it away.

At Francine's block of flats, he helped her upstairs. He put the lights on and led her to bed. She thrashed about, as if the mattress were a runaway horse she had to master.

He turned his back, but she couldn't remove her clothes. He got her into her pyjamas and kissed her on the side of the head.

'Good night, Francine.'

'Don't leave me! You're staying, aren't you? I –'

She was clawing at his chest. She was an awful colour. He ran for the washing-up bowl and held it by her face.

'Is this it? Is this it?' she kept saying. 'Is it now, tonight?'

'Is it what, Francine?'

'Death! Is he here? Has William Burroughs come to call?'

'Not tonight, sweetheart. Lie back.'

Her vomit splattered the walls; it went over his jacket, his shoes, trousers and shirt, and in his hair.

At the end, she did lie back, exhausted. He removed her soiled pyjamas and put her into a dressing gown.

He was sitting there. She extended her arms to him. 'Come on, Brett.'

'You're pretty sick, Francine.'

'I've finished. There's nothing left. You can do what you want to me.' She was shivering, but she opened her dressing gown. 'That's something no one ever says no to!'

'What difference would it make?'

'Who cares about that! Fetch yourself a drink and settle down. I've always liked you.'

'Have you?'

'Don't you know that? Despite your problems, you're bright and you can be sweet. Won't you tell me what you are on tonight, Brett?'

He shook his head and put a glass of water to her lips. 'Nothing. Nothing.'

'There must be someone else you're going to. That's a rotten thing to do to a woman.'

He thought for a time.

'There is no woman. It's a taxi driver.'

'Christ!'

'Yes.'

'The one who fished you out? You won't know where he is.'

'I'll go to the cab office and wait. They know me there. Hell, understand what I want.'

'What's that?'

'Good talk.'

She said, 'You enjoyed sleeping with me last time.'

'What last time? There wasn't any last time.'

'Don't pretend to be a fool when you're not. Get in.'

She was patting the bed.

He walked to the door and shut it behind him. She was still talking, to him, to anyone and no one.

'There's someone I've got to find,' he said.

REMEMBER THIS MOMENT, REMEMBER US

It is nearly Christmas and Rick is getting quite drunk at a party in a friend's clothes shop.

It is a vast shop in a smart area of west London, and tonight the girls who work there have got dressed up in shiny black dresses, white velvet bunny ears and high shoes. When Rick and Daniel arrived, the girls were holding trays of champagne, mulled wine and mince pies. Has there ever been anything so inviting?

The girls helped Rick's son Daniel out of his pushchair, removed his little red coat and showed him to the children's room where remote-controlled electric toys buzzed across the floor. There was a small seesaw; several other local children were already playing. Rick sat on the floor and Daniel, though it was late for him, chased the electric toys, flung a ping-pong ball through the open window and dismantled a doll's house, not understanding that all the inviting objects were for sale.

Rick had begun drinking an hour earlier. On the way to the party they had stopped at a bar in the area where Rick used to go when he was single. There, Daniel, who is two and a half, had climbed right up onto a furry stool next to his father, sitting in a line with the other early-evening drinkers.

'I'm training him up,' Rick said to the barmaid. 'Please, Daniel, ask her for a beer.'

'Blow-blow,' said Daniel.

'Sorry?' said Rick.

Daniel held up a book of matches. 'Blow-blow.'

Rick opened it and lit a match. 'Again,' Daniel said, the moment he blew it out. He extinguished two match books like this, filling the ashtray. As each match illuminated the boy's face, his cheeks filled and his lips puckered. When the light died, the boy's laughter rang out around the fashionably gloomy bar.

'Ready, steady, blow-blow!'

'Blow-bloody-blow,' murmured a sullen drinker.

'Got something to say?' said Rick, slipping from the stool.

The man grunted.

Rick persuaded the kid to get into his raincoat and put on his hat with the peak and ear-flaps, securing it under his chin. He slung the bag full of nappies, juice, numerous snacks, wipes and toys over his shoulder, and they went out into the night and teeming rain.

It has been raining for two days. News reports state that there have been floods all over the country.

The party was about ten minutes' walk away. Rick was wet through by the time they arrived.

His successful friend Martin with the merry staff in the big lighted shop full of clothes Rick could never afford, embraced him at the door. Martin, has no children himself, and this was the first time he had seen Daniel. The two men have been friends since Martin designed and made the costumes for a play Rick was in, on the Edinburgh fringe, twenty years ago. Rick congratulated him on receiving his MBE and asked to see the medal. However, there were people at Martin's shoulder and he had no time to talk. The warm wine in small white cups soon cheered Rick up.

Rick hasn't had an acting job for four months but has been promised something reasonable in the New Year. He has been going out with Daniel a lot. At least once a week, if Rick can afford it, he and Daniel take the Central Line into the West End and walk around the shops, stopping at cafés and galleries. Rick shows him the theatres he has worked in; if he knows the actors, he takes him backstage.

Rick's three other children, who live with his first wife, are in their late teens. Rick would love always to have a child in the house. When he can, he takes Daniel to parties. Daniel has big eyes; his hair has never been cut and he is often mistaken for a girl. People will talk to Rick if Daniel is with him, but he doesn't have to make extended conversation.

As the party becomes more crowded and raucous, while drinking steadily, Rick chats to the people he's introduced to. Daniel is given juice which the girls in the shop hold out for him, crouching down with their knees together.

Quite soon, Daniel says, 'Home, Dadda.'

Rick gets him dressed and manoeuvres the pushchair into the street. They begin to walk through the rain. There are few other people about, and no buses; it is far to the tube. A taxi with its light on passes them. When it has almost gone, Rick jumps into the road and yells after it, waving his arms, until it stops.

As they cross London, Rick points at the Christmas lights through the rain-streaked windows. Rick recalls similar taxi rides with his own father and remembers a photograph of himself, aged six or seven, wearing a silver bow-tie and fez-like Christmas hat, sitting on his father's knee at a party.

At home, Rick smokes a joint and drinks two more glasses of wine. It is getting late, around ten-thirty, and though Daniel usually goes to bed at eight, Rick doesn't mind if he is up, he likes the company. They eat sardines on toast with tomato ketchup; then they play loud music and Rick demonstrates the hokey-cokey to his son.

Anna has gone to her life-drawing class but is usually home by now. Why has she not returned? She is never late. Rick would have gone out to look for her, but he cannot leave Daniel and it is too wet to take him out again.

When Rick lies on the floor with his knees up, the kid steps onto him, using his father's knees for support. Daniel begins to jump up and down on Rick's stomach, as if it were a trampoline. Rick usually enjoys this as much as Daniel. But today it makes him feel queasy.

Yesterday was Rick's forty-fifth birthday, a bad age to be, he reckons, putting him on the wrong side of life. It is not only that he feels more tired and melancholic than normal, he also wonders whether he can recover from these bouts as easily as he used to. In the past year two of his friends have had heart attacks; two others have had strokes.

He guesses that he passed out on the floor. He is certainly aware of Anna shaking him. Or does she kick him in the ribs, too? He may be drunk, but he means to inform her immediately that he is not an alcoholic.

However, Rick feels strange, as if he has been asleep for some time. He wants to tell Anna what happened to him while he was asleep. He finds some furniture to hold on to, and pulls himself up.

He sees Daniel running around with a glass of wine in his hand.

'What's been going on?' Anna says.

'We went out,' Rick says, pursuing the boy and retrieving the glass. 'Didn't we, Dan?'

'Out with Dadda,' says Daniel. 'Nice time and biscuits. Dadda have drink.'

'Thanks, Dan,' Rick says.

Rick notices he has removed Daniel's trousers and nappy but omitted to replace them. There is a puddle on the floor and Daniel has wet his socks; his vest, which is hanging down, is soaked too.

He says to her, 'You think I was asleep, but I wasn't. I was thinking, or dreaming, rather. Yes, constructively dreaming . . .'

'And you expect me to ask what about?'

'I had an idea,' he says. 'It was my forty-fifth birthday yester-

226

day and a good time we had too. I was dreaming that we were writing a card to Dan for his forty-fifth birthday. A card he wouldn't be allowed to open until then.'

'I see,' she says, sitting down. Dan is playing at her feet.

'After all,' he continues, 'like you I think about the past more and more. I think of my parents, of being a child, of my brothers, the house, all of it. What we'll do is write him a card, and you can illustrate it. We'll make it now, put it away and forget it. Years will pass and one day, when Dan's forty-five with grey hair and a bad knee, he'll remember it, and open it. We'll have sent him our love from the afterlife. Of course, you'll be alive then, but it's unlikely that I will be. For those moments, though, when he's reading it, I'll be vital in his mind. What d'you say, Anna? I'd love to have received a card from my parents on my forty-fifth birthday. All day I thought one would just pop through the door, you know.'

He is aware that she has been drinking, too, after her class. Now, as always, she begins to spread her drawings of heads, torsos and hands out on the floor. Daniel ambles across the big sheets as Rick examines them, trying to find words of praise he hasn't used before. She is hoping to sell some of her work eventually, to supplement their income.

She says, 'A card's great. It's a good idea and a sweet, generous gesture. But it's not enough.'

'What d'you mean?' he says. He goes on, 'You might be right. When I was dreaming, I kept thinking of the last scene of *Wild Strawberries*.'

'What happens in it?'

'Doesn't the old man, on a last journey to meet the significant figures of his life, finally wave to his parents?'

'That's what we should do,' she says. 'Make a video for Daniel and put it in a sealed envelope.'

'Yes,' he says, drinking from a glass he finds beside the chair. 'It's a brilliant idea.'

'But we're quite drunk,' she says. 'It'll be him sitting in front of it, forty-five years old. He'll turn on the tape at last and –'

'There won't even be tapes then,' Rick says. 'They'll be in a museum. But they'll be able to convert it to whatever system they have.'

She says, 'My point is, after all that time, he'll see two pissed people. What's his therapist going to say?'

Don't we want him to know that you and I had a good time sometimes?'

'Okay,' she says. 'But if we're going to do this, we should be prepared.'

'Good,' he says. 'We could . . .'

'What?'

'Put on white shirts. Does my hair look too flat?'

'We look okay,' she says. 'Well, I do, and you don't care. But we should think about what we're going to say. This tape might be a big thing for little Dan. Imagine if your father was to speak to you right now.'

'You're right,' he says. His own father had killed himself almost ten years ago. 'Anna, what would you like to say to Dan?'

'There's so much . . . really, I don't know yet.'

'Also, we've got to be careful how we talk to him,' he says. 'He's not two years old in this scenario. He's my age. We can't use baby voices or call him Dan-the-Noddy-man.'

They dispute about what exactly the message should be, what a parent might say to their forty-five-year-old son, now only two and a half, sitting there on the floor singing 'Incy Wincy Spider' to himself. Of course there can be no end to this deliberation: whether they should give Daniel a good dose of advice and encouragement, or a few memories, or a mixture of all three. They do at least decide that since they're getting tired and fretful they should set up the camera.

While she goes into the cellar to find it, he makes Daniel's milk, gets him into his blue pyjamas with the white trim, and chases him around the kitchen with a wet cloth. She drags the camera and tripod up into the living room.

Although they haven't decided what to say, they will go ahead with the filming certain that something will occur to them. This spontaneity may make their little dispatch to the future seem less portentous.

Rick lugs the Christmas tree over towards the sofa where they will sit for the message, and turns on the lights. He regards his wife through the camera. She has let down her hair.

'How splendid you look!'

She asks, 'Should I take my slippers off?'

'Anna, your fluffies won't be immortalized. I'll frame it down to our waists.'

She gets up and looks at him through the eye piece, telling him he's as fine as he'll ever be. He switches on the camera and notices there is only about fifteen minutes' worth of tape left.

With the camera running, he hurries towards the sofa, being careful not to trip up. They will not be able to do this twice. Noticing a half-eaten sardine on the arm of the sofa, he drops it into his pocket.

Rick sits down knowing this will be a sombre business, for he has been, in a sense, already dead for a while. Daniel's idea of him will have been developing for a long time. The two of them will have fallen out on numerous occasions; Daniel might love him but will have disliked him, too, in the normal way. Daniel could hardly have anything but a complicated idea of his past, but these words from eternity will serve as a simple reminder. After all, it is the unloved who are the most dangerous people on this earth.

The light on top of the camera is flashing. As Anna and Rick turn their heads and look into the dark moon of the lens, neither of them speaks for what seems a long time. At last, Rick says,

'Hello there,' rather self-consciously, as though meeting a stranger for the first time. On stage he is never anxious like this. Anna, also at a loss, copies him.

'Hello, Daniel, my son,' she says. 'It's your mummy.'

'And daddy,' Rick says.

'Yes,' she says. 'Here we are!'

'Your parents,' he says. 'Remember us? Do you remember this day?'

There is a silence; they wonder what to do.

Anna turns to Rick then, placing her hands on his face. She strokes his face as if painting it for the camera. She takes his hand and puts his fingers to her lips and cheeks. Rick leans over and takes her head between his hands and kisses her on the cheek and on the forehead and on the lips, and she caresses his hair and pulls him to her.

With their heads together, they begin to call out, 'Hello, Dan, we hope you're okay, we just wanted to say hello.'

'Yes, that's right,' chips in the other. 'Hello!'

'We hope you had a good forty-fifth birthday, Dan, with plenty of presents.'

'Yes, and we hope you're well, and your wife, or whoever it is you're with.'

'Yes, hello there . . . wife of Dan.'

'And children of Dan,' she adds.

'Yes,' he says. 'Children of Dan – however many of you there are, boys or girls or whatever – all the best! A good life to every single one of you!'

'Yes, yes!' she says. 'All of that and more!'

'More, more, more!' Rick says.

After the kissing and stroking and cuddling and saying hello, and with a little time left, they are at a loss as to what to do, but right on cue Daniel has an idea. He clambers up from the floor and settles himself on both of them, and they kiss him and pass him between them and get him to wave to himself. When he has done this, he closes his eyes, his head falls into the crook of his mother's arm, and he smacks his lips; and as the tape whirls towards its end, and the rain falls outside and time passes, they want him to be sure at least of this one thing, more than forty years from now, when he looks at these old-fashioned people in the past sitting on the sofa next to the Christmas tree, that on this night they loved him and they loved each other.

'Goodbye, Daniel,' says Anna.

'Goodbye,' says Rick.

'Goodbye, goodbye,' they say together.

# THE REAL FATHER

It was true: Mal couldn't bear his son Wallace and dreaded see-ing him now. What natural feeling was there between them? They were bewildered strangers who didn't know what to say or do together.

Today, Mal was to take the nine-year-old away for the night.

'We can spend time hanging out,' explained Mal again. 'We can talk – about anything you want.'

'I'd rather go to hell,' Wallace said. 'I'd rather be dead than go anywhere with you!' Loudly he whispered, 'Fucker!'

Wallace had arrived at the house the previous evening. Normally, he stayed the weekend, but Mal was glad to be taking him home tomorrow, after their trip, as he was required at a party. Nevertheless, since he'd woken up, Wallace had been sob-bing and complaining on the stairs. It was nearly lunch time; the taxi was waiting outside.

'We're only going to the seaside.'

'For the night!'

Mal explained, 'I've already said that will be nicer for us, rather than rushing back on the last train.'

'Nice for you, torture for me!'

'For me, too, it looks like.'

Wallace was not only what was commonly described as an 'accident', there had been no necessity for his birth at all. How could he not have sensed that?

Mal's wife came over to them. She was accompanied by their four-year-old, who tried to stroke his hysterical half-brother's swollen, tear-riven face.

'Don't cry, Wally,' he said.

They were all looking at Wallace. His *Beano* shirt ('Look, I'm an advertisement!') was covered with chocolate stains: Wallace used it as a napkin. When he ate, he still spilled his food, and always knocked over his drinks. This was partly because he refused to sit at the table, but ranged about the house looking for things to break and turning the TV off and on. His trousers had a hole where he'd fallen but his trainers were top-of-the-range, with lights in the heel that flashed when he kicked an adult. What annoyed Mal was not his son's resemblance to his mother – the boy turned his head and suddenly Mal was reminded of his eternal connection to a stranger, as if this were a black joke – but to the boy's stepfather, who Wallace called 'Dad' and Mal 'The Beast'.

Mal said, 'Wallace, we do really have to leave – otherwise we'll miss the train.' Wallace opened his chocolate-filled mouth. Mal reached out to pull him. 'Get in the bloody taxi now!'

Wallace sprang back, spitting chocolate over Mal's white shirt. 'If you hurt me, I will kill myself.' He stood up and punched himself in the stomach. 'I will now go and fix my hair.'

Mal was glad of the chance to kiss his youngest son and his wife, who attempted to wipe him down. 'Mal, don't get furious. Try and have a good time with him. Try to talk.'

'Talk!'

'Have you been drinking already?'

'Just the one. I'm petrified he'll do something lunatic during the meeting this afternoon. I wish you would look after him today.'

'I am not yet a saint. I'll have coffee with the girls and we'll laugh about this.'

The boy emerged from the bathroom with his mass of hair – which Mal maintained would one day have to be removed surgically, under anaesthetic – slicked down with water. Mal noticed he had added perfumed hair gel, which sat on his head in lumps, mingling, no doubt, with his nits.

Mal took their luggage out to the car. Wallace had no choice but to follow, carrying a plastic bag which contained drinks, his Gameboy, pens, and many half-eaten Easter eggs.

In the back of the car, Mal stroked him. 'Come on. No one's going to love you if you behave like this. You need charm to get by in this world.'

The boy put his hands over his face as the taxi pulled away. He was wearing the goalkeeping gloves he refused to be parted from.

'Don't ever touch me. Or point at me. Don't do anything bad to me, you bastard.'

Mal noticed the driver's wide eyes watching them in the mirror. Clearly, he was from a country with stricter notions of how children should behave.

'For Christ's sake, shhh . . .'

They were on their way to see Andrea Knowles, a young film director, who was considering using Mal as editor on her first feature film. It was a job he needed badly; it would be a significant step up. Inevitably, Wallace's mother had refused to alter their arrangement. Mal had tried to leave Wallace with his wife, but Wallace had taken to calling her a bitch and had kicked her.

Mal and Wallace's mother had had a 'fling' ten years ago, lasting a few weeks. By the time Wallace was born, they had returned to their separate lives. All Mal wanted was for her to disappear into the mulch of the past. Somehow she had become pregnant and refused a termination.

'How can you kill a baby?' she said.

'There are several methods I could suggest . . .'

What did he remember of their affair? One long conversation – their only real talk – during a party. Later, the girl playing the same jazz records over and over; they were all she could afford. Making love while there was a thunderstorm outside, the branches of the trees striking the windows. It wasn't long before they ran out of ideal moments.

Now she was unrecognizable to him and lived with her husband, an unemployed alcoholic decorator. For years, Mal had hardly been allowed to see or even speak to the boy, though he contributed to his upkeep. When Wallace was six, Mal was given access to him about twice a year. All day they wandered around overheated shopping malls in the Midlands. Sometimes Mal phoned him, but Wallace never volunteered any information. After several silences, he said he had to go – *The Rugrats* was on.

A friend of Mal's once joked about how fortunate Mal was to have at least one of his kids living elsewhere. Mal had reddened with fury; for a week, this jibe marked his mind. Being a father entailed various duties which he wanted to follow, except that Wallace's mother prevented them. The word 'duty' sounded odd to him. It was as unlikely a word, these days, as 'moral' or, to him, 'spiritual'. He liked to think he had a pragmatic mouth. Despite this, in his feelings, Mal had had to let his son go – giving him to another man, admitting how little there was of him in the boy – and semi-forgetting him. This was aided by the birth of his younger son.

A year ago, Wallace's mother and her partner had taken a market stall at the weekends, selling home-designed T-shirts. She didn't like Wallace hanging around the market every weekend. Mal guessed this was the real reason for Wallace's having to 'get to know' his real father, by visiting every three weeks.

Mal was relieved to have got his son back before it was too late. Of course, his wife was afraid of the effect this stranger would have on her family. She argued about the length of time Wallace could stay; she refused to let Wallace share his half-brother's bedroom. It had taken Mal a week to convert his own work-room into a space for Wallace, with a TV, video, Playstation and music system. Wallace hated the room but stayed in it during the day, though not at night. He had 'insonia' and heard moans coming down the chimney. Mal lay awake, hearing Wallace watching movies in the living room at four in the morning.

If Mal thought things were beginning to go well in his life, Wallace was the fate he couldn't elude. He had welcomed the boy, but the boy was a genius at not being welcomed. Mal liked to say he wanted to sue for less custody. Sometimes Wallace would play football with Mal, or let himself be taken to the cinema. But Wallace's passion was shopping in London. Mal bought him things to assuage his furious greed: one big thing, it seemed, every day. Wallace had always insisted Mal buy him toys his mother wouldn't let him have or couldn't afford: guns, lightsabres, Playstation discs, Gameboy games, videos of horror films. Nevertheless, Mal knew that as soon as he dropped the boy off at his mother's house, a two-hour drive away, his mobile phone would ring and he would be castigated for the presents, which would be dumped in the basement. The same thing happened if Mal gave him the autographs of movie actors, or film posters and videos.

Now Mal said, 'I'll buy you something at the railway station.'

A space opened in Wallace's distress. 'Buy me what?'

'Anything to stop you abusing me and give me some peace.'

'That's all you want.'

'Wouldn't you?' said Mal.

'I don't want to be here.'

'But we're going to see a woman called Andrea. It's very important that you be nice to her.'

'Why?'

'She might give me a job and I can earn more money to spend on you.'

'I'll tell her you're too lazy and bad-mannered.'

Mal started to laugh.

'What's funny?'

'You.'

'I can stop you laughing.'

'Don't I know it.'

On his last visit, Wallace had thrown some of Mal's papers on to the floor and wiped his feet on them; later, he'd held a cushion over his half-brother's face and punched him. Mal had ripped his belt from his trousers and raised it. His wife cried out and he rushed from the house. Underneath Wallace's whimpering, moaning and abuse, a child was screaming for help. No one knew what to do, but didn't someone have to do something? In such circumstances, how did you learn to be a parent?

As it was, Mal drank when the boy was around. Wallace destabilized him in ways he couldn't grasp, making him believe he was either incompetent and useless or a monster, a feeling which had begin to poison all areas of his life. On his last job, a television serial, his concentration had failed and he had had to do several all-nighters to complete the job. He was afraid that Andrea had heard about this.

At the railway station, Wallace led his father to comics, sweets and drinks. Then Mal obtained sandwiches for both of them, secured a table in one of the cafés and went to get coffee and a beer. On his return, Wallace had disappeared.

Mal waited and drank his beer. Perhaps Wallace had gone to the toilet. After a while, when Wallace's absence seemed to freeze reality into one stopped moment of horror, Mal had no choice but to gather up their bags and the coffee and shuffle through the shops, toilets, bars and cafés as rapidly as he could, asking strangers if they'd seen a plump kid with a filthy face, wearing a *Beano* shirt.

Wallace was alone at a table, driving a hamburger into his mouth and studying his compass.

Mal sank down. 'Jesus, I can hardly breathe. If you do that again, I'll tell your mum.'

'She already knows you don't want me around.'

'Is that what she says?'

'You never visited me on my birthday.'

'I wasn't allowed to.'

Wallace said, 'I didn't like the sandwiches you got for me.'

'I understand. I'm your father and I have no idea what you like to eat.'

Wallace burped. 'It's okay, thanks. I'm full now.'

In the train, Mal sat opposite the boy and closed his eyes.

'Will we crash?' said Wallace loudly. Everyone in the carriage was looking at them. 'They all crash, don't they?'

Mal put on his sunglasses. 'I hope so.'

'Listen –' Wallace had other concerns, but Mal was squeezing balls of wax as far into his ears as they'd go.

He could tell they'd arrived, the air was cooler and fresh. With renewed optimism, Mal carried their bags down to the front, telling Wallace how he'd always loved English seaside resorts and their semi-carnival feel. Such decay could provide a mesmeric atmosphere for a film. If Andrea decided to employ him, he wondered whether she might let him set up a cutting-room here. The family could stay. Wallace might like to visit.

They were both tired when they arrived at the small hotel, which smelled of fried bacon. They looked through into a sitting-room full of enormous flower-patterned furniture, in which an old couple were playing Scrabble.

Wallace said, 'Are you sure it's only one night?'

'Yes.'

'You've lied to me before.'

'Excuse me?'

'You've lied about this whole thing.'

In their room, Mal opened the windows. He went out on to the balcony and smoked a joint while watching the untroubled people walking on the front. Wallace settled down on the bed with his Gameboy. Mal unpacked a change of clothes for Wallace and a couple of books on psychology for himself. He took a shower, opened a bottle of whisky and took a long draught.

When he could, Mal walked about naked in front of Wallace, showing him the stomach flopping above the thin legs, the weak grey pubic hair, the absurd boyish buttocks. Wallace needed to take him in, to see him, as Mal believed people in complete families did daily.

Lately, Mal had been unable to stop worrying about whether Wallace had something wrong with him. Perhaps a certain drug or psychiatrist might be of benefit. Yet Wallace had friends; he was doing better at school than Mal ever had. You couldn't pathologize him for hating his father. For Mal, the strain was in having to work this out for himself. Recently he had been mulling over a memory from his student days of two acquaintances discussing R. D. Laing. At the time, he had been embarrassed by his ignorance and instinctively regarded what they said as pretentious, as showing off. But something about families and the impossibility of living within their contradictions, which made children mad, had stuck in his mind. Perhaps this was Wallace's predicament. Was he the embodiment of his parents' mistake, of their stupidity? Wasn't Wallace somehow carrying all their craziness? What, then, could Mal do?

Mal lay on the bed next to him. 'Wallace, will you cuddle me? Will you hold me and let me kiss you?' But Wallace was trying to look elsewhere. Mal said, 'Maybe you know your mother wouldn't like you becoming close to me.'

'She certainly thinks you is a great big fool.'

Mal shut his eyes but was too aware of Wallace to drift off. The joint was making him dreamy. He said, 'I was – almost – a fool. I haven't thought of this for a long time. When I was seventeen and my father had just died, I packed a few things and left home, leaving my mum, who never spoke to me, or to anyone much –'

Wallace looked up.

'Was there something wrong with her?'

'I couldn't stay to find out. I had dyed my hair multi-coloured. I wore a slashed leather jacket and dirty trousers covered in straps and zips, and black motorcycle boots. I went to live in the back of a junk shop we'd broken into –'

'Could the police have taken you to prison?'

'If they'd found us. But we hid, smashing and burning the furniture for heat. We drank cider and took –'

'You were drunk?'

'A lot of the time.'

'Did you fall down and hurt yourself?'

'Often, yes. Except that my uncle, my father's brother, who was recovering from heart surgery, climbed in through the window one day while we were asleep.'

'Were you still drunk?'

'He said that had my father been alive, he'd have been killed by how I was living. I guess I was that man's lost sheep. He couldn't rest until I was safe. You know that Bible story about the sheep?'

'Sheep? I've seen *Chicken Run*.'

'Right. The next day, my uncle took me to the local college and begged them to admit me. I didn't want to go.'

'You didn't want to learn anything?'

'I hated learning.'

'At school, I'm on the top table.'

'Excellent. My uncle said I could live at his house as long as I was at college. So I couldn't drop out. One time in class, the teacher showed a film called *The 400 Blows*. I figured watching movies was better than work. This film was about a young, unhappy kid – like me, then – who didn't get along with his mum and dad. I kept thinking it was like looking at a series of paintings. It was the first time that beauty had seemed to matter to me. I realized that if I could be involved in such work, I'd get a crack at happiness.'

Mal sat up and poured himself another drink.

Wallace said, 'What happened then?'

'That's how I trained to be a film editor. It's why we're here today.'

The phone rang in the silence. Wallace answered.

'Mum? Is that you?'

It was Andrea, downstairs. Mal started to put his clothes on. 'Champ, we'd better go.'

'Why should we? I don't want her!'

Mal wanted to plead with the boy to be polite but knew it would make things worse.

Outside the hotel, Mal introduced Wallace to Andrea.

'He's my real daddy but not really,' said Wallace.

'You can only have one real daddy.'

Wallace was staring at her. She crouched down and showed him the ring through her nose.

'You can touch it.'

He stroked it.

'Does it hurt?'

'Nope. Well, it does now. I've got another one, called a stud.' She put her tongue out.

'Yuckie. What if you swallow it?'

'See if you can grab it, Wallace.'

It was a good little game.

'Can we go to the pier?' asked Wallace.

Mal gave Wallace a five-pound note.

'Of course.'

Wallace said to Andrea, 'He's going to start being all nice now you're here.'

Wallace walked in front, doing karate kicks and shooting imaginary people. He made circular movements with his arms and hands which Mal recognized from rappers. Mal said that when he was a kid, he and his friends wanted to be 'hard', like the cockney criminals they'd heard about. Now the kids based themselves in fantasy on Jamaican–American 'gangstas'.

On the pier, Wallace stopped suddenly to get down on his knees and peer through the wooden slats to the sea below.

'Come on, gangsta,' said Mal.

'What if we fall through?' said Wallace. 'We could die down there.'

Andrea took his hand. 'I'm quite a swimmer. I'd carry you to safety on my back, like a dolphin.'

Wallace disappeared into the hot, noisy arcades and began to dispose of his money. As they followed him, Andrea told Mal about the film, for which most of the finance was in place; she was rewriting the script. They had time to discuss the films they were currently thinking about when, to Mal's surprise, Wallace said he wanted to go on the trampolines. His money was gone, but Andrea offered to pay for him. Wallace took off his shoes and jumped up and down, yelling.

'A great kid,' laughed Andrea. 'Where did you get him?'

Mal sighed and described to Andrea what it had been like seeing his unwanted son for the first time. He told her what had happened since, and how things stood between them.

They filled Wallace with ice-cream and chocolate. When an argument developed about candyfloss and he used Mal's phone to ring his mother and began weeping, Mal had to tell Andrea that Wallace was hungry.

They parted and Mal took the boy for fish and chips. In the hotel, Wallace refused a bath but at least got into his pyjamas. Mal set him up in front of the TV, where he became instantly absorbed. Mal would be able to slip the bottle of whisky into his pocket and open the door.

'What are you doing?' The boy was staring at him in panic.

'I'm going downstairs to have a word with Andrea.'

'No!'

'I won't be long. You'll be fine.'

Mal shut the door before the boy could say anything else. He put his ear to the keyhole but heard only the commercials, which, no doubt, Wallace was mouthing the words to.

Andrea was waiting. They walked quickly through the part of town Mal was familiar with, past clubbers and those looking for restaurants, into a more dilapidated area called the Old Town. He was surprised to see working fishermen preparing to take their boats out for the night. Behind this, the streets narrowed; the close houses seemed to lean across the lanes and almost touch at the top. There were red lights in some of the windows here. She pointed at a house. 'You could score here.'

They entered a pub that seemed full of rough, tattooed late adolescents, most of whom looked like addicts. She went round the place, greeting those she knew. They were pleased to see her, but she was not like them.

Outside again, she said, pointing, 'We could put the camera there and the actors could run into that alley. We could follow them – that way!'

He turned, needing to see and feel what she did. He noticed there was a sort of silence or poverty – of inactivity or emptiness, he would have said – which you didn't find in London.

She told him, 'The people here think London's a stew full of foreigners. They hardly go there.'

'It's about time we declared independence.'

Mal's legs ached but he went on, pursuing and, at times, questioning her enthusiasm. At last they stood in a cobbled square where the streets seemed to lead in all directions. Mal heard a shout and Wallace came rushing towards them, wearing his pyjamas, football gloves and trainers.

'I followed you!'

246

Mal wanted to pick him up but the shivering boy was too heavy.

'All this way?'

'You tried to leave me!'

'You were safe in the hotel.' He crouched down and embraced Wallace, kissing his petrified hair.

'Someone was going to steal me!'

'No!'

Andrea took off her sweater and tied it around his neck. Holding hands, they ran back. In the hotel lounge, Andrea ordered hot chocolate and crisps for him.

'You two.' She was laughing. 'You look exactly the same.'

'We do?' said Wallace.

'How could you be anything but father and son?'

Mal and Wallace were looking at one another. Mal said to him, 'I would never leave you for long. We were only trying to figure out how to make Andrea's movie.'

Wallace asked, 'What's it about? You're not going to run away from me again, are you?'

'I'm too tired. In fact, I'm exhausted and broken.'

Mal fetched drinks for himself and Andrea.

Andrea said, 'The story is this. I was nearly grown-up but not quite when my mum and dad said they couldn't live together any more. From then on, I would have to move between them.'

'Like a parcel, like me,' said Wallace. 'You don't want to be posted everywhere all the time.'

'It was worse than that,' she said. 'The film is called *Ten Days* and is set around the time I was sent to stay with dad – quite near here – for a holiday. Mum wanted to be with another man, you see, which Dad guessed. When I arrived, I found that my poor father couldn't get out of bed for fear of falling over. All he moved was his arm, to drink. I would sit with him, listening to his stories or watching films. While he was asleep, or passed out,

I'd roam about the town on my own, making friends with the locals. Kids always complain there's nothing to do in such places. We found plenty to do, oh yes.'

Wallace nudged his father.

'She was so bad.'

'The baddest, me. Back home, when I was asked what dad and I did on our hols, they worked out that dad had gone crazy. I was never allowed to see him again.'

'In your whole life?'

'He liked drink and they thought it made him a sick person, a fuck-up.'

'She swore!'

'Dad died a month later. They didn't tell me properly. I heard about his death from a relative. I ran away from home to attend the funeral and I stayed down here a few more days, meeting his friends and sleeping in a tent in the woods. I got into more big trouble at home. I didn't like my new stepfather and came down here to live.'

'It was naughty to run away.' He asked, 'Did you see your dad's dead body?'

'Not in life.' Andrea took a notebook from her rucksack and wrote, '"Goes to see dead body of father in morgue". In the film, she will, now.'

'Dad looks normal to you,' said Wallace. 'But he was in trouble once. He ran away too and he drank cider. He was a burglar, and he had rainbow hair. Didn't you, dad?'

'Wow,' said Andrea. 'He doesn't look like that kind of guy now.'

Wallace said, 'Will you still let him work for you?'

'What d'you think?'

'I think you should let him. But only if you put me in the film.'

'There might be a small part for you. Have you acted before? Tell you what, I'll pretend to hit you and you have to react.

Remember, the action is in the reaction. The camera and the people will be looking at you. Stand up.'

She pretended to hit him a few times. Wallace was sufficiently histrionic on the floor.

Wallace let Andrea kiss him goodnight. Mal accompanied Wallace upstairs and got into bed beside him. Mal's young son often slept between Mal and his wife, but Mal had never slept beside his first son. Wallace fell asleep almost immediately, his comforter twitching in his mouth. He was still filthy; no water had passed over him on this trip.

Mal cuddled Wallace but couldn't sleep. He listened to the sea through the open balcony door. He got up, dressed and went out, locking the door from the outside. On the street it was dark and windy, but there were plenty of people about. The sea was further out than he thought, but he got there.

He realized that he seemed to breathe more easily with so much space around him. He wanted to drift along the beach, following the lights and voices to a crowded bar, to drink and talk with strangers, to find out whether their lives were worse or better than his. But Mal could still see the hotel and what he guessed was their room, the sleeping child just beyond the open balcony door. He couldn't lose that patch of light in the distance.

Mal noticed a group of kids not far away, older than students, listening to a boom-box and passing around plastic bottles of cider. Mal went over to one of them and said, 'Can I dance here?'

'Everyone needs to feel free,' said the kid, who appeared to have been in a fight. Mal hesitated. The dance he had last been familiar with was 'the pogo'. 'Feel free,' repeated the boy.

Mal offered him a swig of whisky from the bottle he had brought out. 'It's been a long time though.'

The boy left him. Mal moved closer to the music and began to shuffle; he jerked his body and shook his head. He was hopping. He began to pogo, alone of course, jumping up towards the sky with his arms out for as long as he could, until he fell over in the wet shingle, getting soaked to the skin.

The sun came brightly through the window of the hotel dining-room as Mal, wearing shorts and shoes without socks, filled himself with buttered kipper and fried mushrooms and toast, a starched napkin tucked into the front of his shirt. He had become the sort of man he'd have laughed at as a boy.

'I wonder if you'll remember much of this trip,' he said to Wallace. 'I think I'll get the hotel manager to take a photograph of us outside. You can put it next to your bed.'

'Dad . . . I mean, Mal –'

Newspapers were excellently designed for keeping boys' faces from the sight of their father.

They were on the train when Andrea rang to say she liked the idea of helping Mal move his cutting-room and family to the town for the duration of the film. She had been nervous of suggesting it herself for fear it would put Mal off the job.

Wallace was saying, 'I need to speak to her urgently.'

Mal passed him the phone and heard him explain that he was prepared to be in the film only if he didn't have to cut his hair or kiss girls.

'Andrea agreed,' said Wallace. 'But will mum let me be an actor for her?'

'She might if you tell her you're getting paid.'

The house was deserted when they got back. Mal had guessed his wife would want to avoid them. He opened the doors to the garden and cooked for them both.

Over lunch, Wallace mentioned his piano lessons for the first time. Mal hunted out a Chopin piece played by Arturo Michelangeli and put it on. As they listened, Mal tried to say why he loved it, but he began to weep. He carried on talking but couldn't stop his tears. What he dreaded was driving Wallace home. How could any love survive so many interruptions?

Late that afternoon, before they reached the motorway turn-off, Mal stopped at a service station and had a Coke with his son.

He said, 'When we get to your house, you won't want to say goodbye to me properly. But I want you to know that I will think of you when you're at school, or asleep, or with your friends.'

'I never miss you. I won't be thinking about you.'

'You don't have to. I'll do the thinking, okay?'

Soon they were at Wallace's front gate. The boy scrambled out of the car and ran around the back of the house. Mal carried the bags to the front door and returned to the car. He watched Wallace's stepfather and mother appear and take the bags inside, almost furtively, as though they were stealing them. Mal wanted to look at the couple more, to try and put these two connected families together, but he just waved in their direction and drove away, turning off his phone.

Mal returned to London without stopping. He parked near the house but went past it without going in. He walked to a nearby pub, frequented by northern men working during the week in London. 'No children or dirty boots', it said on the door.

Mal bought cigarettes and set himself up at the bar, ordering a pint and a chaser. He was unsure whether he was celebrating his new job or commiserating with himself over what he had just endured, but he toasted himself.

'To Mal,' he said. 'And everyone who knows him!'

# TOUCHED

He shouted and jumped up and down. 'See you soon, soon, soon, I hope!'

He continued waving until they disappeared round the corner, his many aunties, uncles and cousins, packed into three taxis. Ali and his parents were standing on the pavement outside the house. The Bombay part of their family had been staying in a rented flat in Dulwich for the summer. Ali and his parents had seen them nearly every day; tomorrow they were returning to India.

'Come inside now.' Ali's father took his hand. 'I don't like to see you so upset.'

Ali was embarrassed by his tears. His neighbour Mike was standing across the road, shuffling his football cards and scratching, watching and pretending not to. He had been round earlier. After the uncles and aunts had begun their goodbyes, the front door bell had rung and Ali had opened it, thinking it was a taxi. His cousins had crowded behind him.

'Comin' out?' Mike had asked, biting his nails, trying to examine the faces behind Ali. Mike had lost a clump of hair; his father had pulled it out, beating him up. 'What's goin' on? We could 'ear you lot from down the road, makin' a noise all day.'

It was the Saturday of the fifth cricket Test. India had been playing England at the Oval. In the morning, Ali's three rowdy uncles and his father had taken their places in the small front room, pulling the curtains and shutting the door. The men had smoked, drunk beer and cursed the Indian bowlers, while the stolid Englishmen, Barrington and Graveney, batted all day. The uncles blamed the Indian captain Prince Pataudi, who had only one eye. The Indian aunties had been teaching Ali's English mother to prepare several dishes which she promised to make for her husband and son. The women carried the dall, keema and rice into the room, which they had been cooking in huge pans first thing in the morning. The men had eaten with their fingers, plates shuddering on their laps, not taking their eyes from the screen. They had yelled abuse in Urdu.

Ali had been allowed to go into the uncles' room whenever he liked. They had begun to speak to him as another man. One even called him 'the next head of the family'. The oldest uncle owned factories in India, the second was a famous political journalist, and the third was an engineer who built dams. At home, all three were notorious 'carousers' and party-givers. During the cricket intervals, they entertained Ali by betting on tossed coins or on which auntie would come into the room next; they played 'stone, paper, scissors'. Ali's abstemious father had a minor job in a solicitor's office.

Ali was an only child. He wrote down cricket scores next to imaginary teams in a notebook his mother had given him. He spent hours alone in the garden, batting a cricket ball, attached by rope to the branch of a tree, with a sawn-off broomstick. The garden was his kingdom, and he was eager to share it with his Indian family as he had today, opening the windows and back door of the small council house. This was unusual: both his parents disliked draughts, whatever the weather. Today, three of his cousins had played cricket out in the garden; the girls, aged between seven and fourteen, had played chase.

The aunties, after they had washed up, had sat on blankets in the shade, stroking and arranging one another's hair like people in a French painting. Ali was kissed and fussed over, enjoying the sight of his aunties' painted toes in their delicate sandals, even the rolls of fat around their stomachs, where their saris had come loose.

That afternoon, Ali had shown his cousin Zahida his bedroom. She was fourteen, a year older than him. They'd looked out at the view of suburban gardens (where he'd once seen a married couple kissing), and he pulled out his copy of *The Man with the Golden Gun*. They bounced on the bed and then she pressed her lips to his. She said she wanted to be 'secret' with him, and he got a torch and led her up the ladder into the attic where there were discarded toys and dusty trunks which had carried his father's things from Bombay. Her bangles clattered and jangled. They couldn't stop giggling. Zahida was convinced there were rats and bats. Who would hear her muffled screams so far up?

They kissed again, but she placed her mouth close to his ear. His body was invaded by such sweetness that he thought he would fall over. She bent forward, placing her hands on top of the filthy water-tank, and in a delirium he continued caressing, until, making his way through intricate whirls of material, he reached her flesh and slid his finger into the top of the crack. That was all. She made noises like someone suffering. He could have remained with her there for hours, but his excitement was yoked to a fear of discovery and punishment. He said they should go downstairs. He went first, and urged her to follow.

'What's wrong?' she had asked. They were back in his bedroom.

'You're leaving tomorrow. I don't want you to go.'

'When I grow up,' she said, 'I'm going to be a pilot like my dad used to be.' Ali had never been in an aeroplane. 'I'll fly everywhere. I'll come and see you.'

'That's a long time away.'

Ali envied his cousins seeing one another almost every day. They lived close to one another and the family's drivers ferried them to one another's houses whenever they wanted. 'We are being called to weddings and parties the whole time.'

Then Zahida said, 'Papa told me you're invited to stay with us.'

'But that's not going to happen, is it? My parents don't like to go anywhere.'

'Come on your own. There's plenty of room. All kinds of bums and relatives turn up at home! Come for the holidays, like we do here. Christmas would be good.'

He said with shame, 'I would, but Dad doesn't have the money to send me.'

'Why not?'

He shrugged. 'He doesn't earn enough.'

She said, 'Save up. Didn't you help out at the circus last Easter?'

'Yes.'

'It made us all laugh like mad. You weren't a clown, were you?'

'I came on to clean up after the elephant,' he said. 'It made the audience laugh. Mostly I carried props around.'

'But you're so small!'

'I'll get bigger.'

She said, 'You're big enough now to wash cars and dig gardens.'

'That's true,' he said. 'I can do that.'

'You can.'

He kissed her. 'Tell India I am coming!'

He was surprised to see his father standing at the foot of the stairs, watching them both.

It was then the taxis had arrived, hooting their horns.

When everyone had gone, Ali's mother sighed with relief. She was leaving for work. His mother was a nurse who worked nights; when she could, she slept during the day. Now, she and father had a row about what the eldest uncles had said to Dad. In a sulk, Ali's father went into his room and sat at his desk with his back to Ali. He was studying law by correspondence course, which Dad's wealthiest brother, the head of the family, was paying for. He had become angry with Ali's father, who had failed his exams and didn't seem to be making much of himself in England. At lunchtime, he had shouted, 'There are so many opportunities here, yaar, and the only one you've taken is to marry Joan! Why are you letting down the whole family?'

As it was, his mother was already annoyed with the men. A few days before, after she had shown off her new washing-machine, they had given her all the Bombay family's washing to do. 'I'm not their servant,' she said, throwing down the pillowcases filled with dirty clothes. Father, with Ali's help, had to figure out how to work the machine, one reading the instructions, the other fiddling with the dials, as a pool of water crept across the floor. Then they ironed and folded the clothes, pretending it was Joan's handiwork.

Dad might now study for hours, with a furious look on his face. Ali sat down, too. In his father's room, where Ali was supposed to have been preparing for the new school year if he was to keep up with the other pupils and not become like his father, all he could hear was the ticking clock. The house seemed to have stopped breathing. His mother wouldn't return until the morning; she'd make his breakfast, ensure he had a clean towel, and, when Mike knocked, send him to the swimming baths.

Ali slipped out without his father appearing to notice; he didn't want to stay at home if no one was laughing or talking. He was surprised to find Mike still outside, kicking a tennis ball against the front wall.

'Come on out, yer bastard. Bin waitin' for yer,' he said. 'What you bin doin', cryin' and all that?'

He and Mike trudged across the flat park at twilight; goal posts like gallows stood in the mud.

'You took yer time gettin' out,' said Mike. 'Nearly dark now.'

'People were round.'

''Ate it when that 'appens. Yer with yer mates now. Everyone'll be down the swings.'

Ali and Mike always went straight to the swings. If it was

raining, they shared cigarettes in the dank shed where the foot-
ballers changed for the weekend league.

Mike shouted, 'There they are! The scrubbers are out!'

They started to run. It wasn't far. Ali knew all the kids; they
weren't his friends but they lived near by, some younger, others
older. His mother called them 'rough'.

'Where you bin?' one of them said to Mike.

'Waitin' for Ali. 'E 'ad idiots round. There were dozens of 'em,
smellin' the place out. It can't be allowed, so many darkies in a
council 'ouse!'

The girls were on the swings, the boys smoking, spitting and
hanging from the metal uprights. The boys attempted to twang
the girls' braces against their breasts as they swung up and
down, but mostly they were discussing the dance. It was up at
Petts Wood and there'd be a reggae group. At the moment, they
all loved Desmond Dekker's music and were talking about
whether they'd be let in to the dance hall or have to sneak in
through the back way and get lost in the darkness. The girls
would be allowed to slip past the doormen, but the boys were
obviously too young. Ali knew he had no chance.

'There's nothing wrong with my family,' Ali said to Mike.

'You over 'ere now,' said Mike.

The two of them looked uncomprehendingly at each other. Ali
spat and strode away, but realized he didn't want to go home. He
would walk the streets until he was ready to see his father.

At the top of the road he noticed Miss Blake's light on behind
the net curtain. Sometimes he went in to see her on his way back
from the young actors' club or his Spanish guitar lesson. She
always gave him sweets and half a crown. She lived with her
brother, a porter at Victoria Station who was well known for
fighting in the local pubs.

Miss Blake was blind and always at her gate when the children
returned from school and the commuters from work. Some of the

other kids would cry out at her – 'She's playing a blinder today!'
– but she would continue to stand there, a pure, inane smile on
her lips. Sometimes, Ali walked around his bedroom with his
eyes closed and his hands out in front, trying to know what it
was like for her. He had visited her a lot lately, needing a few
pennies. In return, she asked to hear what he'd done at school
and what he thought of his friends. He had begun to enjoy his
monologues; it was like keeping a diary out loud. Whatever he
said, she would listen. It was odd, but he spoke to her more than
he did to anyone else.

He tapped on the front window. 'Hi, Miss Blake.'

'Come on in, Alan, dear.'

She thought his name was Alan. He enjoyed being Alan for a
while; it was a relief. Sometimes he went all day being Alan.

He followed her into the kitchen which had patches of curling
lino over the bare floorboards. The kitchen couldn't have been
painted for twenty years and it smelled of gas. To keep warm,
Miss Blake always kept the stove lit. She knew where everything
was in the house, just by touch. The radio was playing wartime
big-band music.

She got him a glass of water which he tried never to drink, the
glass was so filthy, and he placed it next to the metal box in which
she kept her change. She always seemed to have plenty of coins.
She was meant to have paintings inherited from her family, and in
the neighbourhood it was rumoured that, unable to see them, she
had sold them.

She sat there, waiting for him to speak.

At first, he thought he would tell her about the visit of his family
and the restaurants they'd all been to; how they'd seen the zoo,
Madame Tussaud's and Hyde Park. But he had never mentioned
his Indian connection before. She didn't know he was half-Indian;
she was the only person he knew who wasn't aware of this.

He had no idea of her real age. She could have been in her forties;

she could have been in her early thirties. It was all the same to him.

'Alan, light me one up,' she said.

He pulled out a Players Number Six for her, and she took it and placed it in her mouth. She smoked heavily, and liked him to light her fags so she could hang on to his hand with hers.

'Where you bin?' she said.

'Busy, busy, busy,' he said.

She leaned forward. 'It's good to be busy. Doin' what?'

He told her about the visit of his uncle, auntie and cousins. He told her the whole thing, dropping in the fact that they were from India. She listened attentively, as she always did, with one of her ears, rather than her eyes, pointed at him; he found himself speaking to the side of her head, to her wispy long hair and the lopsided smile.

'Our father was in India for twenty years,' she said. ''E was a tea trader. Said it was lovely. Better than 'ere in all this cold. Now your family are off.'

'They've gone.'

'You're missing 'em.' He didn't say anything for a bit. 'What?' she said.

'Yes. I do, and will.' He added, 'I'm going over there, when I've saved up.'

'Won't you take me?'

'You?'

'Oh, please say yes, you will.'

'To India?'

'Oh, take me, take me,' she said. 'My brother Ernie takes me nowhere. 'E just curses me. I beg 'im, just the day out, and why not? To smell and 'ear the sea, why not! They've got a blind school there.'

'Where?'

'Bombay. I've bin told of it! They might take me in to help the starvin' sufferin' children!'

What an extraordinary spectacle it would be in Bombay, the English Indian boy and the blind woman.

She was holding a chocolate. 'Now, come 'ere, you poor boy. Open.'

He went to sit on the kitchen chair beside her. Her pinafore was stained. Her eyes were heavy lidded, always half-closed. There was no reason, he supposed, for her to go to the trouble of keeping her eyes open. The dark moons of her eyes seemed to have become stuck to the top of her sockets.

'Hot today.'

'Where?'

'All over.' He was flapping his shirt. 'I'm sticky.'

'No,' she said. 'Really? You need some talcum powder over you. I've got some somewhere. Let's do this first, 'cause I know what you've come for.'

'Do you?'

Ali opened his mouth in readiness. Then, he didn't know why, he closed his eyes, as though expecting a kiss.

It was her other hand which reached up to his face; it was this hand which stroked his cheek, forehead and nose, and traced the line of his lips.

'I'm only goin' to feel 'ow big you are,' she said, releasing the chocolate into his mouth. ''Ave you 'ad a birthday recently? You seem bigger. That's what I'm trying to get at, Alan.'

'No,' he said, shaking his head, and thereby shaking off her hand at last. 'No increase in size this week.'

'Just a minute.' Now she was holding up half a crown, which he took and pushed into his pocket.

'Thanks. Lord, thanks, Miss Blake.'

'Now keep still.'

She reached for his throat. Her hand was trembling. She was fumbling at something around his neck and then eased lower. Through his shirt she was feeling his chest as if she had never touched another human body and wanted to know what it was like. Her eyelids seemed to be twitching. He had never been this close to her before. He let the chocolate sit on his tongue without biting it, until it melted and dissolved in the heat of his mouth. He found himself thinking of writing to Zahida. When his father went to work tomorrow, he'd go into his room and take some of the flimsy blue airmail paper on which Dad wrote to his brothers. Ali always kept the stamps, and he'd write Zahida a love letter, the first of many love letters, full of poems and drawings, telling her everything. The letters, he knew, took more than a week to get there. He would start writing tomorrow and await her replies, which he would read on the school bus.

Miss Blake worked Ali's shirt loose; it had come completely open. Nurses, like his mother, had to touch strangers all the time. Mother said it was natural; she had seen some rotten things, but no human body had disgusted her.

Ali was silently counting the money he'd make; at this rate he'd be able to stay with Zahida. There would be time for them to do 'everything', as she had put it. He would go where she went, to the club, to the beach, to parties, in the chauffeur-driven car. The family would welcome him as their own. In the evenings, he would sit around with the vociferous men telling stories and jokes, and talking politics. Maybe he'd get married over there and his parents would join him. He'd have to work out the details.

Miss Blake continued to touch him. She seemed to have several hands which went around his upper body, fluttering like dying birds. He had no idea where they would land next. His stomach? His back? He was unable to move, his eyes closed, and all he could hear was the radio, and nothing on it that he liked. He made to move, and Miss Blake let out a surprised cry and turned her face up to him. There was no alteration in the mushed clay of her eyes, but her mouth was twisted.

'Alan,' she moaned.

He slapped the table, and she slid another half a crown across it. He put it in his pocket and skipped to the door.

'Alan, Alan!' Her fingers grasped at the air.

'You can't make me miss *The Munsters*.'

She knew the house and could move quickly around it. But he was outside before she could touch him again.

Father was still at his desk, and his head was resting on his arms. Ali stroked his hair and then tickled his nose. Father sat up suddenly and looked around in surprise.

'What time is this to come back?'

'Don't know.'

'Don't go out with Mike too much,' said Dad, trying to locate his pen, which Ali could see had fallen on the floor. Ali pointed at it. Dad bent down to pick it up and hit his head on the edge of the desk's open drawer. 'Those boys are useless. They're all going to be motor mechanics!' he added, rubbing his head.

'I want to find better friends. Just like you want to find a better job.'

'That's enough, Ali! We've got to work!'

Ali lay down on the sofa on the other side of the room. He pulled his shirt up; his fingers drifted across his body. He touched himself where Miss Blake had stroked him. He smelled his fingers. She was there on him, where Zahida had been earlier. Her money was in his pocket.

He got up. Pretending he was doing his homework, he began to draft his first letter to Zahida. He was already in movement, already leaving there.

Next morning, when he and Mike went past on the way to the open-air swimming pool, and Mike was singing a football song and kicking his kit bag on its cord, Miss Blake was at her gate, rattling the bolt.

'Mike, Mike,' she shouted. 'Where's Alan?'

''Ere 'e is,' said Mike. 'Can't you see 'is stupid brown 'ead? Can't yer smell 'im?'

'Morning, Miss Blake,' said Ali.

'Alan, Alan!' She was leaning far over the gate. 'Don't you want . . . want something to eat? A chocolate or something?'

'I do, Miss Blake. You know I do.' Mike was laughing. 'Just you wait there,' Ali said. 'I'll be back after I've had me dip.'

'But Alan, Alan!' she called again, more urgently. 'Won't you come 'ere and light me snout?'

Ali looked at Mike, and shrugged.

Ali went back to her, drew the packet of Number Six from her hand, popped one in her mouth, took her lighter and lit it. She grasped his hand tightly as he knew she would. When the wind blew out the flame, he handed the lighter back to her. She slipped her hand through the gate and gave him sixpence, which he pocketed. He ran away up the street, to catch up with Mike.

'Mike, you get going,' he said. 'I'll see yer there a bit later on.'

Miss Blake had already opened the gate; Ali followed her up the path.